FOSSIL COVE PRESS

I0662360

Winnipeg, Manitoba

MURDER CHICKENS

On MARS

and

Other Curious and Exotic Speculations

by

D. G. Valdron

MURDER-CHICKENS ON MARS and other Curious and Exotic Speculations

FOSSIL COVE PUBLISHING, 1301-90 Garry St., Winnipeg, Mb, Can, R3C 4J4

Cover Image of Pyramid by Anna Valdron
Cover Raw Images of Mars and Starfield are from NASA
Images of Silurians and Sea Devils are from Doctor Who, copyright British Broadcasting Corp.
Images of Sleestak are from Land of the Lost, copyright Sod and Marty Kroft Productions
Raw Images of Mars and Martian Surface from NASA
Marked image of Martian Cydonia Region derived from Enterprise Project, Richard Hoagland, All Images used for purposes of review and comment falling under Fair Use or Fair Dealing sections of Copyright Act.

Issued in eBook and print formats
ISBN: 978-1-998453-36-8 (eBook)
ISBN: 978-1-998453-39-9 (Draft2Digital Print Book)

No part of this book, including the text, content, cover or artwork has been made by or with the participation of Artificial Intelligence or Large Language Models.

Text set in Garamond

D.G. Valdron's web site can be found at:

https://www.denvaldron.com

MURDER CHICKENS ON MARS
and Other Curious and Exotic Speculations
Table of Contents

INTRODUCTION

So What the Heck did You Just Buy?

What in God's name are *'Curious and Exotic Speculations'*? Is it fiction? Is it fact? Is it something else?

Yes! All of that!

A while back, I asked myself a question: *What if Lovecraft's Cthulhu was a real god, in the same sense that any other pagan god is real?* That is, that it was part of a religion, a religion that had begun somewhere, that changed and evolved accumulating other gods and traditions, and whose history could be reconstructed by studying its elements and texts. I wrote something. It was nifty and clever, and I put it away.

I started doing stuff like that, purely for my own pleasure. I started taking deep dives into fictional subjects, analyzing imaginary creatures in real terms, exploring forgotten corners of folklore like real and mythical lost continents on Earth or the face on Mars. What if Greenland wasn't covered with ice? How could the Romans plausibly find the New World? What if all those 50s Sci-Fi movies were connected? How would you get to a Bear Cavalry? And why would anyone domesticate bears in the first place? Much less ride them?

It was about exploring history and biology, delving into physics and archeology, the quirks of evolution and civilization. It was interesting in and of itself. It turned into a book, **Dawn of Cthulhu**, and another, **Fall of Atlantis**, and then **Bear Cavalry**. Which brings us to **Murder-Chickens on Mars**. What you're holding is the fourth volume of the *'trilogy.'*

Admittedly, what I do here, treating the unreal as if it was real and diving hard and deep is not for everyone.

I figure for every person that gets into it, there's another throwing the book across the room.

You'll like it or you won't. I hope you like it, and if you don't, I hope it wasn't too traumatic.

Fair warning, this book does indeed talk about Martian Civilizations. And it does talk Murder Chickens, a civilization of them. But they're not on Mars. I just loved the title. Maybe I'll do a short story someday, or a novel.

Anyway, thanks for reading. Hope you like it.

Maybe I'll do more of these things…

Onwards

The Martian Civilizations That Came and Went

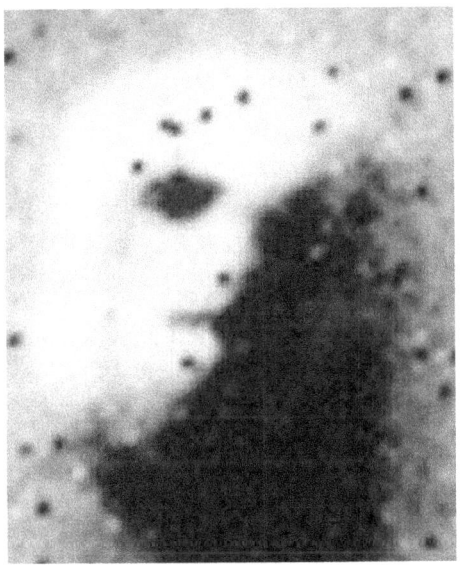

Once upon a time, on the planet Mars, there was a mighty civilization of Humanoids that occupied the planet, building canals, massive Pyramids and monumental sculptures miles across, that somehow vanished away, leaving nothing but a handful of ruins.

Who were they? Native Martians or aliens from another star? Visitors from an unimaginably ancient lost Human civilization? Or time travelers from the future? No one could say.

But what we could say, is that although they'd vanished, their works could still be seen by astronomers, and their titanic ruins became visible with our orbital space probes.

Or so people, some people at least, came to believe. And then, in 1998, it all vanished away. An entire civilization had grown up in our imaginations, blossomed, and then evaporated like the morning dew.

This is the story of the Mars that came and went. An entire Martian civilization lived in our imagination, evaporated away, briefly re-ignited and then faded away forever.

The Canals and the Dying Civilization

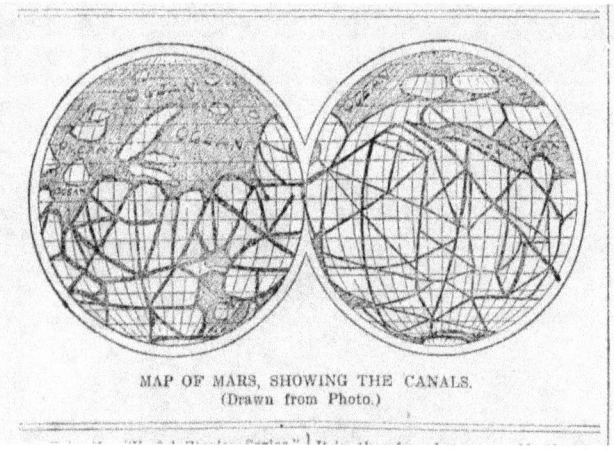

MAP OF MARS, SHOWING THE CANALS.
(Drawn from Photo.)

Mars was always an intriguing world. The first recorded formal observation of it was by Aristotle in 356 B.C.. Galileo turned his telescope on Mars in 1610, recording the phases of the planet.

It was a favorite even in the early days of telescopes, for the 17th century astronomers. Francesco Fontana made the first sketch of the red planet. Christiaan Huyghens in 1666 determined the length of the Martian day, followed in the same year by Giovanni Cassini's description of the polar caps.

Look, it's this way: You're an astronomer, you point your telescope at a star light years away... you're still just seeing a star, a point of light. Big deal. Sure, you could gather more information about the star, color, guesses as to size and characteristic. But it wasn't going to be doing much. Point the telescope at a black spot of space... more stars. Now, I'm not saying it was all dead boring...

But if you ended up pointing your telescope at Mars, suddenly, you had a planet with actual physical detail. Astronomers could train their telescopes upon it and make out actual surface features, and more than that, they could observe changes, marking the progress of seasons. They could discern the white polar caps and watch them swell and retreat over the Martian year good evidence there for ice of some sort, almost certainly water ice. They could occasionally spot clouds, and see when dust storms obscured the entire surface of the planet, clear evidence of a reasonable atmosphere. That made it a favorite subject for Astronomers.

They could make out light and dark features that seemed remarkably consistent, and yet, changed slightly over time and with seasons. The equatorial region seemed the source of an erratic, dark, thick band. The upper hemisphere was somewhat light, the southern hemisphere somewhat dark. It was speculated at first that the upper hemisphere was a continent, the darker areas were seas. Of course it was all guesswork from forty million miles away, and horribly wrong.

Around 1890 evidence of water waned, perspectives changed and the notion arose that the light areas were desert, and the dark areas the marshy remnants of dried seas. The conception of the Martian atmosphere changed, due to the infrequency of clouds and dust storms, the air was thought to be relatively thin.

Notwithstanding this interpretation, it is remarkable how the maps made were quite close to telescope photographs, and even of the maps drawn from the space probes. Genuine features, including Syrtis, Hellas, Argyre and the poles were accurately described, a testament to the fascination the planet held and the diligence of the observers.

Over centuries, Astronomers proved themselves by giving us reasonably accurate, broad descriptions of the planet. Where they fell off, was with fine details, like the canals....

The earliest sketches or drawings of Mars which appear to show canals actually date back to 1840, and appear again independently in 1864, though they were not called canals then.

Giovanni Schiaparelli was the first astronomer to identify the illusory features as canals, in 1877. Producing the first accurate (for its time) detailed map of Mars. This was also the year that Mars' two moons, Phobos and Deimos were discovered. So there was a kind of 'plausibility by association.' If one new feature, the moons, were accepted, why not the other, the canals.

Schiaparelli repeated and elaborated on his observations two years later in another close approach in 1879, eventually identifying some sixty distinct canal like structures. He called them by the Italian word 'canali.' There's an important distinction. In English, canals are artificial waterways, so it might have seemed like Schiaparelli was saying that someone had built them. But actually, the Italian term 'canali' simply meant 'channels' which didn't necessarily imply artificial creation.

But on the other hand, he refused to rule out intelligence and failed to propose any other explanation. He felt that they might be a system for distributing water from melting polar snows to other parts of the planet, a theory which naturally inspires thoughts of intelligent origin. In other words, Schiaparelli was being coy, describing structures which were highly suspicious and suggestive of life and intelligence, but at the same time, reluctant to speculate as to their origins, refusing to either embrace intelligence or to rule it out.

Unfortunately, for the next several years, no one else saw canals on Mars. The next observations were nine years later, by a pair of Astronomers. But indeed, they were observed only infrequently after that. Percival Lowell, in an atypical fit of cynicism, writes in 1895 that the number of people who had seen and described the canals could be counted on one hand. The astronomy community capable of making those observations was small. But not that small.

Now, keep in mind that this was also an age of canals on Earth. The Erie Canal in 1825 connected Lake Erie to the Hudson River, and the Great Lakes to the Atlantic, literally reshaping the American Midwest. The Suez Canal connecting the Red Sea to the Mediterranean and transforming shipping and travel between Europe and Asia had been built in 1860. Between 1879 and 1889, the French had struggled to build a Central American canal to unite the Pacific and the Atlantic. In 1902 the Americans picked up after the French to finally complete the Panama Canal.

Canals, including large ones had been or were being built everywhere in the United States and Canada, France and England, transforming economies and travel, so they were well known. People understood them. But the new giant Panama and Suez canals were literally an order of magnitude greater, transforming continents. The late 19th century was an era of massive construction and colossal scales. The notion that there were similar titanic works on Mars came naturally.

Nevertheless, despite skepticism, the fact that Martian canals were being spotted independently by a handful of observers over a long period of time, the fact that they preceded their official discoverer by a generation, and the fact that they were quite consistent among those who observed them, suggested that there was actually something real there. So the scientific community and general population tended to accept their existence.

Even the failure of these canals to appear in most photographs was not damning, particularly as at least a few photographs under perfect conditions, seemed to show some of them.

Part of this acceptance lay in the fact that observation conditions were often imperfect. Due to inclination, Mars was best observed from the southern hemisphere. The power of telescopes, and the weather conditions and local conditions of observatories varied widely. So it wasn't entirely unreasonable if features so subtle were not universally recognized.

Another part of this was that Mars orbits and Earth's orbits were quite different. Close approaches varied from fifty million miles to an optimum of about thirty-five million. It took several years for the two planets to line up at closest approaches. Following Schiaparelli, the best oppositions occurred in 1892 and 1894, 1907 and 1909 and 1924 and 1926.

The first two sets of dates are particularly important. 1892 and 1894 were the crucial times during which Percival Lowell made his critical observations and wrote his popular books on Mars. – *Mars* (1895), *Mars and Its Canals* (1906), *Mars as the Abode of Life* (1908) and *The Evolution of Worlds* (1910). Lowell, who started out so cynically, became a believer.

It was also likely these books and these same series of observations that brought Mars into prominence. Meanwhile, 1907 and 1909 would have put Mars prominently in the news once again.

The Astronomer, William Pickering, in 1892, came up with the suggestion that canals were not truly watercourses. They were too thick for that, the smallest were estimated to be ten to twenty miles in width, the largest were 150 miles. He thought instead they were bands of vegetation, perhaps fed by watercourses. The actual canals or Martian rivers were too small to see; we were observing the vegetation that grew up around them. This neatly explained why different numbers of canals were seen, and why some seemed to appear and vanish. Some simply would not be in season at particular times. Several other notable Astronomers wrote of Mars canals, including Frederik Kaiser, Richard A. Proctor, Nathaniel Green, J.L.E. Dreyer and Camille Flammarion. These weren't flakes, but serious scientists across Europe and the United States – cutting edge. They were to be taken seriously.

Meanwhile, there was a picture being built up of Mars. The growing consensus in the 1892-1894 period was that its small size and lack of reflections indicated that there were no major areas of deep water on the planet. The lighter area of the north, and in the south, were taken as evidence of continental structure, perhaps worn smooth and reduced to desert. The dark central band which waxed and waned with the seasons was assumed to be a dry sea bed. Vegetation living off residual moisture in the sea bed was considered a likely explanation for the seasonal changes. Life on Mars was the general opinion, the only question was how much life and how far had it advanced.

Mars, Astronomers decided, was a dry planet having lost most of its waters to space or absorbed by the planet's chemical processes. The lack of clouds and the difficulty in observing signs of atmosphere lead to the belief in a very thin and perhaps slowly vanishing atmosphere, perhaps comparable to the mountain regions of Earth. It was believed to be a very old world.

These theories made Mars a world unlike any other in the solar system. It was a world with a past. The moon had always been a rock, we couldn't tell what was under Venus clouds, and the other planets seemed stolid and timeless.

But Mars clearly had a past, a history that included continents and oceans and thick air and probably life. It had been a young world like Earth. And now it was an old world, the seas dried up, the continents worn away, endless encroaching deserts and life clinging on in drying sea beds. It was a vision both romantic and evocative. Disturbing in its hints of our own fate. There was something tragic or disquieting to contemplate life and intelligence trapped on that dying world.

Mars, shared with Earth a uniquely metaphysical distinction of being a world with history written upon it. Something that only made it more compelling to Astronomers and to the public. Romantic, almost mystical notions took hold. The notion of life, the possibility of intelligence was fascinating. The canals beckoned, full of possibility.

Those canals really came into their own with Percival Lowell, who built on Schiaparelli's work. Through painstaking observations, Lowell built up a detailed map, identifying over 180 canals. Lowell's observations, while more extensive, were in general agreement with his predecessors. Subsequent astronomers eventually charted over 500 lines, including most of those seen by Schiaparelli.

Lowell formed a beguiling theory of a dying world, its seas dried up, and its continents worn away. The canals, he concluded, were artificial structures created by the inhabitants of Mars in order to draw moisture from the poles, or from the remnants of the Martian seas.

The canals, as described by Lowell, Schiaparelli and others, were peculiar features indeed. For the most part they were absolutely straight, adjusting only for curvature of the planet. Their lengths varied from 250 miles to 4000 miles. They often joined one another, like spokes in the hub of a wheel, though angles varied. Their thickness was uniform along their length, varying from 20 miles thick small canals, to giants 140 miles thick. There were double canals, structures running parallel to each other. There seemed to be triangular structures joining canals, similar to river deltas. Their 'oasis' or joining points defied explanation.

Lowell's theory that they were the work of intelligent beings was regarded as wild by other astronomers, not because it flew in the face of data. In fact, the work of intelligence was quite a good explanation for what Lowell and others were recording. But the conservative minds of the scientific community simply argued that there might be other explanations for these structures.... Like vegetation. Their problem with Lowell was that they merely considered him premature.

Nevertheless, Lowell's speculative books were read widely, and almost certainly by Edgar Rice Burroughs himself. Lowell's romantic depiction of a dying civilization, struggling desperately to survive by building a network of canals, found its way into popular culture, notably the works of Edgar Rice Burroughs and H.G. Wells. Practically every science fiction writer took their turn at Mars. Mars and Martians made their way into radio plays and movie serials.

Indeed, at the conclusion of his discussions, in *Mars as the Abode of Life*, Lowell dwells at length on the nature of the Martians.

"Mars being thus old himself, we know that evolution on his surface must be similarly advanced. This only informs us of its condition relative to the planet's capabilities. Of its actual state our data are not definite enough to furnish much deduction. But from the fact that our own development has been comparatively a recent thing, and that a long time would be needed to bring even Mars to his present geological condition, we may judge any life he may support to be not only relatively, but really older than our own."

"Quite possibly, such Martian folk are possessed of inventions of which we have not dreamed, and with them electrophones and kinetoscopes are things of a bygone past, preserved with veneration in museums as relics of the clumsy contrivances of the simple childhood of the race. Certainly what we see hints at the existence of beings who are in advance of, not behind us, in the journey of life.

"To talk of Martian beings is not to mean Martian men. Just as the probabilities point to the one, so to do they point away from the other. Even on this Earth man is of the nature of an accident. He is the survival of by no means the highest physical organism. He is not even a high form of Mammal. Mind has been his making. For aught we can see, some lizard or batrachian might just as well have popped into his place early in the race, and been now the dominant creature of this Earth. Under different physical conditions, he would have been certain to do so. Amid

the surroundings that exist on Mars, surroundings so different from our own, we may be practically sure other organisms have been evolved of which we have no cognizance. What manner of beings they may be we lack the data even to conceive."

And there we have it folks. The detailed portrait of an ancient world with an ancient civilization technically more advanced than our own.

The canals on Mars were a done deal. I have a book on astronomy, *The Story of Our Starry Universe*, originally published in 1922, reprinted in 1939, which, despite noting that the canals were still controversial and that some astronomers disputed their very existence, states *"the canals, as far as they are considered to be line-like markings, have been completely verified."*

In short, as late as the 1940's, and likely into the 50's and 60's, the real consensus of Astronomical opinion was that the canals of Mars actually existed, or might actually exist. Certainly, no one was willing to definitively rule them out.

The 'intelligent origin' theory was looked upon with a certain skepticism, it was simply raw speculation. But it could not be ruled out either.

The belief in canals seems to have endured up until 1965 when the American space probe, Mariner 4 had a successful flyby and sent back photographs of the planet's surface. The resulting images shattered that belief beyond all repair with their depictions of cratered moonscapes and not a canal in sight. A few years later Mariner 9 would enter a Martian orbit, and once again, not a canal in sight.

Moonscape wasn't far off as a description, between astronomical observations and space probes we learned that while Mars clearly had an atmosphere, its pressure was only 7 or 8 millibars, compared to Earth's 1000 at sea level - or basically less than 1%, effectively vacuum by Earth standards. Temperatures were cold, approximately 200 degrees below zero, and the absence of a magnetic field meant a surface pummeled by hard radiation.

Nothing could live there. Mars wasn't a dying world, it was dead. And it had been dead a long time.

Since then, with literally dozens of subsequent space probes, we've mapped the surface of the planet carefully, discovering many wonderful features, but only the barest hints of things that might have been ancient watercourses and land forms, at best these were only vaguely reminiscent of Lowell and Schiaparelli's canals, and hardly the source of the sightings.

Certainly, though, there was nothing like the profusion and complexity recorded by Schiaparelli, Lowell and other astronomers.

So what were they? And what happened to them? Some of it was observer error. We were after all trying to see through Earth's thick atmosphere, and peer at an object thirty-five or forty million miles away, at best. These were hardly optimum conditions. Part of it was simply shared expectations, you're looking at a blurry red disk with light and dark patches, you've heard all about canals, they're planted in your subconscious, ticking away at the back of your mind. You unconsciously project them onto a blurry image because you're expecting to see them.

One compelling theory is that Astronomers actually were seeing lines. They were seeing the blood vessels on the insides of their corneas. There's something to that, under the right conditions, the light in your eyes reflects back, and you can actually glimpse these blood vessels projected onto your retina. They're squiggly, but under the right conditions, in brief glimpses, maybe you would see them as channels.

Support for this, is that during this time, Astronomers were also seeing channels or canals on Venus, and given its cloud cover, that was plainly impossible.

Ultimately, we were projecting ourselves onto Mars.

But the space probes also gave that hypothetical Martian Civilization a new lease on life. Because we found... Pyramids.

Carl Sagan's Lost Pyramids of Mars

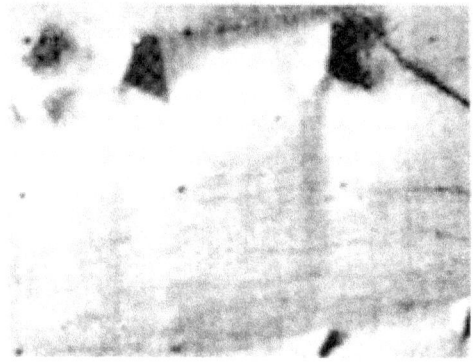

Blame Carl Sagan for starting the ball rolling again.

The speculative Mars of canals lasted from about the 1880s to the 1950s. Maybe longer, but by the end, it was looking pretty far-fetched. It definitely came to an end with the Mariner space probe fly-bys in 1965. These first primitive space probes were aimed towards Mars with a crude instrument package. As they flew by, they delivered the first close up pictures of the Martian surface: A dead, sterile moonscape of endless craters, an atmosphere almost entirely of carbon dioxide, so thin it was a vacuum in our terms, and not a canal to be seen. Old Mars was dead, replaced by a new Mars as sterile as the moon.

Until 1980, when Carl Sagan wrote his book, *Cosmos*, and 'discovered' the Pyramids of Mars. In a very brief passing section of his book, Sagan reproduces a couple of images from Mariner 9 4205-78 & 4296-23, from 1972, which appear to show three cornered objects with straight borders and shadowed sides - Pyramids.

Sagan wrote: *"The largest Mars Pyramids have a base width of 3km and a height of 1km, so they are much larger than the Pyramids of Sumer, Egypt and Mexico. With the ancient eroded shape, they could be small hills, sandblasted for centuries, but they need to be viewed from nearby."*

But look how coy he's being. He actually calls them Pyramids, speculates that they could be natural features, but suggests that we should send a rover to check them out. He doesn't explicitly say that these unnaturally straight, unnaturally angular structures are pyramids, but he's definitely leaving the thought hanging out there in the breeze.

Look, to be blunt, it's not uncommon to find 'Pyramid-shaped' hills or mountains. Here on Earth, people have identified as manmade, apparent Pyramids underwater in the Bermuda triangle, poking through the ice in Antarctica, in Bosnia, in Indonesia and in Russia's Kola Peninsula at the Arctic Circle. They're all just hills and mountains, which is apparent when you look carefully. Natural vaguely Pyramid-shaped hills or mountains are not unusual on Earth, and likely not unusual on Mars. Sagan knew that very well.

But actually, even though he was handling it with kid gloves, he was in tune with the speculation at the time.

Let me explain: High tech Human civilization has been around for a century, Human civilization of any kind maybe 10,000 years. Advanced life on Earth (worms and such) about a billion years. The solar system, four billion years, give or take.

People were seeing UFO's in the sky, and wondering if they were aliens. But there were a group of people who would take that, and wonder "why now?" It was a huge coincidence that we might be visited by aliens at the right time for us to notice.

Perhaps they'd visited in Human history? Or even before? Perhaps they had been other places in the Solar System?

That eventually got us to the ancient astronauts theory, popularized by Erich Von Daniken in his book *'Chariots of the Gods.'* Daniken's book is a whole different bushel of crazy.

But serious speculators went a step further - the vales of time were vast. If aliens did exist, and traveled here, they could have done so at any point in Earth's history, perhaps before Humans had even evolved. If so, there was very little chance their traces would be found on Earth - we have weather, erosion, a very active chemistry and a constantly changing landscape.

But out in space? Park a spaceship or a landing module on the moon, or some other dead world, it might last a very very long time. Not forever, but a long time compared to Earth.

So the thinking was, if we were going to seriously look for traces of alien visitation, we should look out across the solar system, where relics thousands or millions or tens of millions of years might be preserved, waiting for someone to find them.

That's not actually bad thinking, it's definitely got some plausibility going for it. And people like Sagan and others were seriously kicking these ideas around.

The science fiction writer Arthur C. Clarke played with the idea as early as 1948, in the Sentinel, a story where explorers discover an alien Pyramid on the moon, and in 1953, in a story called Jupiter Five, where he speculated that Jupiter's innermost moon was actually a derelict alien spacecraft. These ideas would be picked up and adapted by Stanley Kubrick in his movie, 2001: A Space Odyssey.

The ideas had real currency, so much so that they became a staple of science fiction writers. Kubrick's 2001 A Space Odyssey revolves around a couple of ancient monoliths hidden on the moon and around Jupiter. The television show Doctor Who presciently did a serial - Pyramids of Mars in 1975.

So if Carl Sagan was pointing out a couple of unusually large, unusually symmetrical and triangular Martian pyramids with apparently straight edges... Yeah, that was in the back of his mind. He was definitely raising the possibility.

Now, if that had been the whole of it, it would have never amounted to much.

The Face on Mars

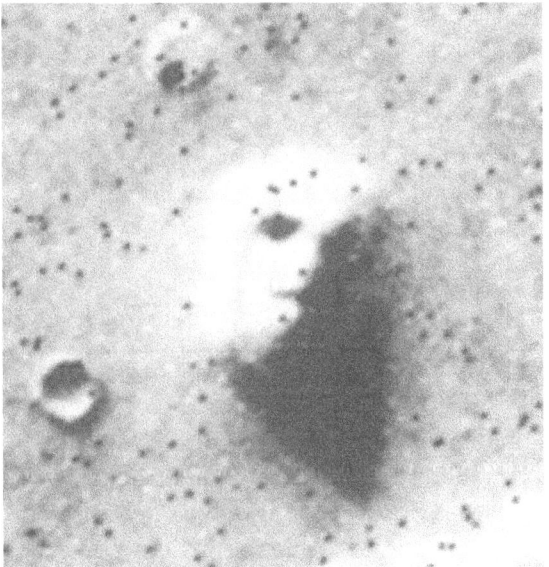

In 1976, there was the Viking mission to Mars. The headline grabbing part of the show was the Viking Lander, an instrument package which landed on the surface, giving us our first pictures of the Martian landscape (gravel and rocks). But the other part of the Viking mission was an orbital satellite that began the process of photographing and mapping the Martian surface in far more detail than terrestrial astronomers ever could, and more comprehensively than the Mariner probes.

Among the images sent back was a stretch of landscape in the northern hemisphere, in a region called Cydonia, which contained a two kilometer long rocky outcrop that suggested a Humanoid Face.

The resemblance was immediately noticed by the NASA personnel at the Jet Propulsion Laboratory who displayed it at a press conference. At that point, there was no thought that it might be artificial. It was just something along the lines of *"Check out this wacky trick of light and shadow, doesn't it look like a face?"*

Then later on Vincent DiPietro and Gregory Molenaar, two computer scientists working at the Goddard Space Flight Center came across it again. They went searching and later found another image of the Face that had been taken under different lighting conditions. That was suggestive. If it was just a trick of light and shadow, then that mirage should vanish when the sun's angle and the light was different. It kept looking like a face.

Eventually, DiPietro and Molenaar, found a total of six pictures, two fairly high resolution, others much lower grade, all at different angles of orientation, light and shadow. It kept looking like a face. That was impressive.

They put the images through computer enhancement which seemed to reveal bilateral symmetry, genuine physical features resembling eyes, a nose, and a mouth, and persistence of these details at different angles of sun and shadow. They eventually published their work as a monograph, '*Unusual Martian Surface Features'* in 1980.

This was followed up by Dr. Mark Carlotto who used single-image shape from shading techniques demonstrating that the Face was not a trick of light and shadow, but a three-dimensional landform. Enhanced image processing by Carlotto suggested the presence of an eye socket in the shadowed side, as well as detail in the mouth that is suggestive of teeth.

Things were getting very strange.

Finding the Great D&M Pyramid

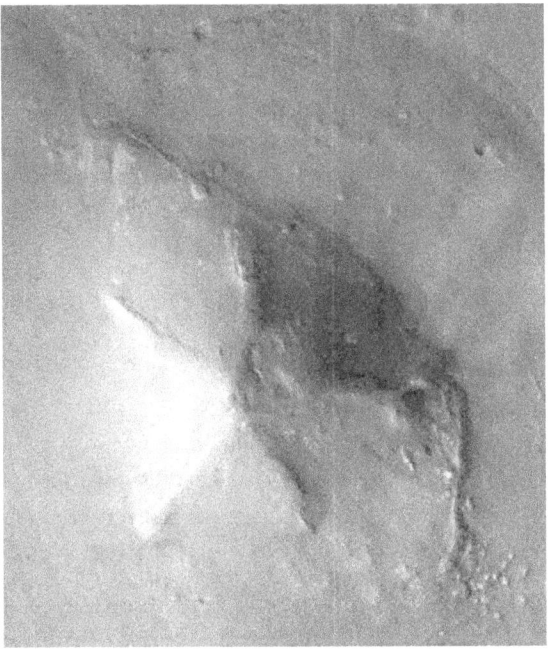

With all the attention on the Face, researchers began to look at other structures in the region. It stood to reason. If the Face was an artificial construct, didn't that imply the possible, even likely existence of other artificial constructs? And if there were, wouldn't the best place to look for them be in the region of the Face? On Earth, massive ceremonial structures like Pyramids or Temples often oriented on each other, cities or temple complexes were organized for sight lines. Would that be true here?

DiPietro and Molenaar looked around the vicinity, and they zeroed in on a large starfish shaped rock or hill, three kilometers across and one kilometer tall, to the south of the face. This object would eventually be called the D&M Pyramid.

The front of the D&M Pyramid, oriented towards the face, features two congruent angles, with two larger congruent angles forming the sides, and a final angle forming the rear. The pyramid appeared to have five straight corners, apart from distortion of what seemed to be an impact crater further to the same side.

It wasn't a perfectly symmetrical pyramid in the sense that each angle was the same. But here is the thing, the different angles of the Pyramid seemed to show a series of mathematical relationships and proportions.

Now, the Face was weird and inexplicable. But the pyramid was something else. An intelligent species will have math, they will employ that math building and operating within mathematical relationships. The D&M pyramid was actually more suggestive of intelligent construction than the Face. Hypothetically, erosion could weather a rock into a face. But it was much harder to explain a series of mathematical ratios incorporated into a pyramid.

The geometric regularity of the D&M Pyramid, together with its apparent proximity to and alignment with other features in Cydonia was strongly suggestive. The Pyramid was the strangest object in Cydonia.

Cydonia Gets Crowded

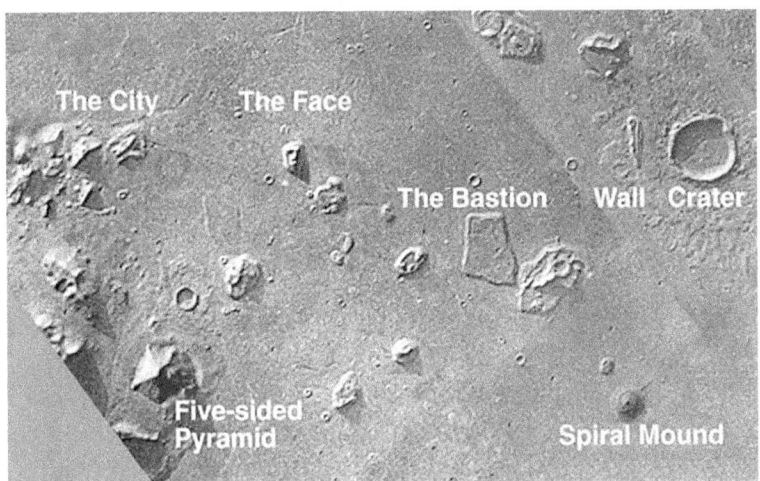

Into the mix came, Richard Hoagland, a science journalist, inspired by the work of DiPietro and Molenaar. He started digging into the imagery himself and noticed a cluster of objects later named the "City", that had a rectilinear arrangement and an apparent orientation to the Face.

The Face's profile seemed to line up with the City's major axis, as if it was designed to be viewed from there. Hoagland claimed that a square arrangement of objects in the center of the City, that he called the "City Square", marked the exact midpoint along the City's major axis, and would have served as an excellent vantage point for a sight line to the Face.

Okay. Maybe. But if you just started looking at rocks on a beach, or in a gravel quarry, you could project orientations and geometric or suggestive shapes. The approach was not too far from shooting an arrow randomly and then running up and drawing a bull's eye where it landed.

But the fact was that there were two very strange objects in the neighborhood, the Face and the Pyramid, and that was very suggestive, so that seemed to warrant taking a close look at suspicious or unusual features in the region.

In 1983, Hoagland organized and led the "Independent Mars Investigation", bringing together specialists in image processing, geology, architecture, and anthropology who studied these objects in greater detail.

Hoagland noticed that another edge of the D&M Pyramid seemed to point towards an unusually shaped round hill that lies to the east of the city on the same latitude as the city square that was named the "Tholus".

Another very unusual structure, which appeared to be roughly triangular with sloping sides was named the "Fortress." All in all, within the local region, Cydonia seemed to be chock full of oddly shaped structures, that all appeared to be in alignment with each other. That was compelling. Odd structures? Okay. Odd structures in alignment? That was suspicious.

Another researcher, Stanley McDaniels came along, noticing small mounds scattered through the Cydonia region, which appeared to have oddly symmetrical geographical relationships to each other, and the various larger landforms. This mound geography seemed strongly indicative of deliberate planning and purpose.

The Cydonia region is adjacent to a lowland formation called the Acidalia Planitae. As more satellites and probes have been sent to study Mars from orbit and with surface probes, the history and shape of the planet has become clearer.

Mars is actually a lopsided world, forty per cent of the planet, the northern hemisphere is a smooth region with very little cratering, roughly three kilometers lower than the southern hemisphere. The southern hemisphere, on the other hand, is heavily cratered, almost a completely different landscape.

Apart from these two halves of a strangely divided planet, there are two colossal impact basins, Argyre and Hellas in the southern hemisphere, a massive uplifted region called the Tharsis bulge, a massive canyon known as the Valles Marinis, and the remnants of dead volcanoes in Tharsis and a region called Elysium.

The current theories harken back to the 19th century, the thinking is that Mars once had a mighty polar ocean in the northern hemisphere, accounting for the lower level and the lack of craters. Mars was once a warm wet world not unlike Earth, billions of years ago. But then, its magnetic field died, and the relentless solar winds stripped the atmosphere and dried up the ocean.

All this, billions of years ago.

Which brings us back to Cydonia. Cydonia literally sits at the edge of a vanished Martian sea. It's a kind of borderland region.

Now on Earth, most of our civilizations and cities have been situated near seas or major river systems. Water is the source of life, after all, and it's also a major means of transportation. So if Cydonia was an ancient artificial complex, it might make sense to be in proximity to a Martian sea.

On the other hand, these sorts of borderlands between land and sea, are also where you'll get a lot of erosion and strange landforms coming into being naturally. Go up the New England and Maritime coasts, where the Appalachians meet the Atlantic, you get a lot of very strange formations - natural arches, flowerpot rocks, etc. So Cydonia is exactly the sort of place you'd get a lot of strange landforms and bizarre or unusual geological features as the receding ocean ate away at the landscape.

Utopia, Inca City and More Faces on Mars

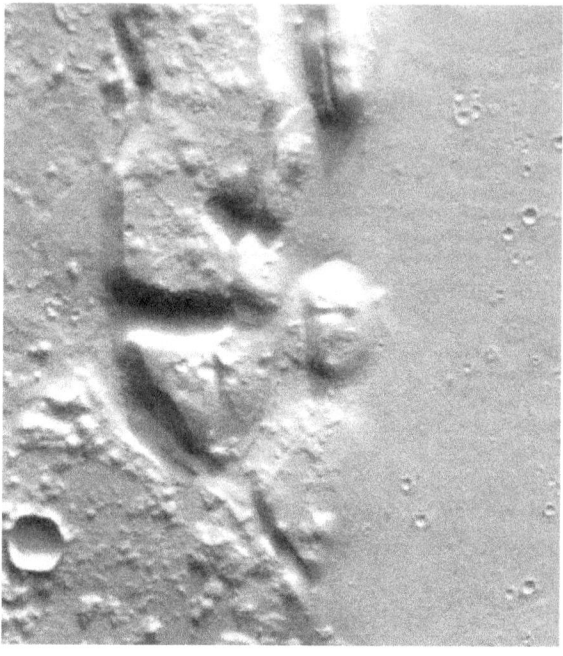

Going on the assumption that the Cydonia site might be artificial, researchers reasoned that if there was one site, there might be others. How to find it though? Mars is a big place. Taking the cue that Cydonia lay next to a lowland, or possible Martian Sea, they opted to follow the 'coastline' - the boundary line between highland and lowland.

This search took them to Utopia Planitae, and what appeared to be a second face, and another anomalous object they called the 'Tie.' This second 'face' resembled the Cydonia face, showing symmetry, and similar size and proportions.

On the downside, it lacked the resolution of the Cydonia face. Neither the image quality, and the 'facial features' themselves were as striking, and unlike the Cydonia face, there weren't multiple images with different angles and lighting to test against. So the quality was lacking.

But it was very suggestive. The way science works is you take data, form a hypothesis, and then look for ways to test it. This is what happened here: They formed a hypothesis, came up with a test, and that lead them to the Utopia site.

The case for a Martian civilization got a little bit stronger.

Attention turned to another unusual feature, dubbed 'Inca City' this was an area of intersecting dunes, crossing each other at perpendicular angles, forming rectangles. It was almost like a city grid.

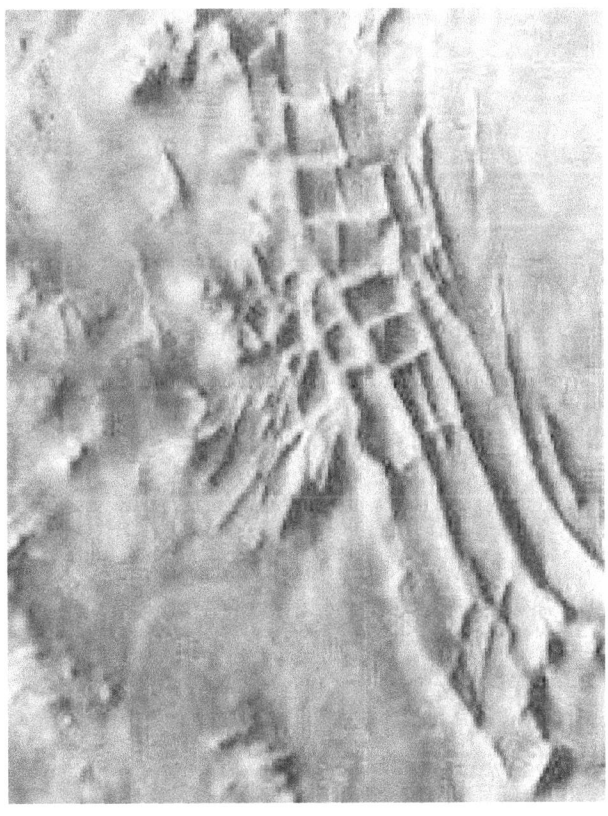

And yes, by golly, in the top left corner of the 'city' there was something that looked like yet another face. If you looked at it just right.

On another location, a mesa was dubbed the 'King's Face' because although it seemed to have face-like features, its forehead projected into and merged with the rock.

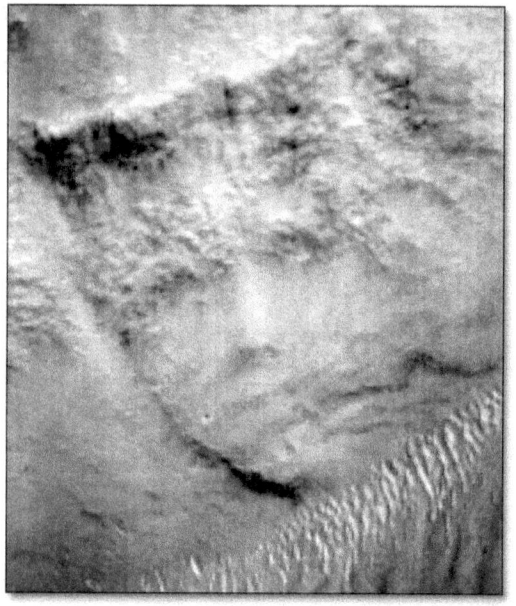

So we were now up to four 'faces' on Mars, all to relatively colossal scale, a kilometer or greater, all similar as if deriving from the same artistic style.

The Cydonia face was by far the best and clearest, the most 'genuine' appearing, and it was the one with the most images. And it led the way. If the Cydonia face was artificial, then each of the other three would need a very careful look. If it was natural, then all the rest were almost certainly the same.

Following on and with all of this was a flurry of researchers, in and out of the Enterprise Project. Some were serious professionals, others were fanciful amateurs, pouring over images from Mars, looking for anything that seemed anomalous. If a hill or mound seemed to show facets or straight angled slopes, it was given a name like 'Citadel' and marked out.

By the late 1990s, interest was at a fever pitch and there was an active movement to get NASA to train its cameras on suspect areas. Luckily for them, Mars Global Surveyor was on its way, to take the most comprehensive orbital mapping of the red planet yet.

The Martian Satellite, Phobos. Artificial?

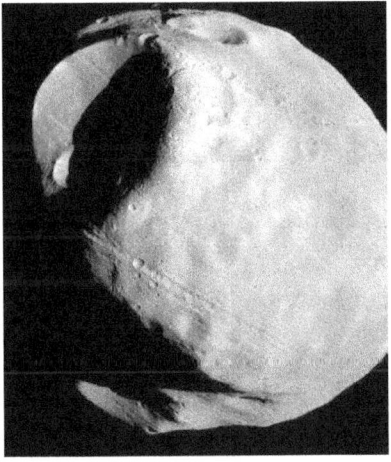

While all the fooferaw was going on with canals between the 1840s and 1950s and then a generation later with Faces and Pyramids on the surface of Mars between the 1970s and the 1990s, the Martian satellites themselves were the subject of attention.

Actually, there are a lot of peculiarities to Phobos and Deimos in popular culture. One of these is that the existence of the two Martian moons was actually predicted by Jonathan Swift in

Gulliver's Travels in 1726, a full 151 years before astronomers discovered them in 1877. In the section on Laputa, a floating city, he wrote in unnerving detail of these moons.

"They have likewise discovered two lesser stars, or satellites, which revolve about Mars; whereof the innermost is distant from the centre of the primary planet exactly three of his diameters, and the outermost, five; the former revolves in the space of ten hours, and the latter in twenty-one and a half; so that the squares of their periodical times are very near in the same proportion with the cubes of their distance from the centre of Mars; which evidently shows them to be governed by the same law of gravitation that influences the other heavenly bodies."

A pretty good guess. Phobos actually orbits 5,827 miles from Mars, or 1.4 rather than 3 diameters, and its orbit takes 7.66 hours, not 10; while Deimos orbits approximately 14,580 miles from the Martian surface, or 3.5 rather than 5 diameters, and has an orbital period of 30.35 hours, not 21.5.

Not exactly close, but definitely in the ballpark.

This seems startling. But Swift didn't have any extraterrestrial inside knowledge. This was post-Galileo, so Swift already knew about Saturn's rings and Jupiter's four large moons. Back then, there were a lot of mystical ideas of symmetry. Venus had no moon. Earth had one. Jupiter had four. Mars was right between Earth and Jupiter, so it just made sense, in symmetrical terms, that Mars should have two. It was a ratio. Presumably, by the ratio, Saturn should have Eight.

And of course, since the Moons weren't visible, Swift decided that they had to be very small and very close. He was a decent mathematician, acquainted with the science of the day. So he just got out his pencil and did some reasonable calculations as to what they had to be like.

Once discovered in 1877, Phobos and Deimos were deemed to be very peculiar moons indeed. Their orbits and their sizes were quickly determined. They turned out to be small fast objects whizzing around their planet. They were ripe for speculation.

Their orbits, their sizes and dimensions, their high albedo or reflectivity all prompted one Soviet astrophysicist named Iosef Shklovsky to speculate that the Martian moons might well be artificial structures. He based this in part, on studies of Phobos orbit which he felt were not sustainable for a natural body.

Now the case for Phobos, based on 'impossible orbital eccentricities' which suggested that it was a hollow body rather than a solid one, seems to be one of those conclusive things. A hollow body would mass much less than a solid one, and its mass would be distributed differently. You could then dope this out by carefully studying the orbital permutations. As pure mathematics, it would admit to no errors. Except they got it wrong, the calculations were discredited.

Among his reasons were, Shklovsky stated Phobos was being *"slowed by electromagnetic drag and tidal friction more than was possible was an actual solid moon."*

Given that Mars no longer has a live magnetic field, I find myself wondering what 'electromagnetic drag' he was talking about. But you know, that's Soviet science for you. They couldn't have known at the time that there was no magnetic field and therefore no electromagnetic drag. He also based his findings on what was then believed to be the thickness of the Martian atmosphere, which seriously overestimated the actual case.

Now, this finding, sometime in the back in 1958, was no big deal. The Soviet scientists were always coming up with goofy theories, including the Lysenkoist approach to evolution, and the notion that Tungaska was a spaceship explosion.

Soviet science of the 50's and 60's seems to be a wilder and hairier place than in the West, largely because Soviet scientists had to spend a lot of time impressing non-scientists in the party establishment, rather than each other. Thus, a wild and flashy theory would get you further politically, than a conservative theory supported by proof.

Shklovsky was right about one thing, though, Phobos orbit is not sustainable. It's slowly spiraling in towards Mars to the point where it will eventually crash. There's some dispute as to how that is going to happen. The best guess is that it will probably break up first, torn apart by tidal forces. So instead of hitting Mars like a 14 mile wide bomb, it may fall as a string of much smaller pieces. Or it may end up as a ring around the world, like Saturn's.

Oddly, Shklovsky found adherents in the west. In particular, a Dr. Fred Singer, science advisor to President Eisenhower, signed on in 1960, supporting the Shklovsky theory of an artificial Martian moon.

Now, I'm not sure what Singer's field of specialty was. But judging from this corker about Phobos: *"Its purpose would probably be to sweep up radiation in the Mars' atmosphere, so that Martians could safely operate around their planet."*

I wouldn't put too much faith in the guy. His conception of a cosmic radiation hoover, while picturesque, is staggeringly illiterate.

Astonishingly, a few years later, in 1963, Raymond H. Wilson Jr., Chief of Applied Mathematics at NASA, climbed on board, stating that *"Phobos might be a colossal base orbiting Mars."*

He also stated that NASA itself was considering the possibility. That's pretty bold. Of course, this was very near the height of Flying Saucer fever, when everyone was half expecting one to land on the front lawn of the White House.

All I can say is that this was before the Pioneer fly-bys, and notions of Martian canals were still lingering, hanging on by their fingernails, but not quite completely dismissed.

Nevertheless, the subject faded away, relegated to the freakier corners of fringe science and mysticism. I can't find any further serious or semi-serious references to possible artificiality of Phobos based on orbital mechanics after 1967-69. Which, coincidentally, would be about the same time that Russian and American space probes were arriving and would to provide accurate readouts on Martian conditions and the best data on orbits yet.

So, my assumption is that the orbit hypothesis simply evaporated. The data was refined, the mathematics were double checked, and voila, it turned out that there wasn't anything patently artificial in Phobos orbit at all.

Meanwhile, a few years later, as pictures from space probes began to come in, it became clear that Phobos was a lot weirder looking than anyone had imagined.

For one thing, there was an immense deep crater in one side of the moon, something that might have looked suspiciously like an airlock. For another, there was a series of reasonably straight, reasonably parallel lines or grooves streaking across the surface.

Unfortunately, these images came out at an inopportune time. Well after the death of Shklovsky's hollow satellite theory, and well before the Cydonia theories. So, for the most part, Phobos remarkable features were considered 'remarkable' and nothing more.

Of course, it was inevitable that Phobos would get swept up in the Cydonia theories, particularly as the fringe theories lost any basis in reality or and became outright projection fantasies.

The favorite loony theory appears to be that there was a possible spaceship or foreign object hanging around Phobos that destroyed one of Earth's space probes. This is less Cydonia, and much more conspiracy theory.

But it all intersects. Other researchers have concentrated on peculiar 'crater chains' or anomalous boulders on the surface of Phobos, looking for signs of artificiality. After all, if there had been aliens building on Mars, it's likely that they were messing around in other parts of the Solar system. Even Earth's moon was the subject of deep scrutiny.

Who Were These Martians?

By 1998, some four regions and perhaps two dozen or more individual structures had been identified that showed features indicating a possibly artificial origin.

These included not one but four apparent faces on Mars, all showing roughly similar features, as if carved by the same artistic tradition. Other structures included several pyramid shaped objects. Some of these objects appeared to consistently express symmetry, pass fractal analysis and even exhibit mathematical ratios. Many appeared to be aligned or related to each other. All of which raised the inevitable, impossible possibility that someone had built them.

There was an anomalous satellite around Mars, Phobos, which might just possibly be showing signs of being artificial.

On Earth's moon, detailed examination and re-examination seemed to show possible artificial structures. Even other objects in the Solar System, particularly moons around Saturn or Jupiter invited scrutiny.

There was a complex of serious people conducting investigations, academics, computer imaging specialists, fractal technicians, attempting a very disciplined examination.

Around them was a penumbra of flakier or fringy types, increasingly less disciplined, more reckless. This was the Martian movement, energized by the prospect that not only had life once existed on Mars, but an actual civilization that had left monuments.

But who?

Or what?

The faces appeared to suggest a Humanoid origin. The presence of Cydonia and Utopia at the edges of an ancient Martian shoreline from its wet days suggested something impossibly ancient. Had there been indigenous Martian inhabitants billions of years ago?

Or perhaps more recent aliens stopping there so much later? Was the Face a message deliberately left behind for Humanity?

If it was artificial, who or what had built it, and why? There was really no way to know, even guesswork boggled.

Who were these alleged Martians?

I suppose the safe answer was that there wasn't enough information to speculate.

Seriously, you can't tell the race, or the hair colour or skin tone of someone who builds a Pyramid. All you can tell is that they built a Pyramid. The only things anyone had to go on were landforms. Any guesses after that were just guesses.

But the more honest answer, I think, was that many of the researchers - DiPietro, Molenaar, Carlotto, McDaniels and others, were pretty serious professionals and this investigation of Martian landforms wasn't doing their careers any good. Hoagland was a bit of a showman, but had some credentials as a science journalist apparently. But their consensus seemed to be it was safest to just stick to trying to analyze the anomalies.

Any speculation past that was likely to get you a short bus ride to crazy town, permanent association with the lunatic fringe, and no hope of being taken seriously.

Still, from our vantage point, it's worth a look. There aren't many possibilities.

One option is that in Mars wet period, billions of years ago, life not only evolved on Mars, but evolved considerably faster, and briefly produced a civilization that left astounding megalithic ruins behind. And somehow, by insane coincidence, they were Humanoid?

That seemed farfetched.

Another possibility is that within the last couple of million years, or the last few tens of thousands, Humans, or a cousin or ancestor species, slapped a civilization together, somehow got to Mars and left a bunch of megalithic ruins, while leaving no trace on Earth. That at least explained why the Cydonia face and its peers looked like us. Because they were us.

That's also pretty far-fetched.

Finally, the guess was that genuine aliens from another star system came along. There's no other place in the Solar System that had any chance at advanced life, so by default, it would have to be interstellar travelers. They built Cydonia, Utopia and potentially other works on Mars, and perhaps possibly on Earth's moon or even Phobos itself. Eventually they vanished, either going extinct or going home. And they built the Cydonia Face as a message to the hopeful primates of the third planet. Which was really nice of them. Their way of saying hello, just in case we ever got civilized enough to find it.

Equally improbable.

It's likely there are other theories, of course, including Murder-Chickens from the PETM, but those would be the main ones.

The thing was, there wasn't sufficient information to even guess as to which theory might be more plausible.

But any such speculation was curiously absent. In that strange land of speculation, somewhere between hard science, and utter fantasy, an entire mysterious Martian civilization had built up, a potentiality that the serious researchers avoided even guessing about.

1998 – Global Surveyor and the End of the Martians

And then, with Mars Global Surveyor, in 1998, just like that, it was gone. The Global Surveyor photographed some 98% of Mars, including most of the anomalous areas, with resolutions reaching down to a pixel for every two meters. That means that if somehow a Bison got loose on Mars, the Global Surveyor would have registered it. If a family went on vacation on Mars in an RV it would have shown up on Global Surveyor.

In fact, Global Surveyor and successors have actually spotted the remains of previous Martian probes, particularly the ones that crashed.

We got to see the Cydonia face in far more detail than ever before, and at that high level of resolution, it didn't look much like a face at all. When the Global Surveyor photographs emerged, what we saw was not just the face under different angles and lighting, but the face at a degree of fine resolution we'd never seen before. The resolution was something like a hundred times more detailed.

Under that level of detail, even though Carlotto's basic structure and contour analysis held up, it seemed much more clear and likely that the Face was simply an eroded mesa that had some face-like features. But there wasn't anything that screamed intelligent construction.

The probability of the Face being an artificial structure dropped substantially to relatively negligible levels.

The Face appeared to be an eroded hill. The D&M pyramid on close resolution simply was not nearly as symmetrical as it had seemed. It didn't have straight sides, or clear angles. All those geometric ratios didn't hold up.

The mounds were not anomalies, but merely outcroppings of underlying geology. It turned out to be nothing at all. Overall, the case is far less persuasive than it was.

I think that we can pretty much dismiss the Face and all the other Martian anomalies at this point. We've got very good pictures at extremely high resolution, and under the current state of technology and knowledge, they don't hold up.

The pyramids weren't pyramids, just hills sculpted by a billion years of wind. The faces and all the other anomalies weren't faces or fortresses or arranged complexes, just products of erosion and shadows.

All those apparent potentially artificial objects? Weren't.

If there were huge artificial structures on Mars, the Global Surveyor would have not only identified them, but a myriad of new structures. With more and more resolution, we would have seen more persuasive detail on the major anomalies, they would have shown more signs of artificial construction. And even more importantly, more detail should have revealed more and more smaller new structures: Roads, grids, baseball diamonds, parks, cyclotrons, spaceports the remains of buildings, harbours.

It didn't.

The closer we looked, the more it was just rocks and gravel.

Phobos is just a rock tumbling through the Martian sky on its way to doom, tens of millions of years from now. We have pictures. It's just a rock.

Elsewhere, satellites have mapped and photographed the Moon to an even greater level of detail than Mars. We can identify the sites of the moon landings. There's no sign of any alien construction, whatsoever, on the moon.

As to the rest of the Solar System, there's a lot that is fantastic and remarkable, but nothing that points to artificiality. We've tracked a lot of asteroids and meteors, but we've never seen anything that's moved in ways inconsistent with orbital mechanics. Everything is drifting, nothing is moving on its own.

There's nothing out there. Or if there is, we haven't found any sign of it. So far as we know, we're alone here, and we've always been.

I remember feeling a slight sadness. There was something romantic and mysterious, even promising, about the Face on Mars. There was something compelling and intriguing to the thought that there might have been someone else out there, a city on another world.

In contrast, a rock is just a rock. But I'll take it. From the right angles, with the right shadow, the Face on Mars is still beguiling and intriguing to me, even if it is just a rock.

Beauty is in the eye of the beholder; it doesn't have to be sculpted by hand. A natural landform which, from some perspectives is a dead ringer for a Human face is to me, marvelous in and of itself.

So marvelous, that I half suspect that if Humans ever settle and colonize Mars, it might end up being a tourist attraction. Perhaps it will even be carved, to emphasize the resemblance a bit more and squeeze out a few more tourist dollars. People are like that.

Or perhaps the religiously minded, now that it's all proven to be natural, will see the hand of God at work, and find it miraculous and a proof of their faith. People are like that too.

But it's all definitely natural. At least, as far as we can currently determine without going there and kicking around gravel looking for the remains of billion year old chisels and bulldozers. Not likely to find them.

The truth of Mars is that the planet's surface area is the equivalent of all the land masses of Earth rolled into a ball - approximately 50 million square miles. That's a lot of territory.

And it's mostly just rocks and gravel. There's some ice in caps at the poles, both water and frozen carbon dioxide. And there's sand dunes, or dust dunes, and craters, lots of craters. But let's be serious, it's just gravel. Rocks. Large rocks, small rocks, all sizes of rocks. Mars is a dead dry world, and it has been for billions of years.

Once upon a time Mars was a geologically live world with a thick atmosphere, an ocean, an active magnetic field. But that was long long ago, it's been a sterile husk for a long time.

There was never a civilization there. Perhaps there had been life there once, but if there was, it's likely long extinct. If anything yet persists, then it's likely no more than bacteria. But no one had ever built monuments there.

Billions of years is a long time, and fifty million square miles is a lot of space, and over all that time and space, out of millions of rocks and landforms, erosion sculpted a few into things that we thought we recognized.

Fair enough. We looked, we thought we saw something, we looked harder, and it turned out to be nothing. The titanic Martian pyramids and monuments existed only in a window in our observations and imaginations. I'm okay with that, actually.

I would say that before Global Surveyor though, the case for the Face was very good.

Part of it was the Face itself which showed consistent characteristics of symmetry and proportion through several photos under different angles and lighting conditions.

Part of it was that it wasn't the only face - there was also the Utopia Face, the King's Face and the Inca City face, all of substantially less quality and persuasiveness, all much more likely to be natural illusions, but collectively all on a similar scale and with an a similar apparent 'artistic' tradition - they resembled each other. One face might well be a fluke.

Recurrence of similar sized and shaped face-like structures, that was just peculiar.

Further, the Cydonia region contained not just the face, but an association of other peculiar landforms. There was the five-sided D&M Pyramid whose proportions appeared to embody mathematical ratios. There was the inexplicable crater pyramid, an apparently impossible structure poised on the lip of a crater. There was the 'Fortress', a three-sided hollowed area. There was the City Complex, a group of five pyramids or faceted structures. And there were the mounds. The apparent alignments of the features with each other. In short, there was a lot of very strange objects which seemed organized together in an artificial way. There was a lot that suggested we were looking at non-natural structures.

The evidence justified not necessarily forming a conclusion, but further investigation, taking a closer look. That was basically the position of DiPietro, Molenaar, Carlotto, McDaniels and others. The hypothesis should be tested.

In 1998, the Mars Global Surveyor in the process of mapping the entire planet in detail ended up taking that closer look.

That's how science works. You take the data you have, analyze it, form a hypothesis and then you test it.

I still think we should actually go and poke around Cydonia. I don't expect to find an abandoned alien base. But Cydonia appears to straddle the boundary lines between the Martian highlands and lowlands, the shores of the hypothetical Martian ocean, and the same geological processes that produced those bizarre landforms are likely to tell us a lot about Martian history and geology. That's worthwhile.

There are still a few diehards running around, poring over Global Surveyor photos. Minutely examining each picture sent back from the red planet by rovers, growing excited over oddly shaped rocks or suspicious shadows. The professionals and serious researchers have departed long ago.

The field is left to excitable amateurs, and rather than megalithic landforms, now they scrutinize ground level photos, hoping to discern a recognizable tool or fossil. No one takes them too seriously. I don't. But I respect their enthusiasm.

And they're right about one thing. Sagan himself was correct, way back in the day: If aliens do exist and have come by, it's far more likely that they passed through sometime in Earth's history, than they just happened to show up now.

So it's not unreasonable to peer at the solar system, looking for anomalies somewhere out there that might suggest there's someone else.

Some of the methods used to find and eventually disprove the Martian cities have been used here on Earth, identifying ancient trading paths in Saudi Arabia, lost cities in the Mayan jungle, the remnants of an unimagined civilization in the Amazon rain forest.

These methods worked on Earth, and they were correctly applied to Mars and legitimately raised the prospect that the structures we saw there were not natural.

Then they were applied in greater degree and more detail, and on further examination, these same methods eventually disproved the hypothesis, well that's just science working as it should.

Recently, there's been speculation from a few astronomers that the Interstellar fragments, 1I/Oumuamua and 3I/Atlas might have been artificial. That's unprovable one way or the other. But there's no actual persuasive evidence to support artificial origin, and claims just don't hold up. So frankly, I doubt it.

The truth is, short of extraterrestrials introducing themselves with a knock at the door, we don't have any clear idea of how we would detect intelligent life. Scanning the skies for radio signals, or for anomalous cosmic bodies like Tabby's Star?

Or maybe somewhere in the solar system, or perhaps beyond, we'll find an asteroid that doesn't move right?

Or some impossible symmetrical structure, or buried anomaly on some world or moon? We're guessing and hoping. That's okay.

If we actually make it to other star systems in any meaningful way, we're much more likely to encounter ruins than live civilizations. The techniques and analysis employed, and the choices that were made, point the way to the sort of tests we'll have to rely on.

Until it actually happens, the odds are immensely against any of that. So I don't expect anything. Still, who knows? But the Martians? They lived only in our minds.

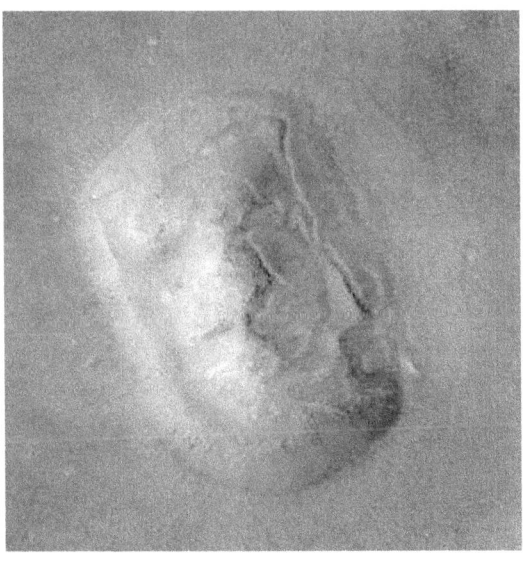

Godzilla and the Original Cinematic Universe

Birth of an Atomic Nightmare

Okay, here's where it all starts. First, you had the Lost World, a silent stop motion epic in 1925. Then you have King Kong - big movie in 1933. King Kong got re-issued every few years, in 1938, in 1942, and in 1952, and for that matter, in 1956 when it was licensed to television.

Why all the releases? It was a different world. Back then VHS, DVD, Blu-Ray, Streaming, none of that existed. Even television wasn't a thing. The only place to see a movie was the movie theater. There was no place else. Once a movie came and went through the theaters, it was gone, unless they'd bring it back after the first run for some reason.

But memories would fade. People's recollections would become sentimental. And there'd be some people who just hadn't seen it the first time around. So if a movie was a big enough hit, then every few years it would be re-released to the theaters to hoover up some more dollars.

In 1952, King Kong got re-released and suddenly, it was a huge hit once again, a top grossing film.

This success inspired the Beast from 20,000 Fathoms in 1953.

That same year, 1953, both Kong and the Beast were distributed in Japan by the film company, Daie. The Japanese were gaga for giant monsters.

In Japan, however, Daie, however, had a rival: Toho Studios. Toho decided to answer Kong and the Beast with their own home-grown giant monster movie, Godzilla. And because they were local, when they were coming up with their monster, consciously or unconsciously, they found themselves looking out their window at the Japan they were living in.

Japan in the 1950s was in a bad place. It had disastrously lost World War II, it wasn't even close, and their antics, when forced to face them, had been pretty shameful. No Empire is nice, but the Japanese in conquering and running their Empire had been brutal. In 1944 and 1945, its cities had been bombed and firebombed to rubble and ashes. The bombing campaigns had culminated in two atomic bombs in Hiroshima and Nagasaki, a terrifying new world-changing technology. After surrender, for the first time in history, Japan had been under foreign occupation, by the United States from 1945 until 1952, another major kick in the collective nuts. Benign but still it was occupation. The Japanese were a people in collective trauma.

In 1954 the Japanese fishing boat, the Lucky Dragon, and its crew of twenty-three were contaminated by radiation and fallout from the Bikini Atoll Hydrogen bomb test. This incident on its own was something of a national trauma, a PTSD flashback to Hiroshima and Nagasaki.

Throw in a front row seat on the fall of China to communism in 1949, the Korean War from 1950 to 1953, the Cold War and the developing specter of World War III and nuclear holocaust... well, that's a lot to deal with.

So yes, the Japanese were a traumatized people, they had some issues to work through. There was a lot of free-floating psychic baggage in the nation, waiting for a concept to act as a lightning rod. The idea of an unstoppable monster coming out of nowhere to lay waste to the country, a monster that could represent everything bad that had happened to Japan; that was a potent attractor, a major lightning rod for psychic baggage.

Godzilla wasn't just a run of the mill monster movie; it was a reflection of accumulated free-floating national trauma.

Godzilla was a metaphor for the atomic bomb, not just in an abstract quoting Hindu scripture way, but in a getting incinerated and having your flesh melting off kind of way. There was a viscerality to Godzilla's terror, an immediacy, which tapped into national trauma. The movie's started with a direct allusion to the Lucky Dragon incident and went on to portray the growing dread of an unstoppable force approaching and the utter despair and helplessness of seeing a city destroyed around you.

Ultimately, Godzilla is destroyed by a remorseful pacifist with a weapon too terrible ever to be used again, an unsubtle allusion to nuclear weapons. It was something that the Japanese, had definite feelings about.

Of course, as a kid, I didn't pick up on any of that, I was just too young. I simply loved Godzilla movies. Destroying Tokyo looked like a lot of fun. It turns out a lot of people did, and not just in Japan. In North America and Europe, where either we didn't feel the same existential trauma, or in a post-war world, we had our own worries, expressed in metaphors and movie monsters.

But there's a thing, I don't know, call it sincerity, call it authenticity. If something has real emotional power, if something is tapping into deep wells, I think you can feel it, even if those aren't your wells, even if you're not directly connected to that trauma or fixation.

There was something ferocious in Godzilla, something honest, and dark and authentic going on with the film makers. It resonated with Americans, particularly with Raymond Burr inserted as a Canadian witness to devastation. In America, there was a flurry of giant monster movies, although eventually they all faded away. But Godzilla stuck around, even the Americans could feel there was something powerful there.

The Stirrings of a Cinematic Universe

Godzilla was a big hit in Japan and America both, big enough that Toho decided to make another one. Godzilla came back.

Godzilla Raids Again, came out in 1955, pitting Godzilla against another giant Monster, Anguiras. It ends badly for both monsters, Anguiras gets its neck snapped, Godzilla is apparently killed by burying it in a glacier. It didn't have the same mythic power as the first.

After that, they let Godzilla rest for a few years. After all, the character had been killed off twice in two consecutive movies. Much more of that, people are going to start to notice.

But hey, Toho had the idea now - giant monsters sold! They followed up with Rodan, a tragic love story about a pair of giant Pterodactyls in 1956. Toho threw a giant robot into 1957's The Mysterians, just to juice it up. Varan came out in 1959, unbelievably, it did not do well. Then Mothra, about a giant moth comes along in 1961.

A name emerged for Toho's giant monsters; they would come to be known collectively as Kaiju.

None of these movies, not even Godzilla Raids Again, tapped into the primordial consciousness of the Japanese the way the first movie had. These weren't atomic monsters mirroring national PTSD, they weren't reflections of the trauma of helpless populations in destroyed cities. Varan was just a big lizard on a rampage. Mothra was a mystical fairy tale of miniature Humans and a giant furry god-butterfly, based on a fantasy novel.

Rodan sort of touched on current issues, a lot of the story builds around deaths in an unsafe mine, reflecting emerging disquiet over industrialization and worker safety, but segues into the story of an aerial destroyer. Compared to Godzilla though, it's unfocused and haphazard. The Mysterians are about encroaching alien invaders and the need for world unity, the giant robot is merely a distraction.

This is significant. Godzilla at its core was really about something: The destructive power of the atom, and in a larger sense, the trauma and destruction of the war. And to a large extent, Godzilla continued to be about something, much more than other monsters, although that 'something' changed over time as attitudes change.

Godzilla was always about the power of the atom, and that gave it a mystique, a presence that nothing else could duplicate. But the Japanese kind of evolved in how they felt about the atom. As the 1950s gave way to the 60s, the national trauma faded, the Japanese became used to a world where the United States was no longer a destroyer but a protector and partner.

Most significantly, the atom was redeemed. Nuclear weapons now protected Japan and nuclear power would come to meet a quarter of Japan's energy needs, reducing dependence on foreigners. As these developments took place, Godzilla moved from a threat to a reluctant defender and eventually to a friend to Humanity.

But arguably, with the exception of Hedorah in the 70s, who clumsily but clearly symbolized toxic pollution in a relentlessly industrializing society, none of the other monsters tapped into any deep well in the public consciousness. Ghidorah might represent China, or Communism, but that was shallow symbolism. There was nothing visceral that haunted people there, it was just an external threat - dangerous but manageable.

Instead, what evolved with Toho was that giant monsters were just... there. Rodan was a holdover from the Mesozoic. So was Gorosaurus, Baragon, Manda, Titanosaurus – all basically prehistoric. Some, like Mothra or the lion-god, King Seesar, were tied to Japanese mysticism. Others like Ghidorah, Gigan, Mechagodzilla were Sci-Fi fantabulous. Creatures like the crayfish, Ebirah or the spider, Kumonga were just out there in lost corners of the world, with no particular reason for existing. Increasingly, in Toho movies, giant monsters were part of the world. Merely holdovers from the deep past or denizens of faraway places.

Of course, if they were all just part of the world in their respective movies, it's not a big leap to see them as all part of the same world. There's the glimmer of a collective universe there. After all, these movies were all set in contemporary Japan. They were, in a sense each pretending to be set in our world, so the same world, over and over.

Also, Toho had all the costumes, the props, the miniature sets just sitting there, waiting to be re-used, home grown intellectual property, with no licensing issues, suit actors, stuntmen and film crews that knew how to build miniature cities and shoot to make guys in suits look like giant monsters. So a collective universe was an easy reach.

Of course, all this was in the future.

King Kong Arrives and Many More Follow

By 1962, Toho figured that seven years had passed, people had forgotten that Godzilla had already been killed twice. Time to bring the Big-G back. The monster-battle shtick had worked reasonably well, time to try it again. This time, the big G faced off against King Kong. And because giant monsters were getting kind of silly, they threw in some comedy. Of course by this time, the audience knew who both Godzilla and Kong were, therefore so did the characters in the movie, contributing to the sense of a monster-filled universe. It was a hit.

A couple of years later in 1964, it was time to do it again. Basically, if you've got a hit, you ride that pony until the legs fall off - and Godzilla had delivered two hits. Toho couldn't walk away from that.

King Kong wasn't available. The rights belonged to RKO. By this time, Toho had built up its own stable of monsters from its other movies, so why not use one of those? Cue Godzilla vs Mothra in 1964, which played in North America as Godzilla versus the Thing. Godzilla was back to being scary and terrifying, there were cute little munchkins, and a giant butterfly. I remember seeing it when I was young and being a bit confused. But the Japanese knew who Mothra was and they loved it. To be fair, it was well made and gripping.

That worked really well, so the same year, they brought back Godzilla, AND Mothra, AND Rodan, and threw in another giant monster - King Ghidorah, a flying, three headed, golden space-dragon, along with an alien subplot. They followed up with pretty much the same movie the very next year, another Godzilla threesome, except with even more aliens, astronauts and Sci-Fi craziness.

This was the mid-sixties, so both the space program and flying saucers were huge in popular culture, there was an almost subliminal sense that actual aliens were just around the corner, and if we didn't meet them here, we were getting ready to go out there to greet them.

More movies followed introducing more giant monsters. Then a few years later, by 1968, Toho released the Avengers movie of its day - Destroy All Monsters, featuring more aliens, more astronauts, and just about every giant monster they'd come up with to date.

Toho's Showa Cinematic Universe emerged, though no one was calling it that back then. It was full of giant monsters, some increasingly friendly to Humanity, some openly hostile. Monster Islands were established where the good monsters would live.

This was a universe with a space program far more advanced than ours and one with Sci-Fi technology, including super-submarines and maser tanks. That turned out to be lucky for us, because this was a universe chock full of lost civilizations and suspiciously Human alien races, most of which were up to no good!

And let's not even mention how we had to save ourselves from the rogue object, Gorath.

No really. Let's not mention that one. It's kind of dumb.

Godzilla, still carrying all its evolving symbolic and metaphoric baggage, was the tentpole character, subsuming all the others and reappearing in movies regularly until Terror of Mechagodzilla in 1975.

Along the way there were more one offs - Atragon in 1963, Frankenstein vs Baragon in 1965, War of the Gargantuas in 1966, King Kong came back on his own in 1967, Space Amoeba was a minor monster mash in 1970. But mainly it was Godzilla, and through the magic of stock footage and recycling suits a recurring pantheon of monsters. Even the one-offs crept into Godzilla's universe.

Yes, Virginia, we had us a cinematic universe, and it was insane.

Now this is the 60s and 70s, the modern Nerd had not been invented yet. So continuity was a pretty loose thing. As one of the producers of Doctor Who used to say back in the 1970s, "Continuity was what we could remember on that particular day."

Like the Marvel Cinematic Universe, it all began with one-off movies for the various characters, albeit in a more unplanned, opportunistic way. But even by the second movie, it was established that Godzilla shared his world with other giant monsters, paving the way for crossovers and implying a monsterverse almost from the start.

In fact, giant monsters were all over the place - on remote Islands, buried in the Earth, the products of mad science, in outer space, all in worlds based on our own, that literally begged for crossovers. This in turn opened the door for other pop-culture Sci-Fi tropes, aliens, astronauts, robots, you name it. The longer things went on, the more opportunity there was to bring them together, building on each other.

Mostly, though, that monsterverse was built on the fact that Toho had all this stock footage, costumes, and their intellectual properties available. And especially because it really sold well. It's not more complicated than that. If the water is good, you keep going back to the well.

Which is what Legendary's monsterverse is doing. Although I suspect that they're much more into selling toys and merchandise than Toho ever thought of doing back then.

Anyway, that's Godzilla's original monsterverse, the Toho Showa era. And now that we're here, let's take some time out and explore all these giant monsters, and the universe they were living in.

First let's look at the monsters, and their common features...

The Properties and Classification of Giant Monsters.

As a bunch, they're a diverse group. At least one, maybe two invertebrates - A giant octopus (or possibly a population of them, they get around), and Hedorah (alternately a space monster).

There are a few arthropods - Ebirah the lobster, Kumonga the spider, Mothra and her larva, Kamacuras a trio of mantises, and Megalon, a sort of beetle.

We have a few Mammals: King Kong, the Ape, whatever King Seesar is (mutant lion?), Maguma the super-walrus, Frankenstein, and the Gargantuas.

One bird type - a super condor from Godzilla vs the Sea Monster, making a blink and you'll miss it appearance, though it returns for a second stock footage appearance in Godzilla's Revenge.

A few robots – Moguera, Mechani-Kong and Mechagodzilla, and a cyborg, Gigan (another space monster).

Mainly though, it's Reptiles: Rodan and Manda, Ghidorah (a space monster) and Godzilla and its ilk.

The Godzilla Style

Actually, a lot of the Reptile Kaiju seem to broadly follow Godzilla's body plan - basically, pseudo-theropods, bipedal with long legs and shorter forelimbs, reptilian tails, long necks, triangular heads, predator teeth, splayed reptilian paws and claws. The pseudo-theropods feature dorsal spines, scutes or fins on their back - upright dorsal plates for Godzilla, wide flat plates for Baragon, spikes spreading out to form a carapace for Varan and Anguiras. Minilla, Gorosaurus and Titanosaurus fit this profile, albeit with minimal dorsal spines.

This profile suggests that either all these animals are from species closely related to Godzilla's. Or possibly that they are all members of Godzilla's species, a species which has a lot of individual variation and diversity.

A few others seem to exist on the edges of the profile. For instance, Anguiras or Baragon are quadrupeds, but their hind legs are significantly longer than their forelimbs, so that they seem to walk on their knees, but overall still fit the body plan.

Gigan is generally considered a cyborg. But there are occasionally mutant 'one eyed' sharks in real life, which are very evocative of Gigan's look. It's possible that Gigan, before he was a cyborg, was a mutant, and his cyclops's one-eye, beak and single digit limbs all relate to a single chromosomal abnormality. In other respects, body plan, dorsal spikes, Reptile tail, triangular head, he's a Godzilla-type.

Another monster, Gabara conforms to many of the features of the Godzilla-type, triangular head, long neck, predator teeth and claws, scaly reptilian form, etc., but has only a vestigial tail, possibly another mutation. Given the extreme diversity of physical expression of Godzilla-forms, Gabara's within the range.

Including the borderline specimens, there are almost as many Godzilla-type Kaiju, as there are other types put together. This is interesting.

We know through almost all the movies that the Kaiju seem to seek each other out to battle. The present distribution of Kaiju types may be the product of long ago conflicts. The Kaiju do seem to love to battle. Did the Godzilla-types wipe out many of their Arthropod, Mammal and Reptile rivals? Perhaps Gigan and Ghidorah are actually refugees from Earth who fled to outer space?

Alternately, maybe there's just something about the Godzilla species, or Godzilla-related species that seemed to be prone to becoming giant monsters, much more than other animals. In-universe Godzilla-types may just have an inherent advantage.

Most likely, in real world terms, it's likely that Godzilla's first movie was just that iconic and influential, sort of the way that once Bela Lugosi did Dracula, movie Vampires for decades kept on wearing tuxedos and cloaks. Or it was the easiest build for a stuntman to wear.

The Kaiju are Big. Really, Really Big.

Insanely big. Ridiculously big. In the Showa universe, Godzilla is 50 meters or 164 feet tall, 100 meters or 324 feet long, and 20,000 tons. Godzilla is at the top end, but not the biggest - Ghidorah is at least a 100 meters tall, has a wingspan of 150 meters and weighs 30,000 tons. Even a relative lightweight, Baragon, stands 25 meters or 82 feet, and weighs 5,000 tons.

Later era versions - the Heisei Godzilla, the Shin Godzilla and the Legendary Godzilla got even bigger, reaching past 100 meters tall. But come on. A hundred and fifty feet and 20,000 tons should be enough for anyone. We'll leave those later versions to their own universes.

Now in comparison cruise ships weigh between 20,000 and 80,000 tons. The Titanic weighed about 45,000 tons. So basically, we have creatures walking around on land in the same weight class as the smaller ocean cruise and freight ships.

That's mind boggling. None of these creatures should even be able to walk. Normal bones and muscle and conventional chemistry can't handle that, that's too much mass to move. Physics and biology aren't just broken, they're mugged, dragged into an alley and bludgeoned with the square cube law until they're bloody messes.

How Many of Them Actually Are There?

Most Kaiju seem singular and unique - literally the only ones of their kind. That's kind of how I saw it as a kid watching these movies. You only see one of each kind to a movie, even where they're crossing over. That may be true, or maybe not. A species of one seems pretty weird.

Godzilla seems definitely killed at the end of its first movie, ending up a flesh-stripped skeleton in Tokyo Bay. But the next movie, there's Godzilla. So either the first one got better, or there's two of them. Minilla is called 'Son of Godzilla' and might be another of Godzilla's species, which would make three.

It's simpler with Mothra who keeps laying eggs and getting killed, the larvae hatch to become the new Mothra. That's one of the very few clear examples of a life cycle in these movies.

We do see Minilla hatch from an egg, and the Kamacuras (giant Mantises), Frankenstein and Gargantuas each start out smaller grow to Kaiju scale.

There are definitely two Rodans in their movie, and an egg, though both Rodans appear to die. So who is the Rodan appearing in the rest of the movies? Is it the egg? Did one of them get better? Both of them recovered and after they just keep trading off in subsequent movies? Was there a third one running loose?

Visibly different and different sized King Kongs appear in Godzilla vs Kong and King Kong Escapes. One lives on Faro Island, the other hangs out on Mondo Island. Maybe they're the same, we never see them in the same room together after all. Perhaps Kong just changed residence and... appearance and... shrank a little? Or maybe there were two Kongs.

Anguiras is killed by Godzilla in the next movie, but then reappears as Godzilla's friend for subsequent movies. Apparently, it got better. Not only that, it didn't hold a grudge for the whole neck snapping thing and worked things out with Godzilla so they became pals? Or was that a second one showing up in some later movies? Did he get killed again, in Godzilla vs Mechagodzilla? If so, he got better, because he's in Destroy All Monsters made earlier but set later in continuity. Or there were three Anguiras.

Varan, Ebirah, Gorosaurus, Kamacuras and Kumonga are all killed, sometimes horribly, in their first movie appearances. But they all appear again either through the miracle of stock footage or re-use of the costumes? Did they all get better, or were these second monsters in subsequent movies?

The Kaiju are incredibly powerful and durable, and let's face it, they mugged physics and biology really hard. So who knows? It's entirely possible that they can recover from apparent death - neck broken, buried in ice or lava, jaws ripped apart, literally have a limb ripped away or getting reduced to a skeleton. No big deal they just walk it off.

Alternately, the population of Kaiju may be small numbers of each variety who tend to stay well away from each other for some reason, so you only ever see one at a time.

Mostly, with the exception of Godzilla Raids Again, Rodan, and the Mothra movies, there's little suggestion that there's more than one of each. In these movies, everyone says "that's Rodan" and no one says "that's another Rodan." As I said, they usually showed up one to a movie, which kind of leaves the impression that each specimen is unique.

In particular, in Destroy All Monsters, the 'Avengers Movie' of Toho's Universe, set in 1999, all the monsters are gathered on Monster Island. One each. There's no suggestion that there's populations of each species or that there's more than one of each kind. Maybe that's all there was? Or the surplus got killed and these are the survivors?

But we don't really know for sure. There's no explanation in the movies as to how Monsters who are apparently killed seem to be back, healthy and hearty, but also no suggestion that there's more than one. Is each unique, are they species? I'll leave it to the reader.

Clearly, we're diving deeper than Toho ever did.

The Kaiju have Superpowers.

That's right, you heard me: Superpowers!

Despite the fact that their size should make it impossible to even walk, several of them - Rodan, Mothra, Gigan, Ghidorah and Hedorah not only walk, but fly, and at supersonic speeds or better. Even Godzilla can sort of fly using his atomic breath. There's no way that wings, even large wings, could lift those weights. Titanosaurus can't fly, but it can whip up hurricane winds with its tail fin.

Gigan and Ghidorah fly in space, which is hard to explain. So at least some of the Kaiju must have gravity negation abilities. Possibly, most or all of them might have. They're all dragging a lot of weight around somehow.

They don't necessarily seem to need to breathe the way we do. Ghidorah, Gigan and Hedorah are just fine in space. Godzilla seems perfectly comfortable on land, underwater, or swimming inside lava. Only extreme cold seems to slow the Big-G down in a few movies.

They're Energy Wielders: Some, but not all of the Godzilla-types have radiant power - Godzilla and Minilla have variations on atomic breath, Baragon has heat beams, so does Gigan. Godzilla and Gabara also seem to have electrical powers.

Of the Arthropods, Megalon and Mothra have radiant powers. Mothra's powers seem more mystical. Among mammals, King Kong and King Seesar seem to have an ability to absorb energy and hurl it back. Kong in his second Toho movie seems immune to radiation, but not hypnosis resistant.

Ghidorah spits gravity beams. I don't even know what a gravity beam is.

Bottom line, across the spectrum, some these Kaiju are wielding or controlling some pretty exotic energies. Atomic blasts, heat beams, gravity beams, gravity negation and whatnot. Crazy stuff.

All this suggests that Kaiju are not biological creatures as we understand biology, but something more like walking nuclear reactors producing or neutralizing radiation, exhibiting seemingly impossible strength and durability, and messing freely with fundamental forces of the universe, including fundamental forces we may not understand, and using it

Oh, and speaking of screwy physics - whatever exotic energies power these Kaiju seems to allow some of them to do size shifting. In Godzilla's Revenge, Minilla can reduce itself to Human size. In Godzilla vs Megalon, Jet Jaguar can grow to Kaiju size. In Space Amoeba, an alien energy causes ordinary animals to grow Kaiju sized. In the Zone Fighter television series, both the Peacelanders and Garoga are able to attain Kaiju size. Mothra's Shobijin are tiny Humans, although we never see them change size. With the possible exception of the Shobijin, these size changes seem to be temporary.

Weird physics are at work, definitely. The Marvel Cinematic Universe had nothing on these guys.

Where Did These Kaiju Come From?

And where did their superpowers come from?

Probably not Atomic Testing: In the original movie, it's strongly suggested that Godzilla and its atomic powers were created by the misuse of nuclear weapons. But if the first was genuinely killed, then there must have been two Godzillas, which is harder to explain with atomic testing. Worse, Minilla, which may be the same species as Godzilla wasn't created by atomic testing and it has atomic blasts of a sort. Most of the monsters, including the flying and energy casting ones don't seem connected to modern nuclear weapons.

The Kaiju, as a group are very old. Possibly insanely old: It's not exactly clear how long a particular Kaiju, or individual Kaiju, have been around before they were discovered. Frankenstein and the Gargantuas only developed within a couple of decades. On the other hand, Ghidorah was active centuries or millennia ago when it devastated Mars. King Seesar's been hiding or hibernating for a similar length of time. Varan was a legendary lake monster known to folklore, but never formally documented in Japanese written history. Some of them, at least, have been around for a long time.

All of them seem to be emerging in the post WWII era, literally within a period of a few decades, almost all of them full grown and ready to fight.

But there's been no significant historical record of them over thousands of years of civilization. This suggests that most or all of them have been mainly dormant for most of Human recorded history. Again, evidence that most of these creatures are almost all ancient on the order of thousands of years. Or perhaps tens or hundreds of thousands?

Maybe millions or more. Or tens of millions. After all Rodan, Manda and the Godzilla-types seem to all derive from the age of Dinosaurs. The insect types might be even older. Given what must be bizarre and impossible physics, they may be near immortal.

Of course, if they are old, and if they've been around that long, and dormant for most of Human history, why are they all waking up now?

Possibly atomic testing?

But most of them don't seem to be near atomic testing sites. Possibly the seismic waves are waking them, but then earthquakes are common. It's possible that atomic or hydrogen bomb testing is releasing a radio 'scream' or some other exotic energy burst that they can detect, and that's what is waking them up and setting them off. It seems to have triggered Godzilla, possibly Anguiras, and Rodan. Mothra is unhappy about it, and it's the direct or indirect cause of Megalon's rampage.

But if they can sense atomic tests, and it's 'loud' enough to wake them up angry, what else can they sense, and how far do those senses extend?

One thing we know for sure, the Kaiju appear to be able to sense or detect each other across great distances. They're always traveling immense distances to fight, and they have no trouble homing in on each other in movie after movie. And they seem to be able to do more than sense each other's locations, they can even communicate...

The Kaiju can Talk to Each Other.

Yes, really. Generally, they just don't want to. Overall, they seem to prefer battling each other or just going off on their own. They'll team up with each other in a battle, but once it's over, they'll put distance between each other. Even on Monster Island, where they're gathered and seem to get along, they seldom hang out.

Where it gets weird is in 1964, in Ghidorah the Three Headed Monster, Mothra seeks out Godzilla and Rodan who are battling, and interrupts the fight to ask them to work with it against Ghidorah.

I'm not making this up.

The result is a brief argument where the monsters have a somewhat philosophical debate whether to let Humanity go hang, or whether to stop Ghidorah.

Still not making it up.

Years later, in Godzilla vs Gigan, we see Godzilla and Anguiras have an actual conversation on Monster Island about something not being right on the mainland, Godzilla sends Anguiras to investigate, and later, they head for Japan together.

That's very sophisticated communication and behavior.

In Godzilla vs Hedorah, another child has visions of Godzilla. Godzilla, especially through its later movies, seems to have an unusual degree of rapport, showing up to fight bad guys and collaborating and coordinating with other monsters. When the Monsters are gathered on Monster Island, they seem to manage to get along peacefully... mostly.

Interestingly, there's evidence that at least some have occasional psychic rapport with Humans. Mothra, for instance, is in telepathic communion with its Shobijin Priestesses through consecutive appearances. In Godzilla vs Mechagodzilla, a priestess seems to have some ability to communicate with King Seesar. Minilla in Godzilla's Revenge communicates with a child, although that whole movie may be a hallucination.

In King Kong Escapes, this version of Kong appears to understand Humans when they speak to him in Japanese or English, languages he almost certainly has never heard before. It gets crazier, he gets hypnotized, and obeys commands in whatever language (Japanese probably?) that Doctor Who and his henchmen are speaking.

Some Humans appear to have a sensitivity to the presence or even the approach of Kaiju. A Martian Princess is able to sense the coming of Ghidorah. In Zone Fighter, the Zone family is friends with Godzilla, to the point of sparring with it.

Add them up, and you have some of the most disquieting revelations about the Showa Universe:

The Kaiju, or at least some of them, are intelligent. Possibly as intelligent as Humans, possibly even more. They have language, or at least complex communication. And they're psychic, perhaps broadcasting psychic energy, which may explain the ability to communicate with each other. Some of them can even understand, influence or communicate with Humans, particularly children. But they can also influence or sense adults with the right genes and possibly the right training.

This, in turn, raises an interesting prospect suggested by a fellow Kaiju fan, Gordon Long:

Several of the Kaiju are worshiped as gods, or supernatural super-beings which would be another way of saying gods. Mothra is worshiped as a god, so is King Kong. Manda is a god/guardian to the Mu-ans in Atragon, and Megalon is a god/guardian to the Seatopians. King Seesar seems to be worshiped as a god/guardian. Varan is well known locally as a nature god/spirit of the lake. Even Godzilla is named after a nature god from the Odo Islands. This suggests a widespread pattern of Kaiju worship, even when they haven't been active, persisting into modern times in some corners.

Interestingly, this worship is also seen in the highly advanced 'lost civilizations' Seatopia and Mu, likely carried over from their earlier root civilization.

If that doesn't creep you out, I don't know what will.

I mean, the notion of a giant, atomic, fire breathing monster is bad enough.

But that it might be smarter than you, and have psychic abilities allowing it to communicate with its own kind and Humans, and being de facto gods for ancient times and lost civilizations?

That's... disturbing.

It suggests that this is their world, not ours.

So What Does it all Mean?

What a mess!

Seriously.

This is what you get when, year after year, for twenty years, you steadily add new details, new characters, and new situations to a shared universe. Eventually, it eats away at its own foundations, consumed by the need for novelty, slowly undermining its own premises.

The original movie was a masterpiece, arising from collective trauma and rooted deep in the collective psyche of a nation, smashed by war, suffering devastated cities, the atomic bomb, foreign occupation and the collapse of its place in the world.

But step by step, the subsequent movies subverted or erased every element, moving away from the mythic power of the original, to something akin to professional wrestling featuring giant monsters.

Then again, the same thing has happened with the Marvel Cinematic Universe, or for that matter the DC Cinematic Universe, to the Universal Monsters both original and their failed reboot, to DC and Marvel Comics, and even literary shared universes like Thieves' World. I think it's doubtful that the Godzilla Cinematic Universe, could have avoided it, even if it had been planned more deliberately.

It always starts off good, with iconic characters and situations, and then more characters thrown in, there's more complexity, new details keep adding to the baggage, leaving new hints and inferences, then it all gets unwieldy. It starts to break down and ends up as something of a mess that's gotten away from its creators.

Toho never really wrestled with or acknowledged the implications of the world it was building. Partly because it all kind of assembled and evolved bit by bit. But mainly, I think because they didn't want to, they just wanted to make movies about giant monsters punching each other.

But they ended up with a world that was almost Lovecraftian in its scope. This was a world whose true rulers were gigantic behemoths, walking nuclear reactors the size of warships, each wielding unimaginable power. These were creatures capable of devastating cities, swimming through lava or existing on the surface of the moon. Their lineages stretched back hundreds of millions of years. It was a world of creatures who were as or more intelligent than humanity, with language and psychic abilities. For perhaps the entirety of life on Earth they had ruled, each a walking empire, ignoring or battling each other as they saw fit.

They'd gone to sleep for a while and our Human civilization had arisen in that absence. Now they were waking up. We were just the turning of a page in an endless book that they owned. It was their world, not ours, a world of primordial inhuman gods.

But was ours really the first Human civilization to arise in an era of prehistoric gods?

Continuity Evolving in and Between Movies

As Toho evolved, pressed to keep finding new plots and situations for new movies, common ideas began to percolate, scooping off the pop culture and Sci-Fi tropes of the time. Aliens, robots, astronauts, amazing inventions and super-vehicles flowed into the mix mingling with giant monsters.

In particular, aliens became a big part of Toho's Showa Universe, as it stitched itself together, becoming more than the sum of its parts.

And the Toho Universe was definitely connecting together. It wasn't just a giant monster's round-robin tournament with each movie standing alone.

Sometimes there were direct references to events that connected the movies. Godzilla Raids Again, the Big G is buried in a glacier. That glacier must have calved into the sea, because in Godzilla vs Kong, the movie begins with it bursting out of a floating iceberg.

In Godzilla vs Megalon, the Seatopians phone up the Nebula M aliens from the previous movie, to borrow Gigan.

Then there are implicit references, things they probably didn't think about, but which make sense in hindsight. For instance, in Ghidorah the Three Headed Monster, Ghidorah simply arrives from outer space to attack Earth, and is beaten back by

Godzilla, Mothra and Rodan. In the next movie, Monster Zero, set much further into the future, we find that Ghidorah is actually under the control of the Xillians, who bargain with gullible astronauts to acquire Godzilla and Rodan in order to attack Earth.

It feels like a pretty obvious connection to assume that the Xillians were operating backstage and out of sight in the first movie, sending Ghidorah against Earth. What's the alternative? That Ghidorah just randomly attacked Earth, got booted back into space, and then coincidentally ended up under the control of the Xillians who unknowingly plotted to get Godzilla and Rodan on board so they could attack Earth themselves? The Xillians were completely innocent the first time around? I don't buy it.

There are two separate undersea/underground civilizations in the Pacific. Mu, featured in Atragon, and Seatopia, featured in Godzilla vs Megalon. Both of them have guardian monsters that they worship. Neither movie alludes to other undersea civilizations. Neither civilization acknowledges the other's existence. But both of them have giant monsters - Manda and Megalon that show up in Godzilla's movies. So the monsters, and presumably their host civilizations both exist in Godzilla's continuity.

Two nearly identical, monster-hosting, underwater civilizations side by side? That's a hell of a coincidence. Or is it? Maybe within the inter-connected universe of Toho movies, it's better to assume that both of these civilizations are related somehow, perhaps they originated from a common ancestor.

What all this means is that there's definitely direct connections and continuity in Toho's Universe. There are very definite explicit references. And then there are events which seem so obviously connected or related it might as well be explicit.

It's not just Kaiju professional wrestling. We can go deeper.

A Survey of Toho's Lost and Alien Races

There are a lot of aliens in this Toho universe. Tons of them. By my count at least eleven, counting the undersea kingdoms.

First, let's go through the roster, otherwise it'll be hard to keep track of them.

First, the **Mysterians**, appearing in the movie of the same name in 1957. The Mysterians' homeworld, an asteroid between Mars and Jupiter, is blown up in a nuclear war, so they show up here looking for new real estate and women. They also based on the moon temporarily. They bring a couple of giant robots – Mogueras, sort of mechanical Kaiju chickens. They end up being pushy jerks so Earth unites against them and they're wiped out.

Next, the **Natals,** from the Toho movie Battle in Outer Space, 1959 but set in 1965. The Natals mess with gravity as part of the attack on Earth, have a base on the moon, and use the same flying saucers as the Mysterians. Earth gets wise, and by this time the space program is far more advanced, so we take the battle to the moon and defeat them. No giant monsters or robots, but they do seem related to Mysterians. Their flying saucer mothership is easily shot down by Earth forces.

Mu: 1963, Atragon, the story of a super-submarine. The Atragon encounters an underground, undersea civilization, Mu, the remnant of the sunken continent of Lemuria. They want to conquer the world and they worship a giant serpent-like monster called Manda.

Martians: 1964, Ghidorah the Three Headed Monster. The first sign of Ghidorah are hijinks with a mysterious Princess from the Selgell islands. She reveals she's really a Martian. Turns out Mars was inhabited until Ghidorah showed up and wiped them out. The Martian survivors fled to Earth and settled on Selgell islands where they blended in.

Xillians are from Monster Zero in 1965, set sometime further in the future and featuring Godzilla, Rodan and Ghidorah. An Earth spaceship finds Planet X out around Jupiter. The Xillians or X-ians, beg for Earth's monsters to help them with Ghidorah, but it's just a trick. An Astronaut and a Xillian girl get romantic.

Kilaaks are the villains of Destroy all Monsters, released in 1968 but set in 1999. The Kilaaks are from a super-hot environment, so much so that their natural form is a sort of metal worms and Earth's environment is fatal, which makes you wonder why they want to conquer it. They wear female human suits to get around. They claim that their world is somewhere between Mars and Jupiter, in the asteroid belt. Their plan for conquest involves taking control of Earth's monsters and employing Ghidorah yet again. Their flying saucer is easily shot down by Earth forces.

Hunter M Nebulans, aka Nebulans, 1971, who are identical to Earth cockroaches, except for being dramatically larger, intelligent and able to wear the exteriors of dead humans as disguises. So the resemblance may be overstated. They invade Earth covertly in 1972 in Godzilla vs Gigan. Their world was originally inhabited by humans or humanoids, but was overcome by pollution, leaving them looking for new real estate. Their monster is Gigan, but they also employ Ghidorah. Interestingly, a pollution monster, Hedorah, showed up in the previous movie, just ahead of their attack. And the Nebulans are from a pollution world. Suspicious?

Seatopians – Godzilla vs Megalon, 1972 the Seatopians are a second underwater, underground civilization. They get upset by Atomic testing and send their monster, Megalon, to smash Japan. The Nebulans lend them Gigan.

Peacelanders and **Garoga**, from the 1973 television series Zone Fighter. The Garoga are imperialistic bad guys, humanoid but with insect features. The Zone Fighter family are refugees from the conquered planet Peaceland, fled to

Earth. The two sides fight it out here. Godzilla helps out the Zone family. Ghidorah and Gigan show up working for the Garoga, who also use temporary Kaiju – terror-beasts. The Garoga claim to have created Ghidorah.

Black Hole Planet 3 Aliens, aka Simeons and Mutants. Godzilla vs Mechagodzilla, 1974, the Black Hole aliens, looking like humanoid apes and calling themselves Simeons, take their stab at conquering Earth with a robot Godzilla. In the next movie, Terror of Mechagodzilla, 1975, the Black Hole aliens are back, looking more like mutants than apes, using Mechagodzilla again, and a second monster, Titanosaurus. They say that their flying saucers can travel from their world to Earth in about a thousand hours, but are easily shot down by Godzilla.

There are a couple of other space incursions – Hedorah begins as a spore or pollution feeding slime from something called the 'Dark Gas Nebula' (possibly Hunter M?) and is allegedly ferried to Earth by a passing comet, which may imply it's from the Solar System. In Space Amoeba, an Earth probe around Jupiter is hijacked by a glowing alien mist and sent to Earth. But we'll ignore those for now.

Who or What are these Aliens, Really?

In Godzilla's universe all these aliens are literally stumbling over each other to invade Earth within the span of a few decades, after apparently ignoring us for thousands of years. At least three groups showed up as refugees. Two groups seem to be home grown and living undersea. In three cases Earth forces go into space to confront them. They're right up in us.

Why the sudden interest? One of the refugee groups has been here a long time, so we can overlook them. And the undersea groups are also long standing but suddenly they're stirring? And out in space, suddenly they're all showing up here, one after the other? That doesn't feel like coincidence.

There are some odd things about these aliens. For one thing, they don't seem very good at conquering Earth. You'd think a full-fledged alien civilization capable of crossing interstellar space would squash Earth's defenders flat. It would be like Europeans with machine guns against spear and shield wielding tribesmen. At least one of them should have us bowing to our new alien overlords. But mainly, the invasions are small scale, attempt to use local resources and take over local monsters and are easily beaten off.

Seriously? Where are the extraterrestrial fleets in the sky? Come on: War of the Worlds, Earth vs the Flying Saucers, Independence Day? They should be kicking our ass. Why are they so puny?

Instead, not only are they generally small scale, but Earth has a pretty good track record of shooting down their flying saucers and battling them on Earth and in space. Those are pretty crap saucers.

Several of them are definitely actually local – the Mu and Seatopians for sure. The Mysterians, Martians, Kilaaks and Xillians are or were all definitely in the Solar system. Both the Peacelanders, like the Martians and Mysterians before them, flee to Earth as refugees, which suggest that they were close by. The Garoga were close to the Peacelanders, so also likely close to Earth. And the Black Hole Aliens claim that their world is only 40 days travel by their saucers, which might suggest they could be local.

Why are they so Human? And by Human, at least five - the Martian refugees in Ghidorah, the Mysterians, the Natals, the Xillians, and the Peacelanders, are completely physically Human. Two more the Garoga from Zone Fighter and the Simeons from Mechagodzilla are clearly Humanoid. Only two, the Cockroach Nebulans and the rocklike Kilaaks, seem genuinely alien, and the Nebulans shared their world with humans/humanoids. But even the Humanoid and alien ones are able to perfectly disguise themselves as Human, apparently sharing the same 'disguise' technology. All the Humans and Humanoids seem perfectly fine with Earth's atmosphere and environment. Only the Kilaaks don't seem comfortable on Earth.

The 'Human' aliens are sexually compatible. For instance, when the Mysterians come to Earth, they want Human women to reproduce with. In Ghidorah the Three Headed Monster, we learn that Mars once had a thriving civilization before Ghidorah came along to smash it after which the surviving Martians fled to Earth and settled in as refugees... and no one noticed! Or in Monster Zero, the next movie with Ghidorah, we discover the Xillians, and in a subplot a male Earth astronaut and a female Xillian fall in love and get romantic.

None of that should be possible - a Christmas tree is more closely related to a Human than a genuine alien, and you don't see people getting jiggy with the local hardwoods. An actual alien should be completely incompatible on a physical, chemical, even molecular level.

If several of these aliens are provably or probably local, if almost all of these aliens are fine with our air and environment, if most of them look Human down to earlobes and eyebrows, if they're reproducing with Humans, or at least having sexy times, they're Human. The question is, what are they doing out there in space?

And if half of the known aliens are actually Human, then it's likely that the Humanoid ones may not be truly alien either. Just mutated.

To really hammer it in, all of the alien races are not just Human or Human-appearing but all appear ethnically Japanese. This includes the refugees hanging out on Earth, the ones who are only disguising themselves as Human, and somehow including the members of two underground civilizations on Earth.

Yes, obviously it's because all these movies are made in Japan, with Japanese actors. But still, within the context of Toho's universe, this does need to be accounted for.

All of the aliens, plus the two undersea civilizations on Earth, seem obsessed with Kaiju. Not only are they invading in the same era the Kaiju are arising, but many have their own Kaiju, or are fixated with controlling Earth's Kaiju. Why this connection to giant monsters?

The Mu from Atragon have Manda, the Seatopians have Megalon, in space the Xillians have Ghidorah and the Nebulans have Gigan. On top of that Gigan and/or Ghidorah are also employed by Seatopians, Kilaaks and Garoga. They're apparently passing them around like playing cards, or the monsters are hiring out. That's just weird.

Both the Mysterians with their Moguera robots and the Simeons from the Mechagodzilla movies create giant robot monsters as weapons, those are weird choices, and it's oddly the same technology. Meanwhile, the Nebulans build a weaponized Godzilla statue (a Mechagodzilla in progress), and turn their monster, Gigan, into a cyborg. This is a fairly distinctive set of technological choices to arise independently across three different cultures, unless all three had inherited the technology and the preconceptions from a root culture.

On that front, the aliens seem to have the same technology and technological styles. They're all ahead of us, with spaceships and force fields, but not so impossibly far ahead that we can't fight back. The non-human ones use the same disguise technology; they all seem to be at the same or similar level.

Oddly, they're all jumping on us within a few years of each other. Thousands of years of civilization, no recorded alien invasions. But suddenly, when the Kaiju start showing up, almost a dozen of them are all crowding Humanity within a forty year time frame. Why now? And why does it seem to overlap with the giant monsters?

It's as if there's a common set of underlying cultural assumptions or tropes. It's as if the aliens and undersea nations, and including the Japanese for that matter, are all the same family tree, coming from the same original civilization.

Let's call it Lemuria, but stick a pin in, and we'll get back to it.

Outer space seems to be a dangerous place - there used to be Martians before Ghidorah came along and wiped them out. It seems like Ghidorah often works for other aliens, so maybe it was a hit job? I would guess that it's most likely the Garoga or the Xillians, as they seem to be the first controllers of Ghidorah. But it could have been someone else, Ghidorah apparently gets around.

The Mysterians report that their world was destroyed by a nuclear war. With who? Was it a civil war? Or did they get in a fight with someone else? The Garoga or the Xillians perhaps?

The Garoga later on wiped out the Zone Fighter's home world, and both sides came to Earth - the Zone family as refugees and the Garoga as invaders.

As we've pointed out, it's likely that they're all local to the System. But if all or most of these alien civilizations are in the Solar System, shouldn't we notice them? Let's be clear - there's not a lot of obviously habitable planets in the Solar System. There's Earth and then there's... well... it's just Earth. Apparently, Mars was occupied, but no more. We've had telescopes and even radio telescopes for a while, we should be able to spot habitable worlds and alien civilizations, if they're local. Unless these aren't habitable worlds like Earth, but more like outposts on rocks.

The Xillians' world is a rocky barren moonscape, with Xillian civilization living underground. That might be the rule for most of the alien races. After all, when we see the Mysterians, the first thing they seem to want to do is dig in underground. So perhaps they're all just based on asteroids or rocky planetoids?

As a general rule, all the Aliens seems small scale. When the Mysterians invade, it's with a small force, suggesting that perhaps they didn't have much of a population to start with. Maybe it's the difficulties of space travel, you can't move huge forces around easily. But the Xillians' home world just doesn't seem to be huge.

If we simply confine ourselves to large objects 90 miles in diameter or so, then we have perhaps eight to ten known asteroids, six Jovian moons, ten around Saturn, five and four for Uranus and Neptune, beyond Neptune there is at the very least, Pluto and its companion Chiron and another handful of planetoids. Essentially, there are, excluding the inner Solar System - the Moon, Mars, Venus and Mercury, at least thirty-five potential planets or planetoids.

Living on small rocky worlds may explain much about the Mysterian and Xillian societies. Their rigorous disciplined quality, their Spartan and mechanistic philosophy, make sense as the products of relatively tiny societies living in isolation in a harsh artificial environment.

Small rocky worlds with self-contained biospheres and small communities would make it easy for mutations to take hold in a population, as with the Black Hole aliens and the Garoga. That's assuming they don't genetically alter themselves to make it easier to survive. That kind of small self-contained system could easily become overwhelmed by pollution as seems to have happened with the Nebulan's world.

The Secrets of the Lost Lemurians

Again, this seems to suggest that all these aliens have a common origin, one shared with the undersea kingdoms: Earth an incredibly advanced, kaiju-focused, super-civilization before our own, Lemuria.

So let's say, theoretically, on a now lost continent in the Pacific, during an age of giant monsters, an advanced civilization, Lemuria, emerges, worshiping Kaiju, and perhaps using or relying on them in technology and war.

The Lemurians achieve unheard of heights and amazing technical prowess beyond our modern civilization, build underground complexes, develop local space travel, and spread out into the Solar system, establishing self-sustaining colonies on Mars and a number of Planetoids.

Or perhaps, it was the Kaiju, intrigued by precocious little Apes, who came together to uplift Humanity into a civilization, telepathically guiding a priest class, and revealing the secrets of their atomic biology, allowing and helping Humans to develop technology and eventually build space colonies.

Then something goes wrong - civil war most likely. Whether it's between the Lemurian City states, or the Kaiju themselves, the result is that the Lemurians and their continent are destroyed. The Kaiju go to sleep, with a few, including Ghidorah and Gigan, retreating to outer space.

On Earth, there are surviving populations - Refugees on the Japanese islands, reduced to rebuilding from savagery, all memories and records gone; Underground kingdoms of Mu and Seatopia, both of which hide from each other and the rest of the world; More refugees or survivors on Infant Island under the pastoral guardianship of Mothra; and isolated bands of worshippers with legends of a great civilization, or stories of sleeping monsters.

Meanwhile, out in space the colonies are cast adrift, developing in splendid isolation, and occasionally warring upon each other. This might explain the Xillian's long term cloaking of their world. Juggernauts don't hide from ants. If they are cloaking, they're hiding, which means they've got something to hide from, and it's probably not from an Earth fallen to savagery. The most likely guess is that there are or were rival Lemurian colonies in the Solar System that posed a threat to them. That or they're hiding from enemy Kaiju.

It seems reasonable to assume that the Martians were the losers in a war where another group, the Xillians or the Garoga or someone else, used Ghidorah. This was after the fall of Lemuria, otherwise, the refugees would probably have rejoined their mother society, rather than simply hiding out.

More recently we have the Mysterian invasion, claiming that their society was destroyed by war, and who are now, like the Martians before them, forced to flee to Earth. Well, why should we assume that the Mysterians destroyed their own world? Perhaps the real story is that the Mysterians and either the Xillians or Garoga were longtime rivals and that the Mysterians were finally defeated.

But what about Nebulans, Black hole aliens, the Kilaaks or the Garoga themselves? How did non-human species replace the Humans? And what of their references to the perils or locations of their home worlds, which seem to preclude the Solar System.

First, in terms of explaining how they came about, we must remember that the Lemurian colonies within the solar system were tightly contained habitats established within or upon rocky, barren, inhospitable worlds. They did not have the luxury of a vast and bountiful world with free water and free atmosphere as Earth did.

Populations were necessarily small, perhaps as little as a few thousand or tens of thousands. Resources were limited, constantly recycled, and the population existed at the limits of these resources. Inbreeding could be a problem. Pollution, mistakes or accidents were far more serious than on Earth, because even a minor problem is huge in a small pool. Things were so tight that their environments had little opportunity to regenerate.

On Earth, if you cut down a forest, there are invariably more trees somewhere else... Except on a vulnerable isolated area like Easter Island, where cutting the trees spelled disaster. Easter Island was so remote that in practical terms, there was no forest anywhere else, or at least, nowhere that could be reached. Thus, losing their forest was an irredeemable calamity.

The Lemurian colonies in space would have been a lot like Easter Island, so remote and isolated, so constrained in resources, that calamity was just around the corner.

For the Mysterians and the Xillians, this resulted in regimented, almost mechanistic societies. For the Martians, this resulted in the eventual abandonment of their home.

We can easily see Lemurian colonies trying to stretch their resources, to do more with less, by either changing themselves or biologically engineering, hardy servants.

The Humans of the Ape-like Simeon's world from Godzilla vs Mechagodzilla may have created a genetically engineered Ape-like servant class to do their hard labor, which eventually resulted in their being displaced by their creations. Or maybe they just added a lot of Ape DNA into themselves for whatever reasons.

Similarly, the Garoga from Zone Fighter may have created similar genetically engineered Insectoid-Humans. Or they may have just added insect DNA. Either way, they ended up with bug eyes and antenna.

The Nebulans, facing a diminishing or deteriorating habitat, attempted to reverse the tide by engineering a servant race of intelligent insects who could tolerate the degraded habitat. As it turns out, their gamble lost, they passed into extinction, leaving only their insect servants to struggle with a world they'd poisoned.

The Kilaaks may have been a manufactured life form constructed for an extremely inhospitable, super-heated environment, perhaps Mercury, or possibly some experimental or industrial complex in the asteroid belt too dangerous for humans, and when Lemuria fell, they simply continued on.

But what about the inconsistencies? The Nebulans claim that their world is in the Hunter M Nebula? There is no such Nebula. The Simeons claim that their world is third from a black hole, and doomed. That doesn't make it sound like they're from around here.

Bad translations, or sloppy terms? Maybe the Nebulans home isn't visible, but was in a section of sky where a constellation or nebula is visible from Earth.

Perhaps with their 'third planet' shtick, the Simeons are hinting that they're from Earth. The black hole reference? That could be Gorath.

Right, Gorath –

I guess we'll have to bite that bullet. Gorath is a Toho movie about a black hole or neutron star object, about 6000 times Earth's mass that wanders into the Solar system and menaces Earth. It's detected around Saturn in 1977, eats a couple of Saturn's moons, and drifts towards Earth. Because it's so heavy, there's no way to stop it, so Humanity builds giant rockets at the South Pole and pushes Earth out of its path (and presumably pushes Earth back). Also a Kaiju walrus appears, because why not. You asked for it.

But the point is that in 1974 and 1975 when the Mechagodzilla movies were set, Gorath, either a black hole, or close enough as to make no difference, was on its way. Maybe the Mechagodzilla aliens knew something, and were desperate to escape to new real estate. Or, if it wasn't, then obviously, it's a hell of a coincidence that Earth and the Ape-mutants world would both be faced with such similar menaces in such a close span of time.

Interestingly, Daie studios, whose Gamera series was Toho's main rival, also made a movie about a rogue planet coming into the solar system to menace Earth. So theoretically, that might connect Daie's and Toho's Monsterverses. But I'm just thinking out loud.

Getting back to the Mechagodzilla aliens, Gorath might explain what happened to them: Gorath got them. Or maybe as it approached closer, they redid their calculations and decided they didn't want our real estate – we were next in Gorath's path.

The Kilaak are almost the only clearly and absolutely non-human race in the Showa universe. But, they share two very strange traits with some of the other cultures that we've now identified as lost Lemurian Colonies. Like all the rest, they're all about controlling and using giant monsters - hell, they even employ Ghidorah, who has previously worked for the Xillians, the Nebulans and the Garoga.

Like the Black Hole aliens and the Nebulans, they are adept at creating Human 'sheaths' or disguises, which have the full appearance of living and breathing persons of apparent ethnic Japanese origin. Obviously, a hell of a coincidence. Why they would have even bothered? Unless it's all the same off-the-shelf technology.

The Kilaaks seem adapted or designed for an extremely hot world genuinely alien conditions. My theory is that they were created by the Lemurians as an artificial life form for Mercury, and got left on the vine, like all the rest.

A word about our two final alien races: I've left them to the end because they feature in a television series that's not really accessible in North America: "Zone Fighter: The Meteor Man." The first alien race occupied an idyllic world whose name translates into English as 'Peaceland'. Once again they they're physically indistinguishable from Japanese Humans, to the extent of being able to blend into the population of modern Tokyo. Just like all the other aliens. And they're likely in the solar system, since they head here as refugees, just like the Martians and Mysterians.

Their world must be in the outer solar system, in a crowded neighborhood where their enemies, the Garoga are able to establish an empire (which suggests at least two or three other worlds). So, most likely, they're parked around Jupiter or Saturn.

Interestingly, the Mechagodzilla aliens, if we assume a connection to Gorath, are probably around Saturn, which makes one wonder if there was contact between the three races. Neither the Garogas nor the Peacelanders seemed particularly worried about Gorath.

As for the Garogas, the evil race in Zone Fighter, they're Humanoids with insect-features, antenna, armored hides and body spikes. Like the other humanoid or nonhuman aliens, they've got Japanese Human-suits. And like other Lemurian offshoots, they're big into Kaiju, using both Gigan and Ghidorah, borrowed presumably from Nebulans and Xillians, and they've managed to create temporary giant monsters - size changing Terror Beasts as weapons.

That's the last anomaly - both the Zone Fighters and the Garoga have size changers. But we saw a size changing robot in Godzilla vs Megalon, size changing in Godzilla's Revenge, with Mothra's Shobijin. The creatures from Space Amoeba. It's just one of those weird Kaiju things.

So that wraps them up - Martians, Mysterians, Xillians, Natals, Peacelanders, Nebulans, Simeons, Seatopians, Mu-ans, Garoga and Kilaak. All unique, but all kind of dipping into the same pot, apparently connecting to each other, having similar or overlapping traits, all likely descended from an ancestral lost civilization - the Lemurians, evidence of a secret common history buried in the history of the Showa Universe.

All of them suddenly become active one after the other, in the same time frame that Godzilla and the other giant monsters start showing up. Coincidence?

Or worshipers returning to resume complicated relationships with their primordial Gods? Resuming an ancient war? Seeking an awakened resource? Or perhaps consciously or unconsciously summoned by the psychic broadcasts of the awakening of the Kaiju, just as the energy of nuclear weapons detonations started to wake the giant monsters?

Or maybe it's something simpler.

Maybe up until the atom bomb, none of the Lemurian offshoots saw Earth as a threat? Once we started dropping atom bombs and testing hydrogen bombs, they started to get worried and decided to start settling scores with each other, bad news for Mysterians and Peacelanders, and eventually start trying to neutralize Earth's potential threat.

The problem was, the more wins we scored, the more worried the other aggressive offshoots got, until, one after other, the Mu-ans, the Natals, Nebulans, Kilaak and so on decided to try us on their own, each Earth win leaving the others more worried.

None of this is explicit in the movies of the Showa universe, and certainly Toho studios wasn't thinking in terms like this.

Mostly, it was probably along the lines of

"We need a reason for our monsters to battle!"

"How about aliens?"

"Great, what will we call them this time?"

They were just trying to make entertaining movies and sell tickets. They weren't trying to be deep.

Almost certainly they kept inventing new aliens because they thought recycling them would get stale and get people thinking about continuity questions. But if so, it kind of blew up in their faces, because we just thought about continuity in complicated ways.

The thing is though, they did create all these aliens, and even if it was laziness, they did give these aliens overlapping tropes and common features. As with the Kaiju, from one movie to the next, they slowly built up a picture, they presented information and details whose implications, even if they hadn't been intended, still formed a picture.

In this case, there's a whole hidden history of a lost civilization and its warring offshoots in space entwined with the history and legends of giant monsters to be teased and inferred out of the various clues and references sprinkled through the movies.

A History of Godzilla's Monsterverse – Movies Included

360 million to 250 million years ago - Age of Insects - the giant arthropods emerge - Mothra, Guardian of Earth, Megalon, Kamacuras, Kumonga, Meganulon, Ebirah and possibly others. Also emerging are the giant Octopuses.

250 million to 65 million years ago: Age of Reptiles - Rodan, Manda, Gorosaurus, Gabara, Godzilla, Ghidorah, Gigan, Baragon, Titanosaurus, Anguiras and Minilla's mother. The Godzilla 'clan' forms and begins to dominate the other Kaiju, either out-producing them, or destroying them. There may have been Kaiju wars off and on through history.

65 million years ago to 30,000 years ago: Age of Mammals - King Kong, King Seesar, as well as the Giant Condor.

Lemurian continent forms and becomes a center of Kaiju activity and residence. The continent is the first 'Monster Island' where the Kaiju battle and form truces, engage in wars, and evolve the first civilization.

100,000 years ago: Humans evolve, spreading across the world, and finding their way to Lemuria, either on their own, or with intervention from some of the Kaiju.

15,000 years ago: The Kaiju begin to uplift Humans, creating a civilization. Humans in Lemuria begin to worship Kaiju, adopting them as totemic gods. As City states emerge, each state worships a particular Kaiju. The Lemurians form a loose confederation, building an advanced technological civilization with the aid and support of the Kaiju.

13,000 years ago: The Lemurians establish two undersea colonies - Mu and Seatopia. After mastering sealed self-contained colonies, they go into space, colonizing Mars and planting communities through the Solar System. Some of the Kaiju, notably Ghidorah and Gigan go into space.

12,000 years ago: The Lemurian Confederation breaks down into civil war with the combatants destroying each other and the continent. Alternately, the Lemurian continent is destroyed by the Kaiju themselves, either in a civil war among themselves or in conflict with the Lemurians.

The space colonies are left adrift, each on their own, to survive or fail. Likely several fail. Others endure to the present, changing as required. Ghidorah, Gigan and possibly Hedorah remain in space.

On Earth, there are four remnants: (1) Infant Island, a pastoral island society under the Guardianship of Mothra; (2) The almost uninhabited Islands of Japan, settled by Lemurian refugees, who lose their pasts and become modern Japanese, King Seesar remains as the protector, but goes dormant and falls into legend; (3) Mu, a warlike Lemurian remnant worshiping Manda; (4) Seatopia, a more peaceful Lemurian remnant worshiping Megalon.

12,000 years ago to the 20th Century: The Kaiju on Earth largely go dormant, possibly as a consequence of the destruction of Lemuria. They either go completely dormant, in long sleeps, isolate themselves, or some combination.

10,000 years ago to the 20th Century: On Earth, Humanity begins its long climb back to civilization. In this new civilization, the Kaiju are barely remembered figures of myth and legend.

In space, the 'Black hole' aliens either create uplifted Apes as servants, or enhance themselves with Ape DNA. Similarly, the Garoga do the same thing with insect DNA, either creating Humanoid-insect servants or simply enhancing their own members with insect DNA.

The Nebulans begin genetically modifying insects, increasing size and intelligence, to act as servants, as their world becomes increasingly toxic.

On Mercury, or in some experimental/industrial complex in the Asteroid belt the Kilaaks, abandoned, begin to slowly rebuild a society in the image of their former masters.

Era of the Space Wars: Ghidorah, acting on behalf of one of the remaining space colonies, likely the Garoga or the Xillians, destroys Mars. Surviving Martians flee back to Earth, establishing themselves on the Selgell Islands.

This may have been the first interplanetary war, and the beginnings of an outer-space arms race/cold war.

Gigan, either as a result of injuries sustained in battle, or as enhancements in the face of external threats, becomes a weaponized cyborg. Most likely by the Nebulans.

The Garoga master the technology to create false 'temporary-Kaiju' known as Terror Beasts, possibly to defend against the Xillian who have Ghidorah, and the Nebulans who have Gigan.

The Peacelanders, also employ 'temporary-Kaiju' technology used by the Garoga, this time to enable temporary super-warriors to defend themselves.

The Mysterians, choose a third path, building giant Robots, at least two, known as Moguera, to defend against outsiders.

On the Nebulans colony, Humans go extinct, finally overcome by their own pollution. The uplifted cockroaches continue their society, but their world is growing steadily uninhabitable, even for them.

On the Black Hole colony, remaining Humans are displaced by Apes and Mutants.

The Garoga begin a campaign to conquer its neighbors, including Peaceland.

The Mysterians get into a war with one of the other space colonies - possibly the Xillians or the Garoga. It will end very badly for them.

20th Century - 1900-1945: Japan becomes a warlike Empire, attacking China, European powers and the United States. The war does not go well and ends with atom bombs at Hiroshima and Nagasaki.

Triggered by the atomic bombs at Hiroshima and Nagasaki, and by continued atomic testing, the Kaiju slowly begin to wake, beginning with Godzilla.

1954 - Godzilla: The Big G emerges, attacks Tokyo, and is apparently killed by the Oxygen Destroyer, being reduced to a skeleton at the bottom of Tokyo Bay.

1955 - Godzilla Raids Again: A second Godzilla, exactly like the first in every way, appears. Or maybe this is the first one, somehow having recovered from being reduced to a skeleton. Either way, it's battling a second monster, Anguiras. Godzilla wins killing Anguiras (who gets getter), but is buried in a glacier.

Presumably between 1955 and 1963, the section of Glacier containing Godzilla calves and falls into the ocean, floating out into northern latitudes.

1956 - Rodan: A pair of dormant Pterosaurs in a mountain in Japan, along with Meganulon insects, are woken or hatched up by a reckless mining operation. They die. Apparently one of them gets better.

1957 - The Mysterians: Aliens lose their war in outer space. Their world destroyed by nuclear weapons, the survivors flee to Earth with two giant robots, the Moguera, and attempt to take over. It does not go well and the Mysterians and Moguera are destroyed.

Off camera: The Xillians are shocked at the handy way in which Earth defeated the remnants of their old enemy. Concerned by Earth's advancing technology, possession and apparent willingness to use nuclear weapons, begin to decide that Earth will need to be dealt with.

Off camera: Meanwhile the encounter with the Mysterians, and reverse engineering of Mysterian technology allows Earth, particularly its space programs, to eventually leap ahead, posing an even greater potential threat to the space colonies. (Note: The suggestion that reverse engineering of Mysterian technology allows Earth to leap ahead is from Gordon Long).

1958 - Varan the Unbelievable: Varan, a dormant monster near a lake in northern Japan awakens and is eventually killed. He gets better.

1960 - Frankenstein v Baragon aka Frankenstein Conquers the World - This takes place over a period of time. In 1945, Nazi Germany sends the heart of the Frankenstein monster to Japan, for study in Hiroshima. Bad decision. Later, in the ruins of Hiroshima, a starving, irradiated Japanese boy finds the heart and eats it. Somehow, whether it's the radiation, or the heart, this transforms him. Years later, as Hiroshima is being rebuilt, a feral boy is found, who begins to rapidly grow Kaiju sized. Eventually, the giant youth, dubbed Frankenstein, escapes into the wilderness, continuing to grow. Meanwhile, another giant monster, Baragon, crawls out of the Earth and starts tearing its way through Japan. Eventually, Frankenstein and Baragon fight. Frankenstein wins, but is either swallowed by an earthquake chasm, or is eaten by a passing giant octopus. Baragon is killed, but gets better. *(Note: This movie is made in 1965, but given that the starting point is 1945, and the starving foraging boy had to be old enough to scavenge, so between 8 and 15, I'm placing it in continuity as between 1955 and 1960, rather than in chronology).*

Off camera: Note the giant Octopus. Giant Octopuses also appear in King Kong vs Godzilla and War of the Gargantuas. Or possibly it's the same one, which just gets around.

1961 - Mothra: Japanese kidnaping of miniature Human priestesses, dubbed Shobijin, from Infant Island rouses Mothra, who hatches into a larval form, and eventually to full form.

1962 - King Kong vs Godzilla: Godzilla climbs out of an Iceberg, and heads for Tokyo. An opportunistic Japanese businessman finds King Kong on Faro Island. After Kong tussles with a giant Octopus, he's kidnaped to Japan and duels Godzilla, with the two of them falling into the ocean. Kong swims back home.

1963 - Atragon: The undersea Empire of Mu, together with its guardian monster, Manda, attempts to conquer the surface world. The world unites against them. A super-warship, the Atragon, puts paid to the attempt.

Off camera: After the Mysterian's attempt, this is the second world uniting threat. We can assume a more unified planet, where the United Nations is a more substantial body.

1964 - Godzilla vs Mothra, aka Godzilla vs the Thing: A Mothra egg washes up on shore in Japan, capitalist hijinks ensue. The Shobijin show up to warn them but no one listens. Godzilla appears, heading for the egg. A flying mature Mothra shows up to battle Godzilla but is killed. But this allows two larval Mothra to hatch and attack Godzilla, cocooning it so that it falls into the sea. Only one of the larval Mothra is ever seen after that, maybe the other is dead, or maybe they just take turns.

Off camera: The Xillians send Ghidorah to destroy Earth. Or Human civilization at least.

1964 - Ghidorah, the Three Headed Monster: A Princess from Selgell Islands appears in Japan. She warns that her people were originally from Mars, and that the Monster that destroyed their world, Ghidorah is on the way. Larval version Mothra intervenes in a battle between Rodan and Godzilla convincing them to fight Ghidorah. After a three way battle Ghidorah flees.

1965 - Battle in Outer Space: Human progress has advanced considerably with a much more unified world, a major space station and space travel to the moon. Unnatural disasters begin to occur, which are eventually traced to enemy aliens, the Natals, who are messing with gravity fields. The Natals have a base on the moon, an Earth expedition travels out there to defeat them. *(This Toho film is made in 1959, but set in the far distant future of 1965. Although no actual giant monsters appear, it's in keeping with other aspects of the Toho universe - a more united world,* *advanced technology, especially space travel, and aggressive but underpowered aliens. Notably, the Natals are using the same flying saucers that the Mysterians used.).*

Off camera: In Destroy all Monsters, the United Nations maintains a moon base. Possibly, this is the Natal moon base, taken over by Earth later on? Or perhaps Earth built its own moon base for protection and to deter the Natals or others from setting up shop. How long does it take to build a moon base anyway?

1966 - Ebirah, Horror of the Deep aka **Godzilla vs the Sea Monster**: Castaways discover a terrorist group on an Island guarded by Ebirah, a giant lobster. Godzilla is also on the Island, sleeping it off in a cave. Eventually, the castaways wake Godzilla, who battles a Giant Condor (who gets better), dismembers the lobster (who gets better), and puts paid to the terrorists. The Island blows up, but Mothra, flying version, appears to carry everyone to safety. *(Originally, this was intended to be a King Kong movie, Toho was working with Rankin Bass who were producing a King Kong cartoon, and the intent was to do a live action version of the cartoon. Rankin Bass didn't like the proposal, so this project was reassigned to Godzilla and instead, Toho made King Kong Escapes, which was closer to the cartoon.)*

1966 - War of the Gargantuas aka **War of the Frankensteins**: Severed tissue or blood from Frankenstein's battle with Baragon regenerates into a hairy child-like Humanoid, dubbed a Gargantua. This child-Gargantua eventually flees into the wilderness where it lives a solitary life as the gold Gargantua, Gaira, growing to giant size. Meanwhile, unknown to everyone, another tissue sample of Frankenstein ended up in the sea, growing to full size as the green Gargantua, Sanda, and beginning to attack shipping and raid the coast. When Japanese Defense Forces attack Sanda, Gaira rescues his brother. But soon they fall out over cannibalism. Also, a giant octopus makes an appearance. *(Note: Frankenstein vs Baragon was released only the year before, it seems* *improbable that both Gargantuas could regenerate and hit full size in a year or less. So this supports putting the Frankenstein movie further back in continuity. In War of the Gargantuas, a child sized Gargantua, is shown in flashback, which is also hard to explain in a year.)*

1967 - Son of Godzilla: A weather control experiment on a Pacific Island is plagued by a giant spider, Kumonga and a trio of giant praying mantises, Kamacuras, who grow even more gigantic. After the insects attack a giant egg, Godzilla arrives, destroying two of the Kamacuras. The egg turns out to be Minilla, thought to be a baby Godzilla (maybe?). Eventually the spider, Kumonga, webs up Minilla and the remaining Kamacuras. Godzilla saves the day, and destroys Kumonga (who gets better). The weather experiment freezes the Island and Godzilla and Minilla nap. No one knows who laid the egg in the first place.

1967 - King Kong Escapes: The evil Doctor Who (no relation), whose secret base is a cruise ship, for reasons known only to himself builds a robot Mechani-Kong to mine radioactive elements. That doesn't work out. So he decides to kidnap a real King Kong to do his mining for him. This King Kong is living quietly on Mondo Island, when he encounters visitors from a submarine. Falling for a sexy blonde, he fights and kills a Dinosaur, Gorosaurus (who gets better), and a giant serpent (which sadly, remains dead). Doctor Who then shows up, kidnaps Kong, hypnotizes him and uses him to dig radioactive elements. Mechani-Kong ends up in Tokyo for some reason. Kong escapes and swims over there, eventually destroying the robot and sinking Doctor Who's cruise ship. *(This is clearly a different Kong than the one that fought Godzilla, which was from Faro Island.)*

1969 - All Monsters Attack aka Godzillas Revenge: Godzilla and Minilla are living on the same Island. A little boy Ichiro, dreams of their adventures, including Godzilla fighting a giant mantis Kamacuras, the spider Kumonga, the lobster, Ebirah, and the Giant Condor (all through the magic of stock footage) until a new monster, Gabara, shows up to bully Minilla. Ichiro communicates telepathically with Minilla, and visits the Island, where Minilla shrinks down to hang out with him. Up to the viewer to decide whether this any of this actually happens or is simply Ichiro's fantasy. Neither option is satisfactory. This was the weirdest Godzilla movie, until Hedorah.

1970 - Space Amoeba aka Yog Monster from Space: A disembodied but sentient alien force takes over the Helios 7 Space Probe around Jupiter. Piloting the Probe back to Earth, it crashes on a Pacific Island which is targeted for commercial development. There, it inhabits a cuttlefish and a crayfish successively, causing each to mutate and grow to gigantic size as Gezora and Ganimes. Plucky Humans destroy the first two, so the alien force in frustration, animates to monsters at once - ca second crayfish into another Ganimes, and a turtle into Kamoebas. Disturbed by bat sonar, the force loses control of its monsters, which battle, and then a volcano blows up everything. More fun than it has any right to be.

Off camera: The monsters here were actually relatively small by Kaiju standards. The disembodied alien force that creates them may be related to whatever power or technology allows the Garoga to create their Terror Beasts and the Zone Fighters to assume their gigantic size.

19?? - Invasion of the Astro Monster: 'Planet X' is discovered beyond Jupiter and space expedition from Earth is sent to check it out. There the Earthlings discover that Planet X is inhabited by the Xillians who live underground. The surface of their world is plagued by Ghidorah. The Xillians convince the Earthlings to let them have Godzilla and Rodan, but it turns out to be a ruse. All three monsters are then used against Earth, until a romance between an Earthman and a Xillian results in Godzilla and Rodan breaking free and defeating Ghidorah. *(released in 1965 but set at some unknown date in the future).*

Off camera: The Nebulan cockroaches in outer space send a spore - a pollution monster, Hedorah, against Earth. While that is in play, they establish a base on Earth, where they make plans to take over, commencing construction of a Kaiju robot, a prototype Mechagodzilla, creating a Godzilla theme park a cover. Given the death toll and damage attributable to Godzilla, a theme park seems... questionable. But they're cockroaches, so maybe good judgment isn't to be expected.

1971 - Godzilla vs the Smog Monster aka Godzilla vs Hedorah: An alien spore arrives evolving rapidly into the incredibly toxic and destructive shape shifter, Hedorah. A little boy has visions of Godzilla fighting Hedorah. Godzilla shows, apparently leaving its new Island home, to battle the pollution monster, eventually triumphing. Weirdest, most disturbing Godzilla movie ever.

Off screen –This is the second movie where children seem to have a psychic rapport with Godzilla or Minilla. The first is Godzilla's Revenge, also weird in its own way. Arguably, Mothra seems to have a psychic rapport with Humans through several movies.

1971 - *Godzilla vs Megalon:* First part - Nuclear testing disrupts Monster Island, sending Anguiras into a chasm, with Godzilla almost following. It also endangers the otherwise peaceful undersea kingdom of the Seatopians, who then plot revenge. Meanwhile, an inventor is drawing up plans for a robot called Jet Jaguar, which the Seatopians are intent on stealing for inexplicable reasons. (*Godzilla vs Megalon is actually released in 1973, but appears to take place over a period of time*).

Off camera: The Seatopians and the Mu from Atragon. What are the odds of two separate undersea civilizations with guardian monsters and ethnically Japanese populations are related somehow?

1972 - Godzilla vs Gigan: The Nebulan cockroach aliens, from their base inside a life-sized Godzilla statue in a theme park, plot to destroy Human civilization, using the monsters Gigan and Ghidorah. By this time, Godzilla and Anguiras are officially pals, and living on Monster Island. Anguiras has apparently gotten over the unpleasantness from Godzilla Raids Again. They realize something is up, Anguiras investigates but is driven off, so then both head for Tokyo. The two monsters face off with Gigan and Ghidorah, the Nebulans Godzilla statue fires a powerful laser at Godzilla briefly turning the tide. Eventually the bad guys are driven off, the aliens defeated, and the Godzilla statue is destroyed.

Off screen: I'm convinced that the alien constructed, life-sized, laser firing Godzilla statue is a prototype Mechagodzilla, destroyed before it could go fully online. Prove me wrong.

Off screen: This is another instance of the Kaiju directly communicating with each other. We saw it in Ghidorah, when Mothra, Godzilla and Rodan have a three cornered debate, and arguably in Ebirah when Godzilla and Mothra cooperate, as well as Godzilla's Revenge, when Godzilla, Minilla and Gabbara converse.

Also Off screen: Ghidorah's working for the Nebulans alongside Gigan. But originally, he was working for the Xillians? Ghidorah gets around, in other stories he shows up for the Garoga and Kilaaks.

1973 - Godzilla vs Megalon: Second part - Jet Jaguar is constructed, and the Seatopians steal it, planning to use it to guide Megalon. The plan works initially, and Megalon goes on a rampage led by the stolen robot. Somehow, Jet Jaguar overcomes the Seatopians programming and seeks out Godzilla for help. Then while Megalon and Godzilla fight it out, the Seatopians call up their friends, the Nebula aliens and borrow Gigan (!). Jet Jaguar grows to gigantic size to help Godzilla. In the end, Gigan flees and Megalon goes home.

Off screen: Jet Jaguar's extremely advanced abilities imply that reverse-engineered Mysterian technology might have been involved in its design. Size shifting was also seen in Zone Fighter, with both the Garoga and Peacelanders, so that might hint at alien technology as well.

Off screen: Here's a wild speculation. The disembodied alien force of Space Amoeba was able to commandeer and control a spacecraft back to Earth. Maybe a portion of it was still around and able to control Jet Jaguar, explaining the robot's sudden sentience, independence, size-changing ability and affinity for Kaiju.

Off screen: The chasms and crevices opening up on Monster Island may indicate that the Island is unstable, and sometime thereafter, the Monsters moved or were relocated to a second Island, again renamed Monster Island, aka Monsterland, seen in Destroy all Monsters.

1973 - Zone Fighter, Television Series: A twenty-six-episode Toho television series, in which Godzilla, Gigan and Ghidorah make guest appearances. Basically, the evil Garoga Empire, Humanoids with insectoid features, attacks the much more Human world of Peaceland. The Zone family flees to Earth, and either because they really hold a grudge, or because Earth is next on the list, the Garoga follow them there. The Garoga are able to grow normal sized henchmen or monsters temporarily into kaiju sized Terror-Beasts. But luckily, the Zone family are able to temporarily grow kaiju sized themselves. They make friends with Godzilla who guest stars now and then. Ghidorah shows up but is defeated and flees. Gigan shows up and is killed dead (for good) conveniently explaining non-appearance in Destroy all Monsters set later in continuity. *(For what it's worth, Toho has confirmed that this series is part of Godzilla's Showa era continuity.)*

Off Camera: Out in Space, the Simeon's in orbit around Saturn discover that the rogue black hole/neutron star Gorath, is on its way and will destroy their satellite. They need new real estate fast, and decide that Earth is looking good.

1974 - Godzilla vs Mechagodzilla: Godzilla shows up in Tokyo to wreak havoc. Anguiras confronts Godzilla, and gets its butt kicked and possibly killed (again). Then another Godzilla shows up. In the ensuing conflict, the first Godzilla's hide is burned off revealing that it's a robot - Mechagodzilla. In the battle, both are injured and forced to retreat. The creators and operators of Mechagodzilla are Ape-like aliens called Simeons, who describe themselves as third planet from a black hole. At the same time that the Simeons are mucking about with Mechagodzilla, they're trying to steal a mystical statue said to be the key to waking King Seesar, the guardian monster of Okinawa, which seems unnecessary. The Priestess awakens King Seesar, Mechagodzilla returns to action, Godzilla rejoins, and things get messy. Mechagodzilla's head is torn off.

Off screen: By specifically saying they're from the third planet, the Simeons may be sneakily alluding that they're originally from Earth. Or possibly third satellite from their primary, which we're guessing is Saturn (see Gorath).

1975 - Terror of Mechagodzilla: An attempt to locate Mechagodzilla's remains at the bottom of the sea is frustrated when a new monster, Titanosaurus appears. Unknown to all, Titanosaurus is under the control of the Simeons, now presenting as mutants, who are rebuilding Mechagodzilla. Godzilla shows up to kick Titanosaurus around. No sooner is Mechagodzilla back online, than Godzilla shows up again to finish the job. Titanosaurus breaks free and helps.

Off camera - depending on where you slip the Xillians into continuity, the Simeon invasions will be the last alien attempts to conquer Earth for the next twenty years. As to whatever happened to the Simeons, that might be Gorath.

Note – the depiction of the Black Hole aliens as Apes and Mutants isn't an accident. They were clearly inspired by Planet of the Apes and Beneath the Planet of the Apes. The Japanese went wild for Ape-men for a while. The Tokkusatsu hero Spectreman fought Ape-Men who could have walked off the movie set, and another Japanese television series, Time of the Apes also ran with the concept.

1979 - Gorath: A United Nations space mission out to Saturn discovers a rogue black hole/neutron star, smaller than earth but with 6000 times the gravity, wandering into the solar system on a collision course with Earth. As it passes Saturn, it eats two of Saturn's satellites. It is determined that in two years or so, Gorath will strike or pass close enough to Earth to destroy it. The only option is to move Earth out of the way with mega-thrusters built at the South Pole. Activating the thrusters wakes up a Walrus-Kaiju, Maguma, which must be destroyed. Earth is saved. Maguma is never seen again. *(This Toho movie was released in 1962, but is set between 1979 and 1982. The presence of a completely gratuitous Kaiju, and an extraordinarily advanced space program and technology places this within the Toho universe).*

Off Camera: Note that by 1970, the Helios 7 Probe had made it to the vicinity of Jupiter. And likely in the 1970s, a manned expedition had been sent to Planet X in the vicinity of Jupiter. So the progression in space exploration seems consistent).

Also Off Camera: Presumably, one of the Satellites of Saturn that got eaten was the home of the Simeons, the 'Black Hole Aliens.' Bad luck for them.

1999 - Destroy all Monsters: Earth has advanced. There's a moon base, a robust space program, and all the active giant monsters are now safely contained on Monster Island. Things go wrong when the Kilaaks invade both the moon base and Monster Island, take over the monsters, and use them to wage war on Earth. This is the 'Avengers' of the Toho Universe, all of the monsters are here, including Godzilla, Rodan, Anguiras (possibly last seen killed), Larval Mothra, Minilla (who has not grown), Baragon (last seen killed), Varan (last seen killed), Gorosaurus (last seen killed), Kumonga (killed in both previous appearances). The monsters break free, the Kilaaks play their final card: Ghidorah, who shows up and is promptly killed (for good?). (Note: Released in 1968, but set in 1999).

Postscript – Non-Toho Giant Monsters

Godzilla wasn't the only spawn of King Kong and the Beast from 20,000 Fathoms. In the 1950s, following the Beast, there was a flurry of what might be best called American Kaiju movies. Mostly, these were achieved through puppets, stop motion, or simply optical processing to mix images, making ordinary sized animals or persons appear colossal.

Although the atomic bomb or radiation would be alluded to, America didn't really have a primordial trauma to work out, it had won the war and dropped the bombs after all. The monsters were just monsters, threats to be defeated by American grit and know how.

Them, 1954, was first off the hopper, featuring giant ants the size of cattle, and animated by puppetry. Not quite Kaiju, obviously, but proportionately a giant monster. In 1957 the same shtick was used for giant grasshoppers in Beginning of the End, not Kaiju sized, but big enough to tussle with, this time with optical printing.

It Came From Beneath the Sea, 1955, featured a genuinely titanic six tentacled octopus that menaced San Francisco, stop-motion animated by Ray Harryhausen. 1955 also saw Tarantula, about a kaiju sized spider, enlarged through the magic of optical printing.

The Deadly Mantis, 1957, like the Beast From 20,000 Fathoms, was a giant ancient creature thawed out from the arctic ice, animated through puppetry. Another less successful puppet was the vulture in The Giant Claw, from 1957. 20 Million Miles to Earth, 1957, alluded to the Beast in its title, with another Harryhausen stop motion creature, the Ymir.

Finally, the Amazing Colossal Man and the Cyclops were resorts back to the optical printer.

1958 saw Earth vs the Spider, and War of the Colossal Beast, the Blob, Attack of the 50 Foot Woman, and the 30 Foot Bride of Candy Rock, all cheaply made. The kaiju sized monsters/people shtick was wearing itself out by that time. 1959's Giant Gila Monster was pretty much the last gasp of the genre in America, although Village of the Giants came along in 1965, and Harryhausen would have a long career in stop motion.

Over in Europe, the genre lasted a little bit longer. In 1959, Eugene Lorie who directed The Beast from 20,000 Fathoms, went on to direct The Giant Behemoth, also stop-motion animated by Ray Harryhausen, it was pretty much a deliberate remake of The Beast. Konga, from 1960, was a suitmation giant Ape, laced with melodrama. In 1961, Lorie went back to the well for a third time, directing Gorgo, often called the British Godzilla. Lorie realized the formula was tired, and tried to liven it up with a mother-son monster angle. 1962 saw the misbegotten puppet production, Reptilicus, shot in Denmark, with a bog standard story.

None of these movies had ever managed to tap into anything primordial or mythic, or access a national trauma the way that Godzilla had. There were allusions here and there to radiation or nuclear weapons creating the creatures, but that was superficial. The formula was rigorous, a monster showed up, caused trouble and was defeated. This quickly exhausted itself.

Unlike Toho, the American and European studios never tried to expand the concept or introduce new wrinkles, such as having the Kaiju battle each other. Of them all, only Gorgo really tried to push the formula. Without innovation, every giant monster movie was just like every other, and none had the mythic power of Godzilla. They grew stale quickly, audiences drifted away.

But while America and Europe were abandoning the genre, Toho was successfully building its Cinematic Universe. By the mid-sixties other film companies in Japan and South Korea were also jumping in. Basically, they were like DC, or Sony with its Spiderman characters, in the modern era, desperately trying to jump in on the Marvel Cinematic Universe bandwagon, either by tying itself to Marvel or presenting a parallel universe.

They were so heavily influenced by Toho, and so closely followed Toho in the look and feel of the monsters, and the Sci-Fi trappings of their worlds, that it's tempting to simply incorporate them into some greater Kaiju Universe.

The most successful was Daie, which had originally led Toho by distributing both King Kong and the Beast from 20,000 Fathoms in 1953. But it was slow to follow up, not jumping in until 1964 with a failed start, Nezura, a giant-rat movie, and a more successful entry, Dagora about a giant space-jellyfish. Listen, I just report these things.

Subsequently, Daie launched, not one, but two successful giant monster franchises - Gamera and Daimaijin. Originally intended to be Gamera's first foe, the concept eventually evolved into Daimaijin, a gigantic samurai statue, which became a trilogy set in medieval Japan shot and released in 1966.

The Gamera series, 1965 to 1980, was about a giant, flying fire-breathing turtle that fights a series of menaces through eight movies, and included aliens and Sci-Fi tropes. Beginning by recycling sets and props from the failed Nezura, Gamera was a surprise hit and spawned its own series of movies and monsters.

Among Daie's other Sci-Fi offerings was Warning from Space about a rogue planet heading for Earth - shades of Gorath. The warning came from friendly aliens occupying a world on the other side of the sun.

Although Warning From Space doesn't connect directly to the Gamera series, in Gamera vs Guiron, Gamera travels to an abandoned planet on the other side of the sun. So either there are two planets out there opposite the sun in the Daie cosmos, or it may be the same planet. So maybe the whole thing - Gorath, Gamera, and Warning from Space really all does just fit into a greater Showa Monsterverse.

Sorry. It's insidious, once you start drawing these connections, it's hard to stop. In my defense, I will say that at some points, Toho and Daie have discussed a Godzilla-Gamera crossover.

A particularly strange mutant was 1972's Daigoro vs Goliath, a co-production of Toho Studios and Tsuburaya Productions. Tsuburaya was the company doing the Ultraman series, and was having its tenth anniversary. Daie productions had gone bankrupt the year before, but former Daie employees from Gamera worked on it, and used practical effects and explosions from Gamera, so it really covered all the bases. It's basically a kid's movie about a lonely giant monster, Daigoro, whose mother dies and who is raised by Humans, until forced to fight the evil monster Goliath. It doesn't actually fit in anywhere, so I mention it here. No relation to Daie's Dagora by the way.

The rest of the Toho clones are all from 1967. That's not an accident. In the previous few years, starting in 1954, but accelerating in 1964, Toho had released seventeen movies featuring giant monsters. Daie had released seven up to 1967. On television, the Ultraman franchise and similar productions were all the rage. On top of all that, Toho was barreling towards its climax – Destroy All Monsters, a Kaiju epic extravaganza for 1968. The Kaiju genre was clearly barreling towards a climax, it was very clearly defined in look and style, and for other film companies it was time to climb on board the bandwagon.

There was the X From Outer Space aka Space Monster Guilala, from Shochiku studios, in which a Mars mission is buzzed by a UFO and returns with a spore which grows into Guilala, looking like a chubby, bloated Godzilla with a beak which can fire or spit up plasma balls. Guilala is mocked as the space chicken.

Gappa the Triphibian Monster, from Nikkatsu, is a heartwarming story about a stolen Kaiju egg and a couple of pterodactyl type Kaiju who come to get it back, reminiscent of the earlier Mothra, Gorgo and the same year's Son of Godzilla.

Meanwhile, South Korea produced Yongary, about a fire-breathing Godzilla-type, who wreaks havoc. In the background is the South Korean space program. So similar was Yongary, that in Germany, the movie was simply billed as Godzilla and the Giant Claw. The Germans often played fast and loose with movie titles.

There's also the contemporary, but unrelated South Korean film, Wangmagwi. In this one, aliens drop off a monster which grows to Kaiju size. Between these two Korean films, they incorporated literally every Toho trope except battling monsters.

None of these knock offs really took hold. Although they followed the Toho mold religiously, they weren't really able to distinguish themselves, and they simply lacked the depth that Toho's cinematic universe afforded. Without a stable of monsters, and without any new directions, they were simply free riders, jumping on the bandwagon but with nothing unique to offer.

Meanwhile, the Kaiju genre was running out of creative steam. The Gamera series ended in 1971, with a 1980 stock footage movie, Super Monster Gamera being a last-ditch effort to stave off bankruptcy. Toho had intended to wrap up its universe in 1968, but, driven by commerce, its monsterverse dragged on until 1975. Toho kept on going strong, continuing to make movies without monsters.

But in 1975, Toho's cinematic universe finally came to an end. They'd literally tried everything, pushed every angle, and had built a sprawling, self-contradicting, albeit impressive lore. But by that time they had largely lost touch with the iconic power of the original Godzilla from 1954. They were creatively exhausted and audiences just weren't there.

Not even a brief revival of Giant-Ape and monster movies around the world, driven by Dino de Laurentis' King Kong in 1976 could push them further. On the heels of Laurentis' Kong came Queen Kong, Mighty Peking Man, A.P.E, and Yeti, Giant of the 20th Century. But Toho and its Godzilla universe sat it out - no returning monster or new monsters appeared to ride the wave.

By 1977, science fiction had taken off in a new direction with Star Wars, and giant monsters were definitely old fashioned. Godzilla and its friends and imitators had a stunning 21 year run of some forty movies, but it was definitely over.

Until 1984 rolled around. That's when a new, bigger, badder Godzilla reappeared in theatres to launch a new cinematic universe: The Heisei Era.

Acknowledgment —In respect of this exploration I want to call out and thank Chris Nigro, a kindred spirit who was kind enough to publish the preliminary versions of this essay online in the Guest Section of his G-Saga web site. Chris has become a good friend and is a writer and publisher in his own right, with Wild Hunt Press. I gratefully acknowledge the thoughts and ideas of Chris, Gordon Long, Vennie Anderson, J.D. Lees and other Kaiju fans, which contributed to the shaping of this the work you have before you now. I treasure their friendship.

The End

Tentacle Overlords and Murder-Chickens

Introduction to the Silurian Hypothesis

Let's talk about the Silurian Hypothesis. It's actually a serious thing. In a nutshell, back in 2018, a pair of Astrophysicists, Adam Frank and Gavin Schmidt, came up with an interesting question.

Basically, what they said is that for at least the last 320 million years, life on Earth has been sufficiently complex to give rise to an intelligent species, and there's been sufficient fossil fuels laying around to support the emergence of an industrial civilization much like our own.

So….Could there be some lost civilization lurking in deep time? And if so, how would we find it? What should we be looking for?

What we learn from these questions is that Astrophysicists seem to have way too much time on their hands. But they had some very interesting points.

The name Silurian, by the way, comes from a Doctor Who serial from 1970 written by Malcolm Hulke, which featured the survivors of a Dinosaur civilization waking up from hibernation and wanting their planet back. Hulke, judging by his other work for Doctor Who seems a little obsessed with the subject, but we'll discuss him elsewhere.

Mainly, what this name tells us is that Astrophysicists are nerds, but we all knew that.

Desperately Seeking Silurians

Could there be some lost civilization lurking in deep time?

And if so, how would we find it? Where would we even look? What would we look for?

It kind of makes sense to at least consider the possibility. Human civilization is about 10,000 years old, tops. And really, it's only in the last hundred or so years that we've been making big moves.

The Earth is four and a half billion years old. We've had life on Earth for maybe three billion years, although most of that is just bacteria or jellyfish and simple stuff. We've had complex life, like worms, for 500 million years. Complex life started crawling onto land 400 million years ago. About 350 to 300 million years ago, things really started getting jiggy.

That's a lot of time. Even if we're only counting the last 320 million years, if you took that, and rendered it as a book, Human civilization would only amount to a hiccup on the end of the period, at the bottom of the last page of that book.

We'd need to last thousands and thousands more years to amount to an actual word in the book, and it would probably be a sappy little word like 'the' or 'if' or 'bye' and not a good word like 'potassium' or 'refractory.' The rate we're going, we'd be lucky to rate even a letter, and it would probably be some lousy consonant.

In all that time, there's a lot of opportunity for an advanced civilization to come and go. So the question the hypothesis poses is: 'If it was there, how would we know?'

This turns out to be more complicated than you'd expect. We haven't found any giant brained turtles with thumbs and power tools in the fossil record. No Super-Lemurs, no Ape civilizations, no smart Dinosaurs, nothing, so far.

But that's not necessarily proof of anything. The fact that we haven't found a Dinosaur with big cranium and a backhoe isn't proof that there wasn't one.

Fossilization is an incredibly rare phenomenon. Maybe one in a million, or one in ten million, of animals that live, manage to get turned into fossils. And most of them haven't even been found. The fact that we find fossils at all speaks to the mind boggling numbers of animals that have lived and died. Every year there are new discoveries, we keep rewriting the history of life. It looks like we've got the big picture down, the broad strokes, most of the major stuff.

But the picture is fragmentary. True enough, in any particular range of a few million years, we've got a decent idea of what was going on. But there's a limit. Realistically, we've identified a fraction of all the species that have ever existed, and it's likely that we'll never identify more than a significantly larger fraction.

It would be very easy for something, even a blip civilization that lasted ten or twenty thousand years, to slip through the cracks. It would be a sliver, a hiccup in a year's record across millions of years, the equivalent of a punctuation mark or a letter or two obscured in the spine of that book I mentioned.

Honestly, we're pretty proud of our civilization, but it's not nearly as permanent as we think. Most of our buildings are constructed to last only a few centuries at most before falling apart. The world is full of lost cities, now only piles of rubble or overgrown jungle, detectable only because the terrain is unusually rectangular. In a few thousand years, Mount Rushmore will just be a weathered series of cliffs. In forty thousand years the Pyramids will be gone.

Basically, if we all died tomorrow, somewhere between ten thousand and a hundred thousand years, almost every trace of our existence would be wiped away.

A civilization coming along a million years from now — hyper-evolved Raccoons or Parrots, wouldn't necessarily know we ever existed.

Now, I'm not going to get too far into the details of Frank and Schmidt's paper. They were deeply interested in the question of what sort of footprints a civilization like that might leave, and how and where we might look for these footprints.

Me, I'm interested in asking: If there were previous civilizations, who the heck were they?

A civilization means that there was an intelligent, tool-using species.

Those don't just grow on trees. They don't spring out of nowhere, fully formed, with no antecedents or forebears.

Look at us, we started from tree rats maybe seventy-five million years ago. Those tree-rats eventually evolved into prosimian like Pottos and Lorises over sixty million years ago, Lemurs fifty-five million years ago, and Monkeys some thirty-five million years back. Apes came along fifteen to twenty million years ago. Then upright walking Apes five million years. The first creatures that could be called Human-like, Homo Erectus two million years ago. Modern Humans are at best a couple of hundred thousand years old. Human civilization ten thousand years, being generous. Technological civilization? Maybe a hundred and fifty years.

Another intelligent species has to start somewhere, they have to evolve from something, they come from somewhere, there's going to be an evolutionary lineage with ancestors and relatives. Even if we don't have proof of the particular intelligent species, by this time, we're likely to have identified relatives or predecessors. Their equivalents of Monkeys or at least tree-rats.

Put yourself in the shoes of some future speculative Raccoon paleontologists. They might never discover modern Humans.

But if they're poking around, and turning up Monkeys and Apes and such, they'd start to think that these little creatures with their forward-facing eyes and big brains and grasping hands might have had the potential to be on the way to turning into something. Even without finding us, they'd have a guess that primates might produce something like us.

So if there were Silurian Civilizations, who would they have been — exotic Proto-Monkeys, Super-Lemurs, some extra-calculating colonial insect, giant Murder-Chickens, smart Dinosaurs? When you get right down to it, the list of candidates thins out pretty fast.

I mean take Hamsters. Hamsters are pretty good, love the little fellows to pieces. But no. I'm not seeing a Hamster based civilization, or any kind of rodents for that matter. Same thing with horses (look ma, no hands!), snakes (no hands, again!), amphibians, or various other entries that for one reason or another, take themselves out of the sweepstakes.

For our Silurian Civilizations, we need some basics: We need candidate species which have, or show a capacity for (1) Large brains/hyper-intelligence; (2) Sensory acuity; (3) Some kind of manipulative capacity; (4) Sociability.

That thins the field.

So let me introduce you to one of the more unusual candidates for Silurian Civilizations.

Cephalopods and the Tentacles in Deep Time

The Cephalopods are by far the most interesting, albeit Lovecraftian, candidates for a Silurian civilization. Possibly several Silurian civilizations.

They've been around for a very long time.

The Cephalopods, the ones around today at least, sport the distinction of being by far and away the most intelligent invertebrates on Earth. That's impressive.

Maybe less impressive when you consider the competition is flatworms, barnacles and mosquitos. But let's not be mean.

Still, there's a lot of evidence for remarkable degrees of intelligence and even some facility with manipulating the environment. Octopuses and Cuttlefish have been shown to be curious and communicative, are able to distinguish different Human beings by sight, and solve relatively complex problems, use tools, build structures, play, communicate and even work cooperatively.

It's hard to gauge Cephalopod intelligence, they're usually classified as better than cold blooded animals. Smarter than fish, snakes, lizards etc., but not quite on the level of Mammals and Birds. Some proponents suggest that some might be as clever as toddlers some not so bright Dogs, which strikes me as a bit optimistic. But sure, why not?

Clearly, they're not on the level of Humans, Apes, Monkeys, Corvids, or Parrots, or even really smart Dogs. But there's definitely something going on with them. There's genuine animal-level intelligence, and that means there's the prospect to build to something more. Possibly, something of Human intelligence, somewhere in the deep wells of time.

Not all cephalopods are Mensa candidates, if Octopuses and Cuttlefish are at the top, it seems that the Nautiluses are the pokey students. It seems reasonable to assume that there's a diversity of intellectual accomplishment in modern day cephalopods — some are likely smarter than others, given size, environment, diets and species. But this is largely unmapped territory.

They have complex neural structures, with ring shaped brains and considerable neural distribution through the tentacles, so much so that some reckless types have described them as having brains in their arms and suggesting that each tentacle has a certain amount of autonomy.

Possibly, their neural architecture is utterly alien to anything in the vertebrate world and we don't have a good handle on how it works. But it does seem to work for them. It's possible that they're at the limits of their particular 'circular brain and tentacles' architecture. Or they could be capable of much more. We don't really know.

On top of that, they've got some of the key pre-requisites. Mainly, highly developed eyes and potentially effective manipulator organs — their arms and tentacles. By the way: Yes, there is a technical difference between arms and tentacles on Cephalopods. No, I'm not going to explain the difference because I don't care.

Looking at the pre-historical record, the Cephalopods go way back. The earliest Cephalopods seem to date back to the Cambrian era, an impressive 530 million years ago. Given that stunning span of time to work with, it's tempting to imagine they might have been able to come up with something interesting and impressive.

Frank and Schmidt were only looking back 320 million years, because they were thinking land-based life and availability of fossil fuels. But the Cephalopod lineage goes back 210 million years further. It took primates 75 million years to get from tree rats to us. The Cephalopods have something like eight times that span to work with. From monkeys to us, 30 million years – the Cephs had almost twenty times that.

Sadly, the earliest Cephalopods seem to have been Ammonites and Nautiloids. We know that the modern Nautiloids are the remedial learning class of modern Cephalopods, so perhaps we shouldn't expect too much from them. Apparently dragging that big shell around means you don't have to be smart.

But then again, we're talking an incredible span of deep time, so who knows?

The more modern lineage of tentacle bandits emerged some 416 million years ago. The oldest Octopus-like fossils date back 330 million years. So basically, right around the earliest time that Frank and Schmidt think a high Silurian civilization was a prospect, the Cephalopods were getting in gear.

Modern octopuses seem to show up in the Jurassic, 155 million years ago, Squids and Cuttlefish, near the end of the Cretaceous, say 70 million years ago.

Now given that these are underwater critters, and soft tissue doesn't usually fossilize, the record is particularly sketchy. But there's no reason to think that the neurological complexity and brain architecture of cephalopods is a recent invention. Or that what we're looking at now is their peak development of these traits, and they didn't reach greater heights earlier.

They may well have been very smart for a very very long time. We can't even say for sure that the Nautiloids of hundreds of millions of years ago may have produced some rocket scientist species. I doubt it, but we can't rule it out.

So hypothetically, we've got a minimum span of say 150 million to 300 million years where a Cephalopod civilization was a real possibility. If we look at the single standard of comparison — us, we went from flinging our poop at Leopards to building spacecraft in about 5 million years. 10 million tops if you wanted to be mean about it.

Now Cephalopods reproduce much faster and in huge numbers, a single female may breed (once) at two or three years and produce 40,000 (mostly rapidly eaten) offspring, and they can reproduce in as little as a few years after being born. Compare that with Humans, producing a mere handful of children, and taking a couple of decades to get going. That reproductive difference suggests a potential to evolve rapidly given sufficient pressure. So we can assume that they could potentially evolve high intelligence much, much more quickly than we did.

But even going by our slow-pokey Monkey standards, the time frame suggests that there's room for as many as thirty separate Cephalopod civilizations could have arisen from start, one after another.

So why aren't we all bowing down to our squishy ink-squirting overlords right now?

Well, they've got some handicaps. A big one is that their blood is copper based (they're just weird!), which is significantly less efficient than our iron-based blood. This is a big handicap since big brains require a lot of energy and particularly a lot of oxygen. And let's be frank, it just takes more work, more energy, to process oxygen out of water than it is to suck it from the air, so double handicap.

Copper based blood works slightly better in cold abyssal environments, so it does give an advantage in certain conditions. But it's a handicap. Maybe they do better in Ice Ages, and there's just not enough glaciation going on. Or at the poles, or in abyssal deeps, which would be hard to reach.

Another huge obstacle seems to be limited life spans; Octopus life spans average three to four years. Cuttlefish live about two and literally fall apart. There's variation, some species life spans are as short as six months, others can live up to fifteen years in captivity, and the giant and colossal squids might make it to thirty. But generally, life spans are very short. It's hard for even a large brained animal to build a civilization if they're dying of old age at about the same time that a Human is being potty trained. We can assume that a Cephalopod Civilization will not go in for long novels or epic trilogies.

But the really big stumbling block is their breeding strategy. Cephalopods breed and then die. They produce massive numbers of offspring which then have to fend for themselves. There's no parental nurturing, no opportunity to pass on knowledge or information, no teaching, no culture. Every single Octopus literally has to invent their version of Octopus civilization from the start, and it dies with them. And they might only have three or four years to do it, tops. On top of that, without any kind of familial or biological-relationship structure, there's no real basis for social complexity, which means no real advantage to organized cooperative behavior.

It seems that the boneless are boned. In the evolutionary sweepstakes, they went down some blind alleys, and took themselves out of the running.

Or did they? Recently, we've discovered Octopus 'nurseries' Something no one suspected, and which frankly astonished scientists.

The first one was discovered only in 2013, and we've only found four so far. Typically, Octopuses are solitary brooders, laying and caring for eggs in isolation, until the young are born and the mothers die. But in the Octopus nurseries, over a hundred females may brood together. This allows for at least a possibility of some kind of social cooperation between brooding mothers, and even something like knowledge or experience to be shared between individuals of different ages, possibly even between generations.

Mind blown! If Octopus 'nurseries' exist, then we have at least a hypothetical possibility that Cephalopods, with the right habitat or environmental conditions might be able to assemble the basic building blocks of culture and civilization as we know it. And if they built it, maybe once they got it running, they could keep it going.

At the very least, it shows that the behavior of modern cephalopods has more potential for complexity and diversity than we imagined.

And that's not the only instances of sociability of Octopuses — look up Octolantis and Octopia online for references.

Or check out the Humboldt Squid, an aggressive pack hunter that seems to go for teamwork. It takes intelligence, social skills and coordination to be a pack hunter, just ask wolves. The potential is there, and it's likely been there all along. So far they haven't amounted to anything lasting that we know of, and truthfully, the Octopus nurseries are likely a transient phenomenon that comes along now and then when conditions are right, have probably occurred thousands or hundreds of thousands of times over thousands of years and have never led anywhere.

It's only a spark, and most sparks flare and die. There are probably millions of sparks that never go anywhere. But now and then, there's one that catches and starts a forest fire.

So we do have the possibility that some past species of Cephalopod might have had the right conditions long enough, that the spark did last, find the right circumstances that it did catch fire. It's a long shot, but three to five hundred million years is a long time.

And lastly, we need to acknowledge that there are forms of complex social organization, like insect colonies, that don't rely on the vertebrate traits of parenting/teaching and building culture on inter generational knowledge transmission.

Colonial insects clearly took a different, fairly sophisticated route. Now the eusociality that insects developed is not a good fit for cephalopods. At least not the ones we know. But who knows, there's room in deep time for a lot of varieties of Cephalopod and life strategies. Hypothetically, anything could happen including potentially marrying ant-like social organization to big Octopus brains.

Colonial Insects by the way, might be another hypothetical candidate for a possible Silurian civilization hiding in deep time. Ants, Bees and Termites all date back to the Cretaceous, possibly even into the Jurassic. That's 150 million years - plenty of time to do something weird. But then again, all the

Colonial Insects have done just fine for themselves without needing a techno-civilization like our own. I think the biomass of colonial insects matches Humanity. There are something like 20 quadrillion ants. Generally, if what you're already doing works just fine, there's no real pressure to evolve.

But the example of Colonial Insects does show us and at least raises the possibility that with three or four hundred million years to keep failing in, the Cephalopods might come up with something allowing for complex social structures of some kind, possibly a linear culture like our own, possibly something eusocial, or something unimagined or even unimaginable.

So maybe there was a Cephalopod Civilization, somewhere in deep time? Maybe there was a whole bunch of them?

But if so? Where's the evidence.

This is the interesting question. We've come to understand that our own civilization is incredibly transient. We've learned that cities abandoned barely a few centuries can end up so completely reclaimed by nature that we'd never know they had been there, except for some oddly rectangular mounds discovered by Lidar. Hell, even the footprints and junk on the moon has maybe fifteen million years before being obscured by micro-meteors and cosmic dust. It's sort of humbling.

Were Homo Erectus elaborate tool users? Did they work with leather and bone? Almost certainly. We know they worked stone and fire, and those are tough ones. It stands to reason that they'd also master materials that were more available and easier to work with as well. It takes a lot of work and skill to chip rocks into a useful tool, or to build or maintain a fire.

Were they wood workers, carpenters, architects? How far could they get? How far did they get? The only bits of their culture that survived are stone tools and some signs of fire. The rest, if there was anything, is gone.

If Homo Erectus had a wooden city it's long gone. If they built a city with clay bricks like Sumer, it's long gone. Even if they built a city with stone, we'd be incredibly lucky to find ruins, and we might not recognize those ruins at all. For all we know, they may have advanced all the way to a space program and gone to Mars.

Of course, if they did, they don't seem to have bothered to settle the Americas, or Australia, or New Zealand, and they'd have probably moved a bunch of animals and insects around, deliberately and accidentally, in ways that would have biologists scratching their heads. We don't seem to find any evidence of a thin layer of pollution, or traces of radioactive elements or exotic molecules that can't exist in nature. We've seen no sign of a spaceport, or even a backhoe. So probably not - scratch Homo Erectus, and the other Homo Whatevers.

If any prior version of Homo built a civilization, and it's not out of the question, they didn't get nearly as far as we did. At best, probably no further than a localized early Iron or Bronze Age level of tech, and they almost certainly didn't last long enough to get widespread or leave a residue.

A deep time civilization might be a snapshot, a few thousand years of needle in a haystack of hundreds of millions of years. Come and gone so fast, that the odds against being one of those one in a million fossils are astronomical, and the odds of us finding it are even more astronomical. Unless you're incredibly lucky, you'd never find a direct obvious relic of a deep time Civilization.

Now admittedly, some very smart people have been thinking about this, people smarter than me, and they have examined our sample size of one (that's us) and speculated that a relatively high-tech global civilization, the stuff we've been doing the last two hundred years, would leave significant discoverable traces in the planetary record.

This would include unexplained global temperature spikes, perhaps changes in atmospheric composition recorded in rocks, unexplained spikes in isotopes, particularly of heavy metals, and perhaps plastics or exotic long-lasting molecules not typically found in nature.

All right, so we've got something to look for. But there are some problems.

First, you have to reach pretty impressive heights to leave that measurable trace. We've had 10,000 years of Human civilization, and only in the last century are we leaving the sort of environmental footprints that would stand out in the geological record.

Second, a lot of the stuff that might signify a possible civilization might also have natural causes — volcanism, solar flares, asteroid impacts, etc. So we'd have to be careful to try and rule that out.

Third, the geological record is not the most sensitive thing around. We measure time by years, decades, centuries, even millennia. But the geological record we're trying to examine is probably sensitive only to a span of a few hundred thousand years at best. So our civilization might only be a few seconds blip in an hours-long program. That makes it hard to interpret.

But the biggest challenge, is that we are searching based on the criteria of our sample size of exactly one. One known civilization, ours, using terrestrial land-based fire and metals technology. That's what we're looking for. We're looking for the sort of traces that we know we are leaving.

I don't have the foggiest idea of what criteria we would use for a water-based cephalopod civilization built on ocean floors, in shallow seas or even tidal zones. What would they do? How far would they even be able to get. How would we even go about searching for something like that? What sort of traces would they leave in the geological record? What would we be looking for?

An aquatic civilization poses real problems. Air moves more quickly than water and is less soluble, so you can escape your garbage by moving away a little bit or moving it away. In water, you'd typically end up breathing your garbage. That's a problem with the population densities we associate with civilization. A lot of 'civilization' things; like monoculture crops, transport, distribution and production will just work very differently than on land. Or won't work at all.

Fire technology is a land-based technology, it's premised on the easy availability of burnable fuel. Without fire, you don't have ceramics or metallurgy. Fire, combustion, is not just our high technology, it's our lifeblood. We use it, directly or indirectly to heat our homes, drive our cars, power literally everything. Sure, we have wind and nuclear, but mostly, we burn stuff.

An aquatic cephalopod civilization obviously has real challenges with burning stuff. They'd find it incredibly difficult to access fossil fuels on land, and underwater it would be a sure fire way to poison their environment.

For fire, even if they used it, they'd have to do things differently. They'd rely on resources, resource processing and energy systems that would be deeply alien. Even if they had a tidal zone or shoreline operation that used fire technology, it wouldn't have the same massive footprint.

We could potentially have a civilization of cephalopods more intelligent than we are, and even more advanced in some ways, but because of their environment, things like fire manipulation and metallurgy doesn't exist. Or exists in marginal fringe technology. Or is developed or applied in such a different way that we'd never detect it. It might develop exotic technologies to build coral cities or manipulate ocean currents and we wouldn't even know what to look for.

A cephalopod civilization could be so different and so alien, I'm not sure we could come up with a test to look for traces of them. Maybe we can formulate tests and apply them, eventually. But I think it would take some careful thinking and a lot of searching.

And honestly, they may not have gotten far enough to leave traces that we could search for. Right now, our search is for civilizations that made it to our level.

But take a look — our ten thousand years of Human culture is littered with dead civilizations. We're the only ones that got this far, in part because we built on almost all of our predecessors.

Having said all that, we might have actually seen a trace of a Cephalopod Civilization. Back in 2011, a husband and wife pair of Paleontologists, Mark McMenamin and spouse Diana Schulte McMenamin, came up with a bold new theory to explain some anomalies they'd noticed.

They noted that the bones of the giant Ichthyosaur, Shonosaurus, a whale-like Reptile that ran up to 70 feet and 90 tons and wandered the ancient oceans, often appeared to be found in unusual configurations, apparently vertebra arranged in double rows, or spirals.

McMenamin suggested that the cause of these strange configurations was a Triassic Kraken, a giant cephalopod big enough to pull down and drown whale sized critters, which would then carefully arrange the bones in artistic patterns, making self-portraits. This implies not only an intelligent cephalopod, but an artistically inclined one, possibly a civilization.

I do have to acknowledge that there are a number of critics and criticism of this theory, such as the almost complete lack of evidence, and the fact that it's nuttier than a rocket ship built by squirrels.

The McMenamin's theory briefly made the rounds of media back in 2011. It was apparently a slow news year, and you heard about it from time to time. Last I heard, the McMenamins are sticking to their guns. Let's face it though, if this is the best evidence for a cephalopod civilization, then we're still looking for it.

But a Roman Empire level civilization, or a Renaissance level civilization in deep time might well pass under the radar and be literally undetectable, unless we get incredibly lucky.

It's possible a Homo Erectus civilization made it all the way to the Iron age in some region, and then vanished without spreading far enough, or lasting long enough, or making enough of an impact to leave traces, and they'd literally be on our doorstep - barely a couple of million years ago, if that.

It's possible that we have had dozens Cephalopod Civilizations, built on particular quirks of climate, geography, biology that reached Roman or Renaissance levels repeatedly and being aquatic, couldn't proceed further, and never left a significant planetary geological footprint. They destroyed themselves, wrecked their ecology, or were simply undone by natural climate change. We might never know or even suspect.

Tentacles in the Outer Darkness?

Even if they reached our levels, space travel and beyond, we might miss them. Even then, their technology and resource use, the way they did things, might be so fundamentally different from ours, that not only would we miss them, we wouldn't recognize them even if we found their traces. We'd literally have to stumble over permanent stone ruins buried long ago. They might have reached space millions of years ago, and we'd never know.

Unless of course, we manage to get out to one of those 'water worlds'

That's an interesting prospect. Satellites around the gas giants — Europa, Ganymede, Calisto around Jupiter, Titan and

Enceladus around Saturn, Triton around Uranus, are believed to be water worlds. What the Hell, there's even speculation an asteroid, Ceres might have, or had, a hidden ocean.

Essentially, all of these satellites are very low density. They're lower density than Earth's moon, which is rock. For the record, Earth's overall density is 5.15, we're a heavy planet with a big heavy iron core. The moon is just mainly plain rock, density 3.3. The density of water is 1.0. The density of the satellites I'm talking about is low, between 2.0 and 1.5. This means that they're basically dirty snowballs, mixtures of water and rock.

Now, the way things work, is that the heaviest elements sink to form the core, and the lighter elements float above. So the thinking is that these worlds are rocky cores sheathed by dirty ice, frozen at the surface. But the way that water works, you might get liquid oceans, powered and warmed by tidal forces, friction or heat decay of the core, covered with an icy, rocky shell.

These are worlds where scientists pontificate that they might possibly have life under the ice, that geological and tidal forces may create pockets or layers of liquid oceans, where conditions might support life. As wild as those theories sound, we've found ice volcanoes spurting water plumes hundreds of miles into space. So yes, around those strange worlds, there are buried recesses of liquid water and heat.

If these Satellites could support life, conditions there might resemble Earth's abyssal ocean depths sufficiently to make them viable colonies for a Cephalopod Civilization, places friendlier to their civilization than Mars is to ours.

It's possible that we may only discover evidence of Earth's lost Cephalopod Civilizations, when one day we knock on the icy shell of those worlds and someone vast, primordial and tentacled goes

"You rang?"

A Smoking Gun? An Emptied Earth and PETM

The search for Silurians hasn't been going on very long. The Silurian Hypothesis itself only dates to 2018, that's barely six years.

Well, assuming we don't find a convenient skeleton with a very large brain case and a collection of power tools, which is a long shot, we have to look for subtle clues.

It can depend on the time frame. Basically, due to erosion, wind, water, volcanism, the simple processes of life, the movement of continental shelves, the average age of the Earth's surface is about 2.5 million years. The Earth is resurfacing constantly. Anything much older than that would be difficult or impossible to detect conventionally.

Sometimes a tell-tale can be an absence. The thing with a stone quarry is that it leaves a great big hole in the landscape. That's a pretty significant tell-tale. It could take a long time for erosion to obscure those traces.

We might look for biological anomalies, say species that somehow exist where they shouldn't be — like Camels in Australia, or Kangaroos in Ireland, although its likely actually much more subtle — small plants, small animals, insects, parasites. Our civilization has been great for spreading things around in ways that would otherwise be impossible. But again, given enough time, it could be hard to spot. Future Racoon biologists might be puzzled by how Camels got to Australia, Hippos to South America and Cats to New Zealand, but they might just assume really good swimmers.

Luckily, we have a sample size of one, that's us, to work with. We can look at our own civilization to guess at what traces we are leaving behind that could be detectable long term. It turns out, we produce a lot of garbage — so you'd want to look for an exotic layer, a lot of traces of plastics, or of complex molecules that don't occur in nature, traces of refined radioactive elements, or rapid climate change (as we're doing right now) that doesn't seem to have a natural or geological explanation.

I don't think anyone's actually carried out any systematic searches for geological markers. There hasn't been a deep dive survey specifically looking for a red flag.

Theoretically, what you would do is identify a bunch of chemical traces, particularly long-lasting molecules and compounds that are hard or impossible to come by naturally, and then you'd start checking sedimentary rocks for a hard to explain layer. There's likely a whole bunch of clever tests we could formulate, and then go searching.

We haven't done that though. That sounds expensive. Instead, basically, what's been done is to give a lot of existing data a look to see if anything jumped out at us.

Something jumped out at us.

It's called the Paleocene-Eocene Thermal Maximum, also known as PETM, try pronouncing it. It was a time, approximately 55.5 million years ago when suddenly, for no apparent reason, global temperatures spiked, jumping 5 to 8 degrees, for a couple of hundred thousand years, before returning to normal. The period that triggered it may have been as short as 6,000 years.

6,000 years is the time frame of almost everything that could be called Human civilization on this planet.

Charted on graphs it stands out massively, as through geological history, temperatures slowly rise and fall, and variation tends to be within a narrow range. The PETM spike is literally shocking.

Definitely, something strange and extreme went on during this period. Something fairly unique.

The only other time we've seen evidence of that kind of weird anomalous spike possibly emerging is... us. We seem to be doing it right now at this moment.

Now, just because there's an extraordinary spike, doesn't mean its actual proof of a Silurian Civilization. That's a potential explanation, but there may be others. Volcanism, cometary impact, methane release, a bizarre shift in ocean currents.

We don't really know. The science of searching for Silurians is in its infancy. And honestly, it's probably not going to be an urgent field of study. We're intrigued by life existing somewhere else right now, we're worried about asteroids hitting us, but the possibility of a fifty-five-million-year old civilization... doesn't seem pressing.

But assuming, just for the sake of arguing, that the PETM really does represent a Silurian Civilization, then that begs the question: Who the hell were they?

Here's the trick: An intelligent species doesn't just come out of nowhere. There's got to be predecessors, there are relatives. Humans are surrounded by Apes, Monkeys and lemurs, and we have progenitor hominids. You don't just jump from Tree-Rat to Tree-Rat-in-a-Lab Coat. That takes time.

You need to look around for species in that ten-million-year window between 65 and 55 that showed signs of moving in the right direction, creatures that seemed to have the potential to develop bigger brains and manipulating paws, predecessors or relatives that show that the capacity is there.

The thing is, 55 million years ago, there doesn't seem to be any good candidates around. The Dinosaurs got waxed ten million years before, so they're not around. The Mammals have only been dominant for ten million years; they're just getting started.

Hulke's original Silurians were long off the stage — unless they managed to hibernate for at least ten million years, surviving the extinction of every other Dinosaur without leaving any traces, and then promptly screw it up. But that seems ludicrously unlikely. So, let's drop that.

The end of the Dinosaurs 65 million years ago literally cleared the biological deck. The period between 65 and 55 million years ago was called the Paleocene. Initially, in those first ten million years, Post-Dino, not much was happening. Mammals, Birds, and various kinds of Reptiles competed — this was when you got the Titanoboas and the super-sized lizards and terror birds. Mostly, for these first few million years, Mammals remained small.

Eventually, in the later part, as we close in on the PETM, the Mammals slowly but steadily began to dominate the ecology, diversifying and towards the end of the era growing larger. But for most of the period, the Mammals were not very impressive. Most of the largest Mammals of the period were probably no bigger than a modern cow. The most sophisticated were probably feebs by modern Mammal standards.

That poses a problem, because you need to be a certain size to host a brain large and complex enough to build a civilization, and mostly, it was the runt era of small primitive Mammals, not too bright, going '*hey, when was the last time I saw a velociraptor?*'

Who is available to rule the world?

Not the primates. Although primates date back to the Cretaceous, basically, they were a far cry from what they are now. Fifty-five million years ago, our ancestors were basically just tree-rats and maybe just starting to experiment with Lemurs.

Yeah, you caught me. There's an outside chance that the PETM was due to Super-Lemurs. Not a big chance, Lemurs had just arrived on the scene, and going by our own example, they probably needed a few more million years to cook. You never know, maybe they could have skipped ahead, but it seems unlikely.

Basically, the issue is that in the ten million years since the Dinosaurs got capped, there's not a lot of Mammals ready to step up, not even Lemurs.

This is the problem generally — an absence of what we would recognize as the baseline of smart critters. The Elephants haven't evolved yet. Neither have cats or dogs. There are no whales. All the big lineages of Mammals, including the ones that might produce an intelligent species simply don't exist in any significant form. Bats are well evolved by this time, but I don't see them producing a civilization.

This was the beginning for the Mammals, they were just starting to come out of the shadows, diversify and find their feet. It wasn't until the later epochs that they would start producing giants and exotic experiments like Apes and Humans. The truth is that we don't actually have any known Mammal lineage from immediately before this time that might have been well positioned to evolve into an intelligent species in time to do the PETM boogie.

I'm not talking about finding an intelligent species here. I'm talking about finding a family whose members might have shown a potential to develop in that direction within the time frame of the Paleocene. Tree rats, pseudo-cows, and whatnot just don't cut it.

So if there was a civilization, then whose was it?

The Giant Murder Chicken Conspiracy

Not Primates and not Mammals.

I think we can rule out super-smart snakes, cerebral tortoises or high IQ lizards. These ectotherms, or cold-blooded animals have slow metabolisms, which means that they'd have trouble with the energy or oxygen requirements of a large high functioning brain. And let's be honest, their metabolisms were slow, their hearts were primitive, their skeletons weren't well built for large and active. They're a wash out.

The Cephalopods are around, but let's leave them off the table for the time being. We already talked about them.

There's only one real candidate for a PETM civilization.

Murder-Chickens.

Giant Murder-Chickens.

There were actually several lineages of giant flightless birds around that time. Think of them as Dinosaurs II, the No-Budget Sequel.

The Gastornithiforms, led by Gastornis, were a line of giant flightless birds with large skulls and powerful jaws. These creatures were built much more heavily and with much larger heads compared to more recent Ostriches, Moa and Elephant Birds. Originally seen as active predators, the current theory is that they were herbivores.

The Gastornithidae started up around the middle Paleocene, roughly sixty million years ago, and lasted until the mid-Eocene, roughly forty-five million years ago. They were widespread through North America, Europe, Asia and possibly even Australia (!). Their largest specimens reached almost seven feet tall and nearly four hundred pounds.

There's also another candidate lineage, the Phorusrhacids, native to South America, definitely predators, whose species ranged from three to ten feet tall, also with heavy builds and massive heads. The Phorusrhacids actually just miss the PETM, the earliest fossils date back fifty-three million years. But this may only mean that we haven't found earlier specimens.

The known Gastornithidae and Phorusrhacids themselves are not the direct candidates for a giant murder-chicken civilization. But what they are is proof of the existence of two lineages of large bodied, highly advanced, terrestrial birds during this time period.

What they do is show us that there were at least two bird lineages around that could have produced a hyper-intelligent, tool-using species of giant murder-chicken.

Yes, I know. Giant yes. Potentially murdery. But not technically chickens. If they were murdering you, you wouldn't be nit-picking like that, would you? So give me a break.

You see, the thing with evolution, unlike the diagrams in high school textbooks, is that it is not a straight line. It doesn't lead directly from one animal, to the next animal, to the next animal, and so on, with only a single species being the result.

Rather, evolution is like a branching structure, species are always branching off, some branches die, some branches proliferate. An earlier species may not result only in a single offspring species. The evolutionary pressure that causes speciation may lead a species in a couple of different directions.

The Elephant ancestor produced Deinotheres (lower jaw tusks), Gomphotheres (shovel tusk), Mammoths, Mastodons and Stegodonts, alongside modern Elephants.

Nowadays, it's just us, but once, there were a handful of advanced Hominids more or less side by side.

Hoofed animals have diversified into everything from Camels, to Cattle, Gazelles and Goats.

The existence of large, relatively advanced flightless Birds, means that somewhere in the evolutionary process that led to them, there could have been side branches or offshoots that evolved towards high intelligence and tool use.

We don't have actual evidence for such a creature, but the possibility of one emerging as a side branch of the Phorusrhacids or Gastornithidae lineage is a lot more plausible than the notion of Tree Rats leapfrogging another five or thirty million years of evolution to produce an Eocene Super-Lemur Pseudo-Monkey or Neo-Ape, or some lizard or tortoise making an incredible number of leaps to the point where it's got its own internet.

Now, to be perfectly fair, neither the Gastornithidae nor the Phorusrhacids really come off as rocket scientists. There's nothing to indicate that they were particularly smart or particularly stupid as Birds go, and definitely they wouldn't come anywhere near the level of Apes or early hominids.

The thing with Birds though, is that today we have several parallel examples of extremely intelligent Birds which are highly social, highly communicative and adept problem solvers — Parrots, Corvids, the Falkland Hawk. These are all Birds that are not related to each other, but which appear to have separately evolved similarly high intelligence and abilities.

Birds were a mature and highly evolved lineage even before the Dinosaurs got their tickets punched, a fifty to a hundred million years before PETM. So they had a major head start on the Tree-Rats. And there's no particular reason to believe that Bird intelligence is a recent development. So potentially, the basic capacity for highly intelligent Birds was there all along, even back in the Paleocene and Eocene. Or even earlier, developing in the Cretaceous or Jurassic periods.

But Bird intelligence as we know it, is probably pretty circumscribed. It takes a lot of energy to fly, and that limits your size. It seems to me that to really fully exploit Bird intelligence, to really develop it, you would need larger brains in larger, heavier heads, which would need much larger bodies than could fly. What you would need to get close to Human intelligence would be a large-bodied flightless Bird, preferably ones heavily built with thick necks and large heads to allow a healthy braincase.

As it turns out, when we go looking back around fifty to fifty-five million years, the time frame of PETM, we actually have at least two major lineages of Giant Murder-Chickens running around at about the right time frame, which could potentially have led to a hyper-intelligent branch line that would get a Giant Murder-Chicken civilization going.

To be completely fair, the startling PETM event is probably natural. I'm not saying it wasn't. I'm not saying Giant Murder-Chickens.

I'm just saying that if it wasn't natural, then it's probably Giant Murder-Chickens.

Primordial Civilizations in Space

Supposing that there was a Cephalopod civilization, or several of them. Or Giant Murder-Chickens really were responsible for the PETM event. Or suppose that sometime in the Mesozoic we really did get a species of hyper-intelligent Dinosaur building a technocracy, or even a few of them. Assume the possibility that somewhere along the line, Lemurs or Monkeys, or Apes or hominids produced an early Human-like intelligence. Or who knows, maybe even a wild card candidate got the jump.

In short, let's assume that with 320 million years to screw around, nature and evolution managed to blunder into creating a hyper-intelligent species that built a civilization like ours.

Well, we've barely begun to think about how to look for them on Earth.

What about in space?

If they reached our level, or beyond, they might well have gotten into space. Maybe they left relics or constructions on the Moon? Or Mars? Or some of the Asteroids? Or on satellites of gas giants?

Maybe it's still there? Preserved by vacuum, immune to erosion. Waiting to be found. Watching us, or staring out at us.

At this point, you're probably thinking about the Face on Mars. That startling image of a Humanoid face looking up at the sky, surrounded by strange Pyramids and possible remnants of a city on Mars. Sadly, the Face is almost certainly natural, as is the rest of Cydonia. But we'll investigate it more thoroughly in another essay.

I think it's only half true that remnants of a deep time civilization would be easier to spot in outer space than on Earth.

There are a few problems. First, while it's true that generally, Space doesn't have the savage erosional processes on Earth — no continental subduction, no oxidization, no extreme chemistry, etc., it's often pretty rugged.

Take Venus for example: A surface pressure 93 times as intense as Earth's sea level — equivalent to being a kilometer under the ocean, temperatures of 860 Fahrenheit, and sulfuric acid clouds. We've sent probes to Venus and they lasted mere minutes before the planet killed them. Anything on Venus is not likely to last.

Mars is also crap, albeit not nearly as bad. Sub-Antarctic temperatures, planetary dust storms, wind and erosion in an atmosphere a hundredth that of Earth. It's not the worst place, but you're looking at real erosion potential over millions or tens or hundreds of millions of years. There's water there, and possible slow chemical processes we don't understand that might shred an artificial object.

Go out to the big Jovian moons, and you have all kinds of craziness. One of these moons, Io is the most volcanic place in the Solar System. Nothing you put there is going to last. Hard radiation, a constant slurry of particles, weirdly active geology? Nasty.

Even if you look at some place that's pretty stable — say the Moon, it's not all sunshine. Actually, sunshine is the problem. The Moon's surface temperature ranges from 250 plus to 200 below zero in Fahrenheit every 28 days. So if you've got any kind of metal or anything else that expands and contracts in response to heat or cold, well, it's going to expand and contract. After ten thousand, or a hundred thousand years metal fatigue sets in. Eventually, a million years, or ten million years, your big high-tech module… it's just a pile of dust, and eventually, no more than a slightly different colored area in the dust.

That's not even considering the punishing effects of hard radiation, cosmic rays and dust, all that stuff. As I've mentioned, it's estimated that Neil Armstrong's footprints on the moon, the lander, the flag, will all be gone in about fifteen million years, give or take.

Even space isn't terribly safe, especially if you're in a planetary orbit. We have a lot of artificial satellites — but you notice that there's no natural space rock sharing those orbits? The problem is that most orbits around a planet or a moon aren't very stable. Orbits tend to decay. Satellites, unless we keep pushing will eventually fall to Earth. Mass is not quite evenly distributed, micro-gravity is slightly different, that tends to pull orbits apart.

If a Silurian Civilization put a satellite or a station or a space-hotel into Earth orbit, or around Mars or the Moon, it will be long gone by now.

Another issue is just how incredibly, mind bogglingly, big outer space is. It's colossal. Mars is 50 million square miles, equivalent to all the land on Earth. We've imaged 98% of it to high resolution. But that's still equivalent to all the land on Earth. That's a lot of landscape to search through.

The moon is 16 million square miles — Equivalent to Eurasia. Also almost completely imaged to a high degree. Mercury or Ganymede, about 35 million square miles, not well imaged at all.

But all that is kids' stuff. You look at deep space, even the inner solar system represents an almost unimaginable volume.

We've done an amazing amount of work systematically cataloguing the rocks floating around in the inner Solar System and the Asteroid belt. We've identified 1.9 million rocks, and have enough data — orbits, masses, to log and track 600,000. But that identification and cataloguing in most cases represents very little information. And then there are a huge pile of rocks that we haven't identified, perhaps more hundreds of thousands.

You could have the Titanic out there, derelict, and we'd never know it. It might be identified and in the catalogues, and we'd never know it. Not unless we got really lucky. It would be a needle in a very big, very difficult, very inhospitable haystack.

Haystacks in Search of a Needle

Is it hopeless?

Not necessarily. Apart from the Face on Mars folks back in the 90s, we haven't really been looking, or even thinking about how to recognize signs of a previous civilization out there.

We've got Mars imaged down to a resolution where a pixel represents a few feet. If there was a bison roving around on Mars, it would be a couple of pixels. We'd have a picture of it. But with billions of pixels, would we find it, without knowing exactly where and what to look for.

But possibly, it's worth running all that satellite imaging through AI looking for anomalous patterns. Maybe fractal analysis could flag possibilities. Search for recurring ratios. Doing it manually, that would probably take a long time. But with current AI and computer technology, we may be able to identify potential long buried or derelict Silurian bases.

If they're there. Odds are, that they're not. But it might be worthwhile taking a look, if we have the processing power and nothing better to do with it, such as generate AI bitcoin porn. Same thing with the Moon.

Then there's the possibility of beacons, or some sort of buried anomaly. That's the whole plot of 2001 — Aliens bury a monolith on the moon, creating a magnetic anomaly that we eventually come to dig up. So far we haven't noticed anything, but who knows?

But so far, if the Silurians were out there, they apparently didn't remember to leave us a message in a bottle. For that matter, why would they have bothered?

I note that there's enough hard radiation out there, that if Silurians existed, they'd probably bury their installations under regolith and rock for protection. That might make things less than obvious, again, unless we were specifically looking and knew what to look for.

There are places in orbit that are actually safe, or might be safe for a while — these are called Lagrange points, they're stable orbital points. There's a handful of them — 60 degrees ahead in orbit, 60 degrees behind. There's a point between Earth and the Sun, a point behind Earth and the sun, there's a point opposite the sun. The moon has its own set, vis a vis Earth. Mars, Venus, Mercury, Jupiter, and Saturn all have them. These are gravitationally stable points — whatever you put in them, could stay there indefinitely.

In fact, there's stuff in them. The points that are 60 degrees ahead and behind in orbit are known as Trojan points. Mars, Saturn and Jupiter all have small collections of asteroids occupying these points — not satellites of these planets, but eternal companions. In Earth's orbit, these points are occupied by at least two asteroids recently discovered in 2010 and 2020, as well as smaller dust and debris. In the Moon's Trojan orbits, there are also collections of cosmic dust and debris called Kordylewski Clouds.

But even these Lagrange points may not be long term stable, not for the inner system. The gravitational effects of the Sun, the Moon, Earth and Venus seem to combine to make the Lagrange points unreliable. One of Earth's Trojan asteroids is believed to only hold its position for another 4000 years, before Venus' gravity slowly destabilizes it and it leaves the Trojan point.

The nearer points around the Earth and Moon may be too mutually unstable for long term occupation — good for a thousand years, but not a million. One thing is for sure — the nearest Lagrange points are all close enough that we would have seen a derelict deep time station there — there's nothing.

At this point, we can say that so far, there's nothing on the Moon or Mars that's so large and unnatural that it's jumping out at us. We've scanned both those bodies to an extremely high degree of resolution. If there was any kind of large artificial structure, something the size of an RV or an Ocean liner, even a seriously deteriorated one, would be visible. We haven't spotted any. Hell on Mars, we've spotted the crash sites of our own probes, and on the Moon we've spotted the lunar landing sites. The things on the Moon and Mars that seemed suspicious in the past have been examined and seem to be resolved. There are no obvious red flags attracting attention.

That doesn't mean that there's nothing out there. Perhaps it's worth thinking seriously about what we should be looking for, how to spot it, and how to distinguish it from natural rocks. Maybe even eventually devoting some processing power to crunch a lot of data and see if anomalies show up.

To me, it's one jump to posit that a Silurian Civilization existed. It's another bigger jump to suggest that such a Civilization made it into space in a big enough way that it left behind something we could find after tens of millions of years. We haven't made it to that point ourselves.

There's a good chance that we won't. Back in the 1960s and early 70s, it seemed like we were going to be all over the solar system. We were supposed to have moon colonies by now. Well, it's turned out to be harder than we expected. Personally, I'm hoping, but more and more, I think we need to fix ourselves and our own planet first.

But who knows? It's worth speculating about.

Maybe They're Watching Us Now?

But wait, if the hypothetical Silurians – Cephalopods, Smart Dinos, Murder-Chickens, Super Lemurs or whatever - actually made it into space... maybe they're still out there now? Maybe they're watching us! Maybe they're the source of all these stories of ancient astronauts and unidentified flying objects.

Well, here's the picture: We've been seeing UFO's pretty steadily now for at least seventy years. They've shown up on radar, been seen by everyone from farmers and salesmen to astronauts and pilots, by people who are gumps and people who ought to know better. Many, even most of these can be cleared up. But there's always some residue that's hard to figure.

Along with that comes baggage — lore and stories about crashed spaceships, reports from people who believe they've been contacted, or worse, abducted. There are dives into history and claims of pre-1950s UFO records, reinterpretations of old claims and reports, and there are ancient astronaut theories of various stripes.

And with all of that, we've been slowly coming to grips with how incredibly vast and empty the Universe is, the likely impossibility of Faster Than Light travel, and the ginormous challenges of sub-light travel. The prospect of travelers from another star system coming to visit us just feels more and more unlikely.

Among other things, how would they even know we were here? We've only been producing detectable amounts of artificial radio for a hundred years. At most, our signals have only spread out to a sphere a hundred light years in diameter. Assume that there's aliens in the neighborhood, then assume that they travel at the speed of light, and assume they jumped in their cruiser right away to come see us, they'd have to be within a fifty light year distance - signals out, travel back. We started seeing UFOs in the forties, that's only twenty years or so of radio emissions, so twenty light years. For the signal to get out, and them to get it and come running at light speed. They would have to have been within ten light years.

It strikes me as incredibly unlikely that advanced aliens would be coincidentally so close and we haven't found any other sign of them. No radio? We actually have scanned most of the nearby stars, started finding planets. It's seeming very unlikely.

Of course, maybe they, or their robot probes have been just parking somewhere in the solar system for a while, watching for us. 2001: A Space Opera, stuff. Maybe. No real sign of it, and no way to assess the possibility.

So, UFO believers have been opening up a bit to other theories as to what the 'aliens' really are. Possibly they are dimensional travelers, whatever that means, visiting from other planes of reality. Possibly, they're time travelers from the future checking us out.

But for our purposes, one of the theories is that they're Silurians, or the survivors of a deep time, Silurian Civilization.

The Silurians, or so the theory goes, whatever they were, died out on Earth millions of years ago. But out in space, they've managed to make a go of it. They've been out there all along and now they're buzzing around checking out the new kids on the block.

And apparently being passive-aggressive mofos playing peek-a-boo while they're at it. They spend seventy years buzzing us, but at no point do they ever actually stop and say hello. What's up with that?

This by the way is the single greatest challenge to any kind of UFO theory: Why are they being such dicks about the whole thing?

So we make the big jump to assuming a Silurian Civilization, and the even bigger jump to assuming they got out into space in a big way, what's the likelihood of them still being around?

Not good.

Look, outer space is incredibly difficult country. It requires a huge commitment to survive out there. Right now, we've got a handful of people on a space station, living in conditions that are basically shacking out in a high-tech bus shelter. To keep those people up there and to keep them alive requires steady resupply and the constant efforts of hundreds of people on Earth. One big screw up, or even a moderate screw up, up there or down here, and they're all dead.

To build something out there that's self-sustaining and permanent, where people could live full-time we'd have to move thousands or tens of thousands more tons of material and equipment up there, and that's even if we're able to access resources up there, like water or metals on the Moon or Mars. The scale of the effort is likely more than the economies of Earth combined, and certainly much more than we're willing to spend.

And arguably, the technology for a long term, viable self-sustaining space station — in orbit, the Moon, or even Mars, just isn't there for us. Back in the day, enthusiasts on Earth kept trying to build biosphere projects. Self-contained habitats that could form a prototype for space colonies. Every single one of them failed. It's just not easy.

The point is, that maybe it could be done, but it wouldn't be small, and it wouldn't be easy. A self-sustaining space base would be monstrously huge.

If it was on Mars or the Moon, we'd have spotted it already, no matter how derelict it became. If it's out there in orbital space, it's likely been tagged and logged. It would be very, very hard to miss, although theoretically we might not recognize it.

Even then, building something with a real shot at long term survival would be exponentially more difficult.

Right now, if we build something rated to last a few hundred years, we're thrilled. Building something engineered to last millions of years? It would be colossal.

And it would need to maintain a population in the thousands, just to maintain genetic viability, and to keep all the requisite skills that were needed to keep the place going — remember, right now on Earth, for every person in space, there are hundreds on the ground working to keep them alive.

What we keep coming back to on each go-round of thinking this through, is that any surviving Silurian complex, tentacles or Murder-Chickens or Super-Lemurs, just keeps getting bigger and bigger, and harder and harder to miss.

One more round — so if there were Silurians, and if the Silurians got into space, and if they got into space in a big-time way to be self-sustaining, and if they actually survived thousands or millions of years to the present... there's no way we'd miss them.

Right now, the atmosphere of Mars is one hundredth that of Earth, for most practical purposes, that's kissing cousin to vacuum. Yet we are sniffing that atmosphere for infinitesimal traces of methane. We are literally analyzing the Martian atmosphere on a molecule basis. We're mapping fossil magnetic fields there that died three billion years ago.

Do you seriously think if there was a live base out there, that we wouldn't detect it? A live base would be huge, it would be leaving some kind of detectable footprint — a thermal signature, radio, radiation, hell even fart gas. The size of an installation required to survive millions of years, and the activities that it would have to carry out to function as a live installation would literally be blaring out at us like a foghorn. The same with the moon, if anything, the footprint, the waste products, the emissions, would be even more obvious.

If there was something in the Asteroid belt, we might overlook it. But again, the likely emissions footprint of a live installation might be easy to spot. Most Asteroids aren't generating electro-magnetic noise, aren't emitting radio, don't have solar panels or whatever to change their profile and keep messing with their albedo and light reflection. If there was one like that, for instance one whose light reflection profile was funny or kept changing, or seemed to have too much or too little heat, or was bouncing off electromagnetic static, we'd notice.

And here's the kicker — no known Asteroid is moving funny. And we're getting to know most of them. If there is a live installation out there in the Asteroid belt, then for at least as long as we've been observing — some for long as centuries, it's been maintaining a dead orbit. That is to say, it has the same orbital mechanics as any dead asteroid, it never moves on its own.

We've mapped lots of Comets and Asteroids, including Comets from the outer Oort cloud and beyond. There is literally nothing out there that we've tracked that is moving around on its own. It's all following the dead mechanics of Newton and Einstein.

When we picked up 1I/Oumuamua, we measured its orbit and determined immediately that it came from outside the solar system. Same deal with 3I/Atlas. If anything asteroid or comet sized was moving funny, we'd be spotting it.

Hell, we're spotting meteors the size of giraffes or Volkswagens if they come close enough. So why aren't we spotting flying saucers. Presumably they're bigger than giraffes.

We would have noticed if something showed independent motion.

So where are they? Everything out there is dead. There's nothing that's moving funny, there's no giant lumps, there's no strange molecule traces, radiation readings, magnetic anomalies, radio noise.

If they managed to get out there, they didn't make it.

They died millions of years ago, probably same time frame as the home team on Earth.

Oh and by the way, if they did survive whatever destroyed the home team, their first order of business would have been to get back to Earth and re-establish. It is literally the only habitable real estate in the solar system.

In space, everything is exponentially expensive to even survive. On Earth, breathing is free, and fresh water just falls from the sky.

Apparently, over the millions of years they've been parked out in space, it's never occurred to them to come back and re-occupy the home planet. They've just been sitting out there, while entire new species like us were evolving on Earth. Yeah, not buying it.

The counter-argument is that they can't because they don't have the resources. But if they have the resources to buzz us with flying saucers, then they probably had the resources and technology to resettle Earth. So why didn't they?

Unless it's the Cephalopods and they've colonized ever snowball water-world with a hidden ocean under ice, and are minding their own business.

But the point is, if they're out there, realistically they're dead. Any Silurian relic out there is just a frozen million year old hulk. A giant tomb.

This is the point where it gets frustrating, because if you explain it to the UFO fan, they just go "*Well, they could be hiding!*"

To survive out there, they'd have to be operating on a scale that would be impossible to hide. There would be no hiding. You can't hide radio emissions, or thermal profiles or fart gas, and you definitely can't hide an Asteroid piloting around like an ocean liner.

But anyway, that raises the problem: Why would they be hiding? What's the motivation?

Well (and this is a conversation I've actually had) maybe they're hiding from Humanity?

Sure. That's why all the UFO buzzing and general passive-aggressive dickishness is going on. They're hiding from us, but they're regularly buzzing Pinata farmers and Airline pilots. Yeah, sure.

But the hiding from Humanity thing poses its own problems. Like when did they start hiding out there? The last twenty years? The last fifty? The last eighty? We've been looking with telescopes pretty hard for a few hundred years now. Did they start hiding from Galileo?

They just kind of quickly shut all the doors and boarded up all the windows? And they'd do it on the sort of installations of the size and magnitude that they'd need to survive tens of

millions of years? It would be like trying to hide a planet —
there's no way you'd patch up that much leakage.

It would be the equivalent of hiding New York City. On Mars,
the Moon, out in its own orbit, it would be literally impossible.
You certainly couldn't do it in a hurry.

And why would they care? So far, our best efforts are
unmanned robot probes. We're not any kind of issue here for
them, and we wouldn't be for centuries more. And
presumably, with that kind of time frame to deal with us,
they'd come up with something better than being passive-
aggressive dickheads.

Maybe they've been hiding all along?

Again, why?

Were they hiding in the Renaissance era? The Roman era?
Were they hiding when the Scots attempt to invent pants went
horribly wrong? When French architecture was the mud hut?
Why? Were they afraid of Haggis? Terrified of our mighty
hammered copper arrowheads? Were they hiding from Homo
Erectus too?

Have they spent the last tens of millions of years hiding all
their installations and emissions, on the off chance that maybe
another intelligent species would eventually evolve on Earth?
Or that such a species would eventually stumble into building a
civilization after more millions or hundreds of thousands of
years? Would then spend more millennia or centuries building
that civilization up to the point where it gets into space and
becomes scary?

But after hiding for tens of millions of years, once their
dreaded nightmare finally appears, they send fleets of saucers
out to play footsie in the most obnoxious peek a boo way
imaginable.

That's crazy! Who does that?

If that's who they are, I want to nuke them on general principles first chance we get. They'd deserve it.

Well, maybe they're hiding from someone else? Some other Silurian Civilization in space? Which is also mysteriously hiding pointlessly?

Or some real extraterrestrial aliens from beyond the solar system, who would presumably be so scary that those genuine ET guys would have no reason to conceal themselves, their activities, their emissions, but nevertheless, have no presence, and are themselves hiding? Is space chock full of intelligent species all of whom are hiding out from each other, apart from joyriders who like to come here and go peek-a-boo.

By the way, the notion that space is full of intelligent races hiding from each other is called the 'Dark Forest' theory. I believe it came up in Liu Cixin's novel trilogy, the *Three Body Problem*. I don't buy it, but we'll talk about it elsewhere.

It's the peek-a-boo crap that gets me, honestly. Every train of speculation derails on the foundation that UFOs are all just really annoying dickheads. Because apparently, Space is some sort of cosmic game of passive-aggressive tag? I don't know, maybe everyone's playing for points? Bonus if you can anal probe a trout fisherman?

Look, here's the deal. All this UFO phenomena, all of it, even the crazy stuff, there may or may not be something to it. It could be nothing. But if it's something, the one thing I know for sure is that the available information is insufficient to draw any inferences or conclusions whatsoever about anything. So I'm inclined to just let it sit there until it blows itself out, or one of them finally decides to do something sensible.

You have to have a big long chain of 'maybe' to get to Silurians in space, and another long chain to get them surviving out there to our time. That's just too much of an ask.

The thing with Silurians in space though, is that we're going into space anyway. We're micro-surveying planets, we're sniffing molecules around exo-planets, were photographing, telescoping, orbit-charting, radio-mapping, and all that jazz. We're collecting massive piles of information.

So as far as it goes, it's all just sitting there. All we need is a working hypothesis, set up some rigorous tests to screen for possible artificial structures out there, feed it the existing data and crunch away.

That's pretty reasonable. Not much in the way of extra effort, and either way, we'll know.

I think it's worth taking a look.

The End

Famous Reptiles of Television

Serpent Men, Horribs and Reptilians

What if Humans weren't the first? What if there was someone before us? An intelligent species, a technological civilization? Is it really so impossible that across hundreds of millions of years of deep time, the Earth might have belonged to someone else?

The Reptiles ruled Earth for some 250 million years, that's a hell of a long time. While they were around, they produced some amazing and terrifying specimens, T-Rex, Mosasaurs, Pterodactyls. They produced a stunning diversity of forms on land, sea and air, and the largest land animals ever. They did everything but produce a civilization, and even there, maybe they did and we just haven't found it.

But what if there was a Reptile civilization? Who would they have been? What would they have been like?

Science fiction writers occasionally played with the concept - Robert E. Howard and H.P. Lovecraft referred to surviving Serpent Kings. Edgar Rice Burroughs had his Horribs of Pellucidar. Isaac Asimov wrote a story about it.

Even scientists got into the act. Back in 1982, Dale A. Russell speculated that if the Dinosaurs hadn't been wiped out, one of them might have eventually evolved into something Humanoid, vaguely (very vaguely) reminiscent of a Gray space alien.

Crazy people got into it, with theories of hidden Reptilians, either from outer space or home-grown, mucking about with Humans. The most famous of these is David Ickes, a former sports broadcaster and holocaust denier who around 1999 discovered that shapeshifting Reptilians, including the Queen of England, were secretly ruling Earth. I'm not going to get into that. Not even a little bit.

In 2018, a couple of Astrophysicists, Adam Frank and Gavin Schmidt, came up with the Silurian Hypothesis, named after the Doctor Who monster created by Malcolm Hulke, speculating on the possibility that an intelligent species could have arisen, and if it did, how would we go about detecting it? Frank and Schmidt still watched Doctor Who, where Hulke's Silurians are recurring monsters. They're not one of the big recurring monsters, but they've shown up now and then.

Of course, Malcolm Hulke was not the first or only writer to come up with the idea of deep time civilizations lost in Earth's past. As we have pointed out, it's been around. It was probably all over the pulps, lost civilizations were a staple of the genre after all. Hulke's just notable for popularizing it.

Now, Hulke, himself, was an interesting person, a card-carrying communist, back in an era when that was still a respectable thing to be, he was a major figure in the show's early history. In addition to writing the Silurians, he followed up with the Sea Devils, another Dinosaur civilization waking up from hibernation and wanting their planet back, and Frontier in Space, featuring the Draconians, who are essentially space traveling Dinosaurs, Colony in Space featuring suspiciously reptilian indigenous aliens, and then Invasion of the Dinosaurs, featuring time traveling Dinosaurs (albeit not with their own time machines). Oh, and he worked on a series called Pathfinder to Venus, which featured, you guessed it, Dinosaurs on Venus. Obviously, he had a thing going.

But technically he got it wrong. Although Hulke's Silurians are definitely from the Mesozoic era, more or less. They have an actual Dinosaur as a pet/sidekick, which is a big clue. The Mesozoic was 65 to 262 million years ago. The real Silurian era was much earlier, 419 to 426 million years ago.

Honestly, Hulke probably thought Silurians just sounded cooler than Cretaceans or Jurassians or (God forbid) Triassians, all of which inspire very different and possibly unkind associations. Silurians sounds reptilian and slimy and slithery, vaguely reptilian and creaky. It's got a ring to it.

Oddly, the Silurian Era has nothing at all to do with lizards or snakes, not directly or indirectly. There wasn't actually that much going on during the Silurian era. In the oceans, fish were busy inventing jaws and actual bones. Up on land, insects and arthropods were giving it a try. It would be at least another hundred million years before Reptiles showed up.

The name actually comes from a Scottish geologist named Roderick Murchison in 1830, who named the geological era after the Silures. They, in turn, were a Roman-era Welsh tribe that had nothing to with Reptiles either. Hulke really struck out. But from a Welsh barbarian tribe, we get a geological era, which becomes a handy, albeit misleading name for an ancient Dinosaurian civilization, which in turn becomes the term for pre-Human civilizations lost in deep time.

But the idea is intriguing, isn't it? What if there had been intelligent Reptiles? The Reptile family tree has all kinds of branches and endured for hundreds of millions of years. Where would they have sprung off? Why would they have developed intelligence? How would they have evolved?

Well, there are actually three major races of intelligent reptilians in our media who have left substantial track records. I'm sure there are many other examples, Star Trek had the Gorn, and V had the Visitors, as examples, but they're mostly extraterrestrial or so thinly sketched that there's not much to say. Not really good material for an in-depth examination.

But these three are interesting and odd enough that they're worth dissecting and exploring: The Silurians and the Sea Devils from Doctor Who, and the Sleestak from Land of the Lost. So what I want to do here, is take my own deep dive. I want to do a sort of dissection and analysis and try and figure out who and what these creatures were, when they stepped out of our television screens. So join me. It could be fun.

The Original Silurians

The Silurians were the original Reptile race. Or they are for our purposes. I've mentioned that Science Fiction writers had kicked around the idea of intelligent reptilians at least as far back as pulp authors like Lovecraft, Howard and Burroughs.

But the 1970 television serial Doctor Who and the Silurians really introduced the public to the idea of a previous Reptile civilization, and made enough of an impression to inspire guys like Frank and Schmidt. Seriously, it's not the Gorn Hypothesis for a reason.

Hulke's serial depicted a reptilian race in hibernation for eons, waking up and confronting the Doctor and the Human race and wanting their planet back. The Doctor desperately tries to make peace between Earth's two intelligent races. But the military decides to solve the problem by just blowing them up. In the era of the cold war and the counterculture, Doctor Who had a lot to say about coexistence, communication and genocide.

A couple of years later, 1972, Hulke went back to the well with the Sea Devils, who had essentially the same backstory - ancient reptilian race, hibernating, wakes up, and hijinks ensue.

The Silurians and the Sea Devils teamed up to trouble Doctor Who in a serial called Warriors of the Deep, back in 1984, where, once again, things ended badly for them. That was it for them, on television at least, the classic series ended in 1989.

The Silurians themselves lived on. They weren't a typical Doctor Who monster, they had a sympathetic backstory, and a genuine claim to be prior owners of the real estate, and the Doctor never saw them as an enemy. They had a unique cachet.

Malcolm Hulke novelized his script, publishing as Doctor Who and the Cave Monsters in 1974, developing more extensive backstory for the Silurians, including providing a Silurian point of view. They would show up in original Doctor Who novels and audio adventures as a relatively popular recurring race.

Then in 2010, they came back to the revived Doctor Who in the episodes The Hungry Earth and Cold Blood, albeit dramatically redesigned for a much more Humanlike appearance. Between their original appearance and the modern era, the television philosophy had changed. Instead of trying to create something alien as we would see in the 1970s, the new millennium wanted relatable. An even more Human version of a Silurian was Madame Vastra, who became a recurring character, starting in 2011.

For what it's worth, within Doctor Who's continuity, radically different versions of Silurians are not implausible. This is a species that has endured hundreds of millions of years, so even without genetic modification, they'd likely have evolved and diversified. And there's a likelihood of genetic manipulation. There may be a hundred variations on Silurians, including some that are Human-ish, and some that are badass nightmare fuel.

For the hell of it, we're just going to go with the original monsters from Classic Doctor Who, ignore the new show revisions, and hopefully make the best of it. I think that's a more interesting exercise.

What we're going to do is examine their anatomy closely, and try and figure out how they live, what they do, how they evolved and where they came from. It should be fun.

Okay, so let's take a look.

My first impression?

Wow, what crap costumes.

By contrast, the Sea Devils are a study in elegance. The Silurians are their half-assed, clunky, costume cousins. You can easily tell it's a Human inside the suit; the proportions are exact. You can also tell it's a heavy goddamned suit, unwieldy, bulky with poor visibility and that the actors are struggling to move around in it. They do a good job, but there are moments where you can tell. The features are completely inexpressive, and the stiffness of the suits restricts even basic body language. It's no wonder they did a redesign for NuWho.

But onwards... Forget that they're men in really heavy poorly fitting costumes stumbling around awkwardly. Pretend they're real critters, with biology, form, function, evolution and whatnot. What do we got? What does the anatomy tell us about what kind of creature they are?

Start with the head. You can tell a lot about a critter by its head. What kind of jaws or mouth does it have? What sort of bite does it have? Are the teeth sharp? Then it's a meat eater. Big fangs? Badass meat eater. Flat grinding teeth? You've got a herbivore! Big jaw gape? That's a bad news design for unaliving with great prejudice. Mix of teeth? Then the creature is fairly well developed. Only one kind of teeth? Most likely an early or primitive species. Eyes - focusing on binocular vision or peripheral, diurnal or nocturnal vision, large eyes to look around with peripheral vision, or tiny beads to see up close - it all tells you something. Other sense organs tell us things about a creature- a long snout means a sniffer. Big ears are a listener. Basically, we can learn a lot about who and what the creature is, and what it does, just by examining the head.

Okay. Now let's take a look at a face only a Silurian mother could love: Catlike eyes, vertically slit pupils. Largish eyes, but not crazily so. No nose to speak of.

No visible nostrils, that's peculiar. Nostrils evolved with semi-amphibious fish. Breathing through nostrils was an early evolutionary advantage. We'll have to assume that they're there, just hidden, or not obviously visible.

Small mouth, lips, no visible teeth.

What's this I see? External ears, and not just any external ears - Big wide sound collectors, and rigid structures just like Human ears. Very impressive.

What else? Looks like armored cheekbones, that's very unusual.

Not much of a neck. But check out those ring ridges around the neck and shoulders. We see those sorts of striated ridges in other species. That's significant.

Huge head, a ridiculously sized head in proportion to basic alignment of facial features and in relation to its body, and weird looking, with two sets of paired bone ridges going up to the central crest.

And get this, an honest-to-god third eye! Wowsers! That's pretty rare in biology. It's mostly an obsolete trait, not seen those in a dog's age, pretty much out of fashion nowadays.

What a mixed bag of weird. So what does this all tell us?

Let's start with the third eye. In modern Reptiles, only the New Zealand Tuatara really has a third eye. This was known back in the 1970s, so Malcolm Hulke was almost certainly aware of it.

The Tuatara is a lizard-like Reptile, but not actually a lizard. It's called a Rhynchocephalian, a primitive order that emerged around 240 million years ago and were pretty diverse in the Mesozoic.

The Tuatara's third eye is at the top of its head, it has features resembling a cornea, retina, rod-like structures and a neural connection directly to the to the brain. It's mainly visible in the young, and gets covered over as the Reptile ages. It's not very effective, it can only really distinguish light intensity, probably can't register movement or form an image.

A few lizards and salamanders, and some primitive fish, still have vestigial structures which were once a third eye. But the Tuatara's are by far the most developed in the modern era. Mammals, Birds, Dinosaurs, Turtles and Snakes all lack the parietal third eye. It seems to be a primitive feature with limited use.

Back in the very old days (as if I was there) it looks like among early tetrapods (four limbed critters), the third eyes had distinct sockets and may have been much more functional. If the Silurians have a third eye, then they're ancient, evolving when such a feature was common and more developed. Before it was abandoned by evolution.

This also tells us is that the Silurians are definitely not Dinosaurs or for that matter, Birds, Crocodilians, Snakes or Turtles. None of them have Parietal eyes.

Instead, they must be descended from a line of evolution from before the Parietal eye became useless - so they're Pre-Dinosaur Reptiles. They've taken a feature that was still a viable significant organ to their ancestors and dialed it up to eleven as a sense organ or weapon. That's a hell of a divergent evolutionary pathway.

Okay, let's move on to the normal eyes. Large eyes, means that they're gathering a lot of light, which can mean they're operating in low light conditions, or taking in a lot of detail.

Vertically slit pupils, like cats. That's associated with nocturnal behavior, also shifting, sometimes rapidly shifting, light levels, and an up and down peripheral vision associated with hunting.

Animals like horses or goats will have horizontally slit pupils, rather than vertically slit. If you're a herbivore worried about getting snuck up on or about running away, horizontally slit pupils gives you an extra wide peripheral vision. Vertically slit means you need to worry about up and down, above and below, and zeroing in on your target.

Notice that with Silurians, both eyes face forward? That's binocular vision, very good for focusing, examining detail, judging depth. Not good for peripheral vision. Found in predators, primates, and critters that need to pay attention, but aren't worried about being snuck up on.

The binocular vision and catlike pupils suggest predator, but as you'll see, a lot of the evidence is going the other way. I mean, come on, there's no predator teeth, no predator jaws, no claws, that's not a hunter/killer bod. The Silurians got reptilian Dad-bod.

What we're seeing, I think, is an animal with a lot of highly specialized visual acuity. Its major sense is sight, and it's seeing in very specific ways. It's likely nocturnal, or at least orienting towards low light dusk and dawns. Binocular vision and slit pupils means it's strongly focused on what's in front of it, probably very good depth perception.

No snout and no nostrils visible. It's almost certainly not operating by scent to any significant degree. That implies that scent isn't a significant factor. It likely is inferior to Human.

But hey, check out those big ears! This is an animal that has biologically invested very strongly in sound collecting. It's possible that like Humans, it has high sound directionality. In Humans, our thick heads make for a dead space, the ears placed on opposite sides of the head catch sounds at microsecond differences - the time it takes to cross the dead space between our ears. From that, the brain can process the differences and figure out where an object is.

The big ears, together with the large eyes and slit pupils are all adding up to a Nocturnal creature. There are other constructions - low light or twilight conditions, perhaps dusk and dawn. Or maybe they are prone to dark places like forests under dense tree cover. Or to dwelling in caves or dens.

What else? Let's look at that jaw/mouth structure. No way is that a carnivore! No visible teeth at all, small mouth, flexible rubbery lips, the sort seen in some herbivores, looks like a small weak jaw.

I don't know if they have teeth or not. You can get by without teeth - Chickens do, a lot of Dinos, Birds and Crocs swallow grinding stones called gastroliths (literally 'stomach rocks' - gizzard stones) which mangle up food and saves on a lot of chewing. So this may be what's going on. But still, most herbivores, including herbivorous Dinos use teeth to rip up plants, tear pieces off to swallow.

Is the jaw small and weak though? Hard to say. Doesn't look like heavy bone structure in the lower jaw, nor does there seem to be much in the way of muscle attachment? Heavy chewers will have the jaw attach to powerful muscles that can run all the way up the side of the head sometimes anchoring at a bone crest at the top, called a sagittal crest. It just doesn't look like it's got much going on though so whatever it's eating, it's not tough or woody, no grasses, no fibrous material. Soft, non-fibrous plants only, possibly leaves. It may have also been eating soft bodied arthropods and mollusks.

Fruit? Unlikely. The thing with fruit is that there's a lot of nutrition in fruit. Not a lot of nutrition in leaves. Leaf eaters have to be bulk loaders, they have to eat lots, spend most of their time doing it, and poop lots to get nutrition out of it. That's why gorillas are often pot-bellied, they're more leaf than fruit eaters. Animals like a Koala or a Panda will spend most of their day eating.

But the advantage of fruit is that it's so nutritious and high energy it can support larger brains and smarter animals - Monkeys, Parrots, Apes, Humans. Leaf eaters? Not so much. Koalas and Pandas are not smart, trust me.

Best guess is that fruit and flowering plants evolved approximately 100 million years ago in the Cretaceous. The Silurians, on the evidence of a functional third eye, are probably way older than that, and evolved before these became available.

But we don't really know what the plant ecology was like in the Permian (the Silurians likely era). We know seeds were around during this time, seed ferns were pretty dominant. As were trees or tree-like woody species, either narrow leaf or broad leafed. But there's no way to guess at the nutritional value of anything, or the nutritional value of life stages of leaves or ferns.

In the Canadian Maritime provinces where I'm from, there's a delicacy called 'fiddleheads' - these are basically newborn or newly sprouted ferns, still curled around like a fiddle's head. They're good eating. So it's possible that Permian fiddleheads, leaf buds, etc., delivered a lot of value.

Who knows? What we know for sure is that the Permian landscape, whatever there was to eat in it, at least some of it must be delivering up enough high value nutrition to power a big old brain.

But there's a paradox. Generally, a lot of nutrition translates into a big old body - big bodies are in a general sense more evolutionarily beneficial than big brains. Big bodies give you biological economies of scale, protect you from predators, get you preference in mating through running off rivals or attracting females and generally allows you to push your way around.

In evolution, as in civilized life, so goes biology, big brains are really only useful for nerds who make their living being sneaky and clever.

But the Silurians managed to achieve high intelligence even before Dinosaurs showed up, and at a time when their fellow critters were all pretty feeble-minded. There's a mystery there. Let's come back to that though.

What about the rest of the cranial anatomy? The Silurian head... There's some tough stuff, and some easy stuff.

You know what's easy? Those neck rings. We've seen them before. On the bellies of whales for instance. Those are stretching folds. Baleen whales swallow massive quantities of water as part of their feeding strategy, so much that their stomachs balloon out. They push all that water out, past filter teeth, their baleen plates, and lick off what's left behind.

But these are horizontal stretch folds right around the neck. What this tells us is that the Silurians, either currently or in their recent evolutionary history, were able to dramatically stretch out, or maybe balloon out, their necks. What an odd feature, given the fixed number of vertebrae? How would they extend it? But if the Silurians had a long neck stretch capacity, maybe they are related to Sea Devils? Who knows? The feature seems persistent - the NuWho Silurians also have the neck-ring folds. A retained ability, or a lost ability with a long term cultural/biological relic feature... like Humans having earlobes.

Now for the hard part - what are those facial ridges? We have lot of good possibilities for the Sea Devil fins. For these? Not so much. Here are my best guesses.

Sound channels/baffles? I'm drawing here on leaf nosed bats, who have a wide variety of exotic facial structures that seem to be connected to their echo-location ability. I don't think that the Silurians were echo-locators. Maybe? In the stories there's no evidence of them clicking or using sonar or radar. But elaborate facial structures, particularly hard ones, might have helped to channel sound, or bounce it, to allow for more accurate sound-location as noted above. It's a possibility.

The lower ridges might serve as anchor points for jaw muscles, but they're hyper-developed for that, and the jaws just don't seem very strong, so nope.

Head butting? Don't laugh! Head butting seems to have been prominent among a variety of horned Mammals from antelope to goats to cattle, was found among Pachycephalosaurs, Tyrannosaurs, and Ceratopsians. Ramming your head or face into your buddy's is a time-honored tradition from Dinosaurs to modern day Scotsmen. Maybe? But it doesn't really feel right - the ridges look too delicate and convoluted for serious face smashing.

It might be simply ornamental, god knows, we have a variety of horned Dinosaurs and Mammals that invest a massive amount of biological energy into horns, crests, flares, that are less to ward off predators and mostly to secure mates or bully rivals. Evolution does strange things when the biological imperative is to look sexy and get laid.

Social/Sexual selection? Maybe. A lot of strange things happen when folk are looking for sexy. This is a good one, because these features are really most prominent on the face - where Silurians are looking at each other, but less prevalent on the backs of their heads, where they don't look at each other, as most social interaction takes place face to face, apart from back stabbing.

Here's something interesting - the lower cheeks look like boney shields, so the first and second upper ridges might offer protection against predator attacks? There might be something to that. The cheeks armor shields definitely suggest that here was an animal armoring up against predators. But the most vulnerable spots - the eyes and ears, seem to be left open.

Maybe it's not an evolutionarily productive development at all. Obviously, if it was negative, they'd have bred it out. But it may be a relatively harmless by-product of another development?

We know the Silurians got really smart, and probably did it relatively quickly. That means that those brains needed to get bigger, inside that skull. But a regular skull size has limits. So the Silurians had to re-evolve their skulls to make more room. Or to put it another way, the Silurians whose skulls were shaping up funny had more room for brains, were smarter, and more likely to reproduce and pass on those traits. So what we may be looking at are the by-products of evolution deforming skull architecture for large brains.

I like the skull deformation theory. And I'll note that if skull deformation was a by-product of an evolutionary beneficial trait - bigger brains, then it might well have been selected for socially, reinforcing the trend, and also resulting in more pronounced or elaborate deformation.

On to Silurian morphology - the body or body plan.

What do we have? Sadly, the Silurians weren't going around naked. They're one of those unhelpful critters that wear clothes. So there's a limit to the information we have and the inferences we can make.

In broad terms it's basically a Humanoid configuration - arms and legs of proportionate length, head (albeit oversized) in the right place, no visible tail, bipedal stance and posture, relatively flat or barrel-chested torso.

Looks like three clawed hands, with an opposable digit and thick curving claws. Feet? Likely wearing booties so we can't actually tell. But it seems to be plantigrade, with basically Humanoid structure and dimensions. It's difficult to tell, but the ankle/upper arch structure seems thicker and more sloping, which may imply less flexibility and a significantly slower running speed.

Skin/hide? What we see of it looks heavy, textured, and there are signs of what may be osteoderms (bony nodules in the skin, an early form of armour plating). The skin seems relatively loose, not a lot of muscle definition (by which I mean - none at all) or fat deposits. There's a very noticeable bony ridge of short spines running down the back, again resembling the Tuatara and some lizards like the Iguana. They're not large enough or prominent enough for heat regulation, and even for defense their utility would be pretty limited.

One thing we don't see is any obvious external genitalia. Either they're shy and keeping them covered, or they're all females, or like birds, they just don't show off their junk. And on that point, there doesn't seem to be any apparent sexual dimorphism.... that we know of. In Classic Doctor Who we meet at least four Silurians but we no idea whether they're all female, all male, or if mixed which is which. We don't get enough of a window into Silurian biology or society to make any guesses.

One of the problems with them wearing clothes is that we potentially have a hard time distinguishing what might be their actual body, as opposed to coverings they're wearing, and where they are wearing clothes, whether what we see - such as their boots, reflects actual anatomy. Overall, the anatomy seems to reflect an odd mixture of 'advanced' and 'primitive' features, and contradictory traits.

For instance, there's some evidence to suggest a lifestyle where they don't really worry about predation (no peripheral vision for predators sneaking up, relatively slow moving) and yet we've got armored cheeks, head ridges and osteoderms in the skin, even a short row of dorsal spines to deter attack from behind. Are these archaic leftover features from an ancestral form?

The most interesting feature is that they're bipeds. Biped tail-less Reptiles. That's a puzzler all by itself. How does something like that develop?

Let's move on and try to explain some of this anatomy. We can start to make some educated guesses about what this anatomy means.

Heavy emphasis on vision and hearing suggests either a nocturnal or crepuscular (dusk and dawn) lifestyle. Or potentially, something adjacent - for instance deep forest cover where low light prevails, or a polar region where high elevation can mean long periods of night and midnight sun. The poles during this period would have been tropical or subtropical.

The persistent limited armor features means that there must be some degree of predation, either currently or in their evolutionary history. But that they're not tormented by big predators with overwhelming size and power. They're not that fast, they're not heavily armored and they're not naturally aggressively equipped with weapons. But they're still surviving.

So they may have other tricks up their sleeves - inaccessible refuges or habitats, tunnels, dens or difficult forest cover. Or social structures allowing them to deter danger. Or they're building weapons like spears. Non-obvious defenses like a Parietal Eye flash? Or perhaps the predators aren't that ferocious - they've facing the equivalent of wolves or coyotes, not leopards, tigers or T-Rex.

It's possible that lifestyle itself is a defense. Nocturnal and crepuscular animals often switch to these times because predators are mainly day walkers. Hunting and killing is tough enough without having to stumble around in the dark. If you avoid the times when predators are most active, you avoid most of the predators.

But we come back to two things - why are the Silurians intelligent? And why are they tail-less bipeds? There aren't actually perfect examples for either of those things, apart from us.

Let's go back to the example of Monkeys, Parrots and fruit trees - sophisticated mental mapping. Basically, not every tree is a fruit bearing tree. Even the fruit bearing trees only have limited seasons. So you develop intelligence to build a mental map of all the fruit trees in the accessible landscape, which ones are in season when, and you can make a nice living showing up at the right trees at the right time.

A complex environment with multiple food sources available at different times scattered through the landscape requires a high degree of complex memory and planning to get to it. Doesn't have to be fruit trees. Raccoons might be as smart as Monkeys, and they seem to employ similar skills, possibly in a more complex seasonal environment where they have to find and eat a lot of different things available at different seasons of the year.

But that only gets you Monkeys, Parrots and Raccoons. Maybe Apes. Australopithecus had about the cranial capacity of a chimp and probably wasn't much more sophisticated. We don't really have a good answer for how we Humans got so much smarter and bigger brained than anyone else out there. Maybe we got into tools and fire and that started a feedback loop?

It's complicated by the fact that we went bipedal well before we got super-smart. So whatever evolutionary process drove walking upright, it wasn't the same process that drove intelligence. Although maybe once we were established biped walkers, perhaps that contributed to further intelligence development.

For the Silurians at least for baseline smarts - Monkey/ Raccoon/ Ape level, we need to assume specialization and complex environments. They started accessing easy to process, high value food, which required a lot of remembering, time focusing and geographical mapping. If we can't get those last few steps for Humans, I don't know how to explain the Silurians being super-smart. We can work out an evolutionary pathway for baseline smarts, and hope that it trends upwards to Human levels of intelligence on its own.

And for the hell of it, let's assume that standing upright, helped them access resources, selecting for both intelligence and bipedalism. Which meant that they needed to be tall and reach up. So possibly they were clipping off the soft tips of branches - seeds, buds, shoots, and the early equivalent of proto-fruit. Maybe even doing some climbing, those hooked claws we see look like they're better suited as climbing hooks than weapons. They were likely forest dwellers. Perhaps deep forest dwellers, with thick canopies. Possibly that explains low light situations, or partial protection from predators.

The Silurians start off as regular quadrupeds, and they evolve bipedalism and gripping claws that can reach up, to access high value food. And they evolve intelligence to consolidate that food basket. In this model, bipedalism and early intelligence go hand in claw, which may not be incompatible with the early evolution of Hominidae. They evolve Sloth-like hooked claws for climbing, or gripping hands for climbing and feeding. They develop extendable necks to reach higher branches.

So your Proto-Silurian, the equivalent to Australopithecus, would have been a transitioning to biped, forest dweller, with a very specialized, finicky diet. Their cat-eyes with slit pupils orient up and down, allowing them to scan trees, and strong binocular vision lets them zero in on interesting items.

Meanwhile hyper-directional hearing allows them to be wary of predators trying to conceal themselves for ambush. Out on the plains, it's hard for predators to sneak up, no cover, so they concentrate on running down their victims. In that environment, good eyes and good peripheral vision keep you safe. In the forest, there's lots of cover, a lot of places to hide and creep for an ambush. Hearing is much more effective than sight.

In low light conditions, that parietal eye might have come in very handy - giving an extra advantage in the sensory department. A feature that's on its way out everywhere else starts becoming useful and developing. The Proto-Silurian already has two useful eyes, so the parietal eye is additional capacity, it can be adapted and redeployed for other uses with no loss of visual acuity.

In Warriors of the Deep, we see the parietal eye flash when they communicate - handy for the showrunners. But maybe also an effective signaling and even a communication device. Since it wires directly into the brain, a signaling parietal eye might trigger further brain development and intelligence development, as the Proto-Silurians exchange increasingly complex information by light exchange. Light can carry much more information than sound, the Silurians may experience something similar to light-based telepathy.

In the Doctor Who Universe, psychic abilities are a real thing, which seem to center on the brain, and on communication parts of the brain. Hyper-development of the brain areas relating to the parietal eye triggers the evolution of psychic ability, and possibly intelligence. So the Proto-Silurian evolves to a full Silurian, developing intelligence, psychic powers, technology, civilization and eventually ruling their planet.

Their civilization over a hundred and fifty million years continually rises and falls. There's no evidence that it was continuous. They preside over several mass extinctions, which may or may not be their fault. And their cities may go into extended periods of hibernation before re-emerging... typically to find that their only real competitors are other waking Silurians, and maybe Sea Devils.

Over this vast time, they speciate somewhat, explaining the small divergences between the original Silurians, the versions from Warriors of the Deep, and the vaster differences between them and the NuWho Silurians.

So where did the Silurians come from? Who were the candidates? I have just one in mind.

These guys. The Pareiasaurs. Notice please, the protruding cheek plates, projecting beyond or overhanging the mouth, very similar to Classic Who Silurians. That's a very distinctive trait, very common to the clade, the name Pareiasaur actually means "Cheek Lizard."

The Pareiasaurs were a very successful lineage of herbivorous Reptiles or Parareptiles that appeared in the middle Permian and came to dominate the ecology. They were characterized by shortened tails and heavy limbs, with size running from two feet in length to ten feet and over two thousand pounds.

Interestingly, many species of Pareiasaurs skulls were often elaborate, heavily ornamented with bosses, bumps and ridges. And their bodies sported osteoderms, bone nodules in the skin as early armor. Oho! Sounds like someone we know!

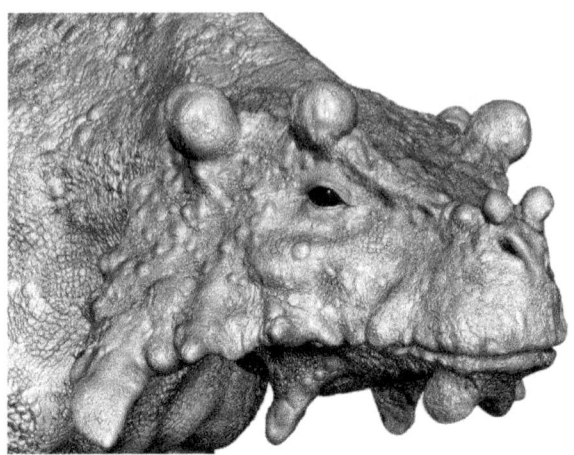

The Pareiasaurs started out as sprawlers, but as they evolved they adapted and switched to upright posture, which means that within the clade, the posture and weight placement seems to have been fluid and bipedal stances could have evolved.

The Pareiasaurs became extremely widespread and diversified in different sizes. Later Pareiasaurs tended to be increasingly heavily armored, suggesting ongoing heavy predation from Gorgonopsids driving natural selection.

Pareiasaurs were very well known in Malcolm Hulke's time, by the way, when he was writing the Silurians. They were actually discovered and described as early as 1876, and between then and the 1930s, a number of species had been identified all over Europe and Asia.

It's likely that Hulke was at least partially inspired by the Tuatara and its third eye. But I suspect that the designers of the actual costume were also directly inspired by Pareiasaurs - those cheek plates are a dead giveaway.

My guess is that they probably went looking through a book of depictions of ancient Reptiles looking for ones that they might adapt to a face and settled on this one. That said, I'm just guessing, they were out there and well known. But even if the Pareiasaur was the inspiration for the design, odds are that no one thought 'hey, Silurians evolved from this line' because I don't believe they were thinking that way. They just thought it looked cool enough to adapt to a costume.

For my money, and for our little exercise, the Pareiasaurs fit the bill for a short tailed, strong limbed, upright (as opposed to sprawling) posture, Pre-Dinosaur diverse and widespread herbivorous Reptile with primitive features like a parietal eye, cheek plates, ridged skulls and osteoderms. Those are all the characteristics of our Silurians.

We know that the Pareiasaurs in real pre-history evolved into dozens of species of all sizes occupying a multitude of niches. It's not implausible that one particular species could have ended up in deep forests, developing a specialized rich diet, and evolving both biped posture, dexterity, communication and eventually high intelligence, sufficient to build a civilization and conquer primordial Earth.

Perhaps the rise of the Silurians coincided with the massive climate change and mass extinction that ended the Permian era and ushered in the age of Dinosaurs... or caused it? Maybe only the Doctor knows for sure.

The Sea Devils of Doctor Who

Honestly, I've always liked the Sea Devils - their ultra-long necks, their turtle faces, large staring eyes and head fins, all of it suggests an entirely non-Human but, somehow organic, physicality. It was successful in a way that few generic monsters are.

The trouble with monsters on movies and television, at least up until computer generated imagery, is that there are only a few ways to do it. You can do stop motion, which is time consuming, incredibly expensive, and has a distinctive jerky look. You can do puppets of various kinds, which can be iffy.

Or you can stick a man in a suit. Which, 99% of the time, looks exactly like a man in a suit. That's just hard to get away from. There's a Human profile, long legs, shorter arms, a torso and head, that's easily recognizable no matter how you dress it up. Even Ridley Scott's Alien was a man in a suit, albeit an ultra-tall, ultra-skinny Somali guy, and they had to do a lot of careful shooting to make the alien seem inhuman.

It's a thing, over and over. You just have to get used to it. The more you try to avoid the Human silhouette, the more complicated and cumbersome the costumes become. Look at some of the designs that came out of Jim Henson productions in the Dark Crystal, amazing, but... dubious. Most producers don't even bother much, stick a rubber mask on and the job is done.

But the Sea Devils? They were something special. By the simple expedient of wearing the Monster's head as a hat and dressing the rest of it up a bit, the designers escaped the Human silhouette, and produced something that was non-human, but elegant and organic.

The Sea Devils were another creation of Malcolm Hulke, card carrying communist and Dinosaur fanatic. They appeared in the 1972 Doctor Who serial of the same name. Basically, it was the same story as the Silurians - they wake up, look around and go *"It's our damned planet, Monkey-boys!"* The variation was that this time, they hooked up with The Master, a renegade Time-Lord and the Doctor's nemesis for the season.

They were an immediate hit for their distinctive look, with iconic images of a band of Sea Devils rising up out of the ocean as they invaded the land. That unique headpiece, worn like a hat, with its turtle face and side fins was popular with fans. You can see home-made Sea Devils in Doctor Who parade floats from the 70s and 80s.

The Sea Devils, together with the Silurians, actually made a comeback in 1984. The two races teamed up in Warriors of the Deep. Set in the near future, Earth is divided into two militant nation-blocks armed against each other, and Earth's prior owners unite to start World War III and get the Humans to wipe each other out. It's a dark and pessimistic serial, despite being over-lit and shot flatly. But its reputation is worse than it deserves, mainly because of an incredibly bad sea monster, the Myrka, which was actually a sort of pantomime horse costume.

After that, the Sea Devils moved on to novels, audio adventure and fan-fictions as regular supporting characters in the Doctor Who universe. The show was rebooted in 2005, and recycling the classic monsters became a thing. By 2022, their number finally came up again with the Whittaker Doctor episode, Legend of the Sea Devils. On the positive side, the iconic look was kept and even refined. On the not-so positive side, the episode was... dire. Very, very dire. In the end, apart from the look, everything that made the Sea Devils potentially interesting was jettisoned, and they just ended up being generic monsters.

Coming up in 2026, is a spin off miniseries, The War Between the Land and the Sea. From the trailers, it looks like the Sea Devils have come in for a substantial redesign, becoming basically sexy, muscular Humans with some token scales and fins, except for the sexy female Sea Devil, who is slender and girlish, with token scales and fins. It looks dire. We're not going to talk about it. I'm just going to ignore it.

For this exercise, we'll focus on the classic serials. So let's break down that anatomy first, and see what we can figure out from it.

First up - Sea Devils are almost certainly not carnivores or carnivore descended. No sign of predator teeth. No sign of teeth at all, actually. They seem to have wide mouths, small or reduced jaws, and beaks. You can have toothless predators of course - look at Eagles and hawks, but those have sharp beaks and claws. Sea devil beaks are not sharp, they're more like turtle beaks. No sign of claws.

This is not an obligate carnivore. There's no real sign of predatory adaptations. So not meat eaters, and likely not fish eaters.

What are they eating? Well, beaked sea turtles eat jellyfish, but there's not a lot of nutrition there, and Sea Devils with their bodies and big brains probably require a high value diet. I would suggest water plants, particularly soft water plants, mollusks, soft bodied invertebrates, likely small, relatively slow moving or sessile life forms. The Sea Devil larder is probably quite diverse.

They're definitely not going after fast swimmers or big game hunters, not with what nature gave them. Although they may have developed nets or fish spears that expanded their diet. They may or may not have gone after hard shells, though they might use their hands to pry mollusks open, or to smash small shells with rocks.

Also, Sea Devils have poor binocular vision. They've got some, but their eyes tend towards placement more towards the sides of their head. They have a huge range of peripheral vision but likely a poor binocular overlap range. These are the sorts of eyes you have when you don't want things sneaking up on you, and when whatever you need to be focusing on isn't that good at getting away.

Large eyes though, comparatively larger than Human, and apparently fixed, suggesting that they're adapted to low light, possibly nocturnal, or possibly dim environments like under water. They don't seem to have eyelids that I recall, but perhaps Legends of the Sea Devils CGI'd some blinking eyelids on. The size of the eyes suggests that they're processing a lot of visual information. They may see differently from us, but they're seeing a lot.

It's possible that while they seem to tolerate normal light, their preferences above ground are night and twilight. I'm also willing to bet their vision is shifted downward towards reds and greens, they may see into the infrared. I wouldn't be surprised if they can detect very subtle graduations of light and dark, or are adapted to see into or assess turbidity.

Eyes seem to be the primary sense organ - there's no indication of sonar domes, as in dolphins and whales. Nor lateral lines as used by sharks or other fish. Ears don't seem prominent. Small nostrils indicate scent is not a major asset.

Nostrils give them away as habitual air breathers. Two nostrils, in the beak, just about the mouth. That suggests the presence of a palate, so that they can breathe without opening the mouth, or while the mouth is swallowing or open. It's not obvious, but I assume the nostrils are able to seal when underwater. Whatever they are, we can rule out fish-men - fish don't have nostrils.

Nostrils are located forward on the face. In a lot of fully aquatic critters, Whales, Dolphins, Phytosaurs, nostrils migrate further back on the head. Even semi-aquatic forms like crocodiles often have raised nostrils. This indicates that the Sea Devils are, at best, semi-aquatic. Of course, there's a lot of other physiological evidence for that. They're really not well adapted as full time swimmers.

There are a couple of anomalous head features - those head fins, and the inflatable throat sacks, both of which are hard to evaluate.

The head fins seem particularly difficult to understand. It would produce nothing but drag underwater. So what could it be? Let me offer some wild guesses

* A thermo-regulation organ - the Sea Devils are clearly non-Mammalian, thermal regulation might be a problem, as it is for lizards, turtles, snakes, etc. Trickier for Sea Devils because to be intelligent, they need big brains, the function of those big brains might require stable temperatures. Actually, this is a problem even for Mammals - stable brain temperatures - and its one of the reasons for artiodactyls (cloven hoofed animals) success - it's called Selective Brain Cooling. If the Sea Devils have problems with thermal regulation, particularly for the brain, then radiant fins that can be extended and furled, and which can have their blood flow regulated, might be the ticket.

Again, temperature regulation is why Elephants and Desert foxes have huge ears, and polar bears small ones. Possible.

* Sexual/social display - Maybe the big fins get the girls. Or get the boys. Or just signal health, social status, etc. to potential reproductive partners. Far from impossible. The world is awash with sexual and status displays in the form of boobs, butts, biceps, beards, horns, antlers, colors, feather display, swelling throat sacks, you name it. The Sea Devils are highly visual, a really good set of head fins would call attention, maybe the right kind of attention.

* Oxygen collector/external gills -Not without precedent in the animal world Turtles can extract oxygen from water through their anal cavities (I bet you did not want to know that), and the Axolotl amphibian retains external gills as feathery structures. It's possible that the head-fins are blood vessel rich oxygen exchangers, delivering just a little bit more oxygen and hyper-charging that big Sea Devil Brain. Big brains by the way, consume a lot of oxygen and a lot of calories, they're an energy intensive organ. So the Sea Devil's may have co-evolved the head fins as a way of providing a boost or getting extra oxygen. Impossible? No. Likely? Who can say?

* Signaling/communication - kind of related to social display, but it's possible that moving them, or even changing pigment like a cuttlefish or chameleon would allow the Sea Devils to communicate effectively underwater. Think of it as walking around with a pair of semaphore signalers bolted to the head. Any evidence for this? Actually - negative evidence, we've never seen the fins move or change color. But then we've never seen them underwater. So maybe on dry land, they're inert, but underwater they're used to silently talk up a storm.

* Underwater sense organs. It's tempting to see them as something like ears. But ears, external ears, are just sound cups. They're designed to funnel sound into the actual ear. From the pictures and videos, there's no actual sign of them connecting to an ear structure. But that doesn't mean they're not some

other kind of sense organ. They may function underwater as a kind of thermal sensor array, or be good at picking up and assessing vibrations in the water, or perhaps a form of electro-sensitivity like a shark's lateral line, or even chemo-sensitivity similar to smell. Again, we don't ever see them used on land, and we don't see them underwater.

* Swimming structures, actual fins for propulsion or stabilization. No, just no. Absolutely not.

* Something else/ Combination - possible. Who knows? All we really know for sure is that these are extremely well developed, physically prominent structures. Evolution wouldn't put that much effort into them, unless there was a strong selective driver.

Although they're extremely prominent in the Sea Devils and Legends of the Sea Devils, they're not mobile, and don't manifest any particular obvious use. In Warriors of the Deep they're not visible, so either cropped, or covered by the helmets. And who knows what Russell T. Davies is going to do, in his War Between the Land and the Sea miniseries.

So food for thought. But any of these explanations would make the Sea Devils more interesting, more complex, would have some effect on how they evolved, how their civilization developed, and who they are. Therefore, I expect Doctor Who will ignore it.

Let's do the throat sacks?

Obviously, there's a simple rational explanation. The Sea Devil necks/throats are where the actors head goes, and they wear the Sea Devil's head like a hat. Actually, it's a wonderfully clever conceit that breaks up the Human outline and gives them their compelling alien/non-human look.

But we're pretending the Sea Devils are real animals. So... extended neck, and prominent, potentially inflatable throat sacks.

A lot of animals have long necks compared to Humans, so we won't worry too much about that part of it.

Is the throat sack inflatable? Does the apparent throat sack have a purpose? Well, it's not clear that it inflates or is inflatable. But in some of the pictures from Pertwee's Sea Devils, it does look more puffed out. So let's assume it does inflate, what does that mean?

* Might be an oxygen thing, inflating it like an air sac / spare lung. If you're floundering around underwater, that might make a big deal an extra five or fifteen minutes of moping around underwater before you need to come up.

* Could be a pseudo-gill. Basically, a heavy folded, blood vessel rich internal structure, used to suck in water, extract oxygen, and expel it. Doesn't mean they're fish; it's not a particularly efficient gill structure compared to fish. But having learned about turtle anuses, we can't put anything past the bounds of possibility.

* Could be a social/sexual signaler, like with bullfrogs and some birds and lizards.

* Might be a feeding/storage structure. If Sea Devils are primarily plant/soft-bodied-animal eaters, they might need storage capacity, and fill their throats as they feed.

* Or a hunting structure - Walruses hunt with jets of compressed water, so do belugas, turtles hunt by sucking water inside. The Sea Devils may use throat inflation to suck in water and eject a concentrated pressure stream to stun small prey, or maybe they inflate it to suck in prey.

* Or on that front, maybe an underwater sonic cannon? Some whales stun prey with concentrated bursts of sound. In which case, it's helping generate sound. We've seen no indication of that, however.

Unlike the head fins, we don't actually know for sure, based on what we've seen, if there really is actually a significant structure here, or what its purpose or function might be. But any of these would reveal interesting things about Sea Devil life.

What about the rests of the morphology? The rest of the body?

Well, let's dive in.

No apparent tail. Either it's absent, relatively small, or docked. This is a very anomalous feature for Reptiles or amphibians. The Plesiosaurs and Placodonts had reduced tails, mainly because they were swimming by paddling. Turtles have minimal tails. We can assume some sort of evolutionary pressure to reduce tails. It wasn't helping the Sea Devils or their ancestors.

Long limbs. Way too long. Generally, aquatic animals' limbs reduce. There's two good ways to swim - tail wagging (Dolphins and Whales, Itchthyosaurs, Crocodiles, Manatees) or paddling (Sea Turtles, Sea Lions, Plesiosaurs, Placodonts). But water is a very thick medium, you get a lot of return from very small motions, long limbs provide drag. Aquatic limbs are short and tend towards paddles.

Even semi-aquatics will tend this way - look at beavers, otters, etc. all short limbs.

There is an exception to this rule - Frogs. Semi-Aquatic, long hind limbs, shorter fore-limbs, swimming mainly by the hind-limbs. Not great swimmers, but semi-aquatic nevertheless and very good leapers.

We can say very definitely that the Sea Devils are not fully aquatic. At best, they're semi-aquatic, functioning in water and on land. Definitely well built for land locomotion, but also clearly spending a lot of time in water. Webbed hands and feet, which still remain hands and feet, contribute to the semi-aquatic conclusion. From the original Sea Devils it looks like they have opposable thumbs, and at least three or four fingered hands. The number of fingers may vary from story to story, but is probably not significant.

No indication of foot structure, except that it seems able to orient perpendicular to body and support their weight on land. It's likely that there's at least one load bearing toe structure, and the foot is able to spread out for walking on muddy or soft ground or swimming, and the ankle is able to reorient laterally for swimming, but this is guesswork. It's likely that the foot and ankle structure are complicated, given the diversity of environments it has to function in.

There is likely a trade-off for this. I don't think we see the Sea Devils running. Their best gait seems to be a fast walk. I doubt that they can run efficiently. It's likely that the fleeing strategy amounts to escaping land predators by going into the water, and water predators by going onto the land, or otherwise collectively standing and fighting.

But what else is new. Hominids traded speed for slow walking/running with our own foot structure, and it worked out just fine for us.

Bipedalism? How did that develop? Now here's the rub. They're tail-less (or short-tailed) bipeds. Because, obviously, the actors inside them were.

But we're just pretending they're real animals. So how do we explain bipedalism? There are plenty of biped Birds and Dinosaurs, but that's a very different thing from what Humans do. If Silurians were Dinosaurs, sure they'd be bipedal, but the body plan, even with a short tail or no tail, would be more like a murder-chicken, and not a Jenga tower like us.

In fact, Human-style bipedalism seems incredibly rare - there's us, and our fellow Hominids, there's Oreopithecus, and finally, there's an extinct species of Monkey, Paradolichopithecus, maybe. And... That's it.

To compound things, we don't even know with any certainty why Human bipedalism evolved (or how or why it evolved in the other noted primates). At this point, the best guess is that Humans evolved as a Savannah Ape, habitually bipedal to see over tall grass, and to walk long distances. So we're up against the wall on this one.

But there is another theory.

The 'Aquatic Ape Hypothesis." This is a bit of fringe paleontology which hypothesizes that bipedal walking evolved because of living in marshlands, tidal zones, shorelines, and rivers and swamps. The idea was that the need to wade or walk in and around water opened up many feeding opportunities, but also encouraged standing and walking upright as a means of taking maximum advantage, up and down, in that environment.

It's a fringe theory, but it's fairly detailed and well developed, and ties together a lot of different bits of information from all kinds of sources. I'd recommend you look it up. Even if it's not accepted by standard paleontology, it makes a good read.

But even if it doesn't apply to Humans, this may be an explanation for Sea Devil bipedalism. If they did evolve as shoreline and marsh dwellers, particularly in tidal zones, perpetually going in and out of water, then that might explain their two-legged walking stances. They're following the Aquatic Ape model.

This would also be consistent with a lifestyle that emphasized wide peripheral vision, but relatively less long distance or binocular vision, and a feeding strategy that involved a diversity of soft plants and small slow prey. The turtle faces, and the frog/Human body proportions might well be a workable plan for this kind of environment.

We can see the idea of the Sea Devils evolving as a quadruped marsh/tidal Reptile, slowly evolving frog-like proportions and a biped stance, and developing intelligence in response to a complex environment.

Let's assume this is the case - that the Sea Devils evolved as short tailed shoreline Reptiles, plant feeders, and/or slow soft prey omnivores, maybe an ecological niche loosely similar to Raccoons or Muskrats, who gradually become upright in a Human-like way.

Intelligence and larger brains evolve to cope with a very complicated ever-changing environment and a diversity of food sources. The Proto-Sea Devils are munchers or snackers, always looking for something different, their diet is an ever-changing basket of small meals, not focusing on a narrow range like browsers/grazers or predators. They're generalists not specialists. They're driven towards curiosity, you never know when some new thing might be good to eat, or a pain in the ass, best to find out.

They're driven to complex memory and time fixing. One reason Parrots and Primates got so smart was mental landscaping. Not every tree in the forest is in season for fruits or nuts at any particular time. Only a few are. You start to need a mental map of when and where the fruit bearing trees are, and not just at a particular time, all year long, and from season to season.

The better your map is for time and space, the better you're able to find the fruits or nuts you need at a particular tree at a particular time, and to navigate the best routes from one to the other, and to make sure you're around for the ones that are coming into season, and leaving the ones going out of season. There's a lot of complicated mental mapping.

But you don't need to be a Parrot or Monkey, or a fruit eater, for sophisticated mental mapping. Raccoons are opportunists and generalists, living in an equally complex environment, and surviving with a complex basket of small meals. They're considered as intelligent as Monkeys. So there's different pathways that work - the point is diversity and complexity, and the need to be smart.

For the Sea Devils - with a hundred different food sources and species going in and out of season, with seasonal tides, difficult shorelines, marshes and rivers with their own flood patterns, they'd develop similar complex mental maps of space and time, locations and seasons.

They'd probably exist in small family groups and tribes, but during spawning times, there'd be a lot of food all in one place, far more than a tribe could hoard, so they'd likely have to develop complex social structures, including for dealing with strangers and neighbors, and when it was good to hang out and when it was best to be on your own.

And likely, because habitable zones are probably narrow and fluctuating, Proto-Sea Devils were constantly crossing and intruding on territory, so they likely would develop complicated social behaviors as well.

What about technology? Cutting tools probably came from sharpening clam shells and shards of wood or rock. Good cutting tools would make up for poor teeth and make harvesting and hunting, even fighting and defense easier. Hammer stones for breaking open shellfish. That's common, both otters and birds will use stones to crack open shells. Pointed sticks would come in handy for fish spears, spearing small prey and even medium prey and warding off predators. There are a lot of fibrous plants in the environment, so knots and knotting, small ropes and ties would be pretty easy. Gorillas are observed to make primitive knots for their nests.

The huge game changer? Nets. If you can make twine and knots, nets are an inevitable step and once you have nets, your food availability skyrockets. All those fast moving fish and amphibians, fast lizards, that were too small and quick to catch - suddenly, you're harvesting a cornucopia. But using nets takes cooperative labor, it's not a one person or small family operation. The more participants, the bigger and better the net harvesting, the more people contributing labor, the bigger, more professional, more thorough nets are built, mended and replaced.

Suddenly, the Sea Devils can support villages, whole communities, labor specialization. Big harvests lead to food storage, which requires more complex structures, food processing, and a manager class. Civilization is starting up.

Sea Devils probably are not unfamiliar with construction of homes or nests. They may well have adapted like Beavers or Crocodiles, building lodges or dens accessible only underwater. It may be that Sea Devils are just biologically driven to feel safest when their homes are surrounded by water.

Larger stable populations living in secure villages and using nets for harvesting mean that there's now a lot of available labor for tasks, spare labor that can be put to use to make life better. The Sea Devils occupy niche zones - shorelines, tidal flats, river littorals. They need water, but not too much, not open sea, not deep, just near-shore water, and land but not too dry, not too far from water.

Well gosh - with all that spare labor, we can do landscaping. They already have the basic rudiments from constructing their lodges. Water-ponding, dams, limited flooding, tidal channels. Slowly, an extensive incremental program of landscaping maximizes Sea Devil habitat. A niche species slowly expands, dominating more and more of the landscape. As the Sea Devils grow smarter and smarter and more versatile, intelligent and technological, they go even beyond their preferred habitat. Like Humans, they come to dominate every environment on their world.

There's enough clay along the water zones that they probably master ceramics and pottery, sun hardening. Fire comes along much later than with Humans, but proves to be a useful tool. Metallurgy follows much later.

Next thing you know, you've got a civilization.

So what exactly are they, these Sea Devils? I mean, assume Reptiles. But there are all kinds of Reptile lineages, extinct and current.

Which lineage though?

Let me throw out a thought. I think the Sea Devils were an evolutionary by-blow, not a main event species. I think that they were a transitional species that took an off-ramp.

Basically, the Sea Devils were like Otters or Beavers, they were a borderland species, similar to ancestors of Whales or Seals, they evolved in the transition from Land back to the Sea. It's likely that the main line of evolution for their genus or their relatives, was towards a fully aquatic Reptile species.

So basically, my theory is that the ancestor of the Sea Devils was a semi-aquatic Reptile that branched in two directions. The main direction was to keep doing what it was doing, become increasingly and eventually fully aquatic, until they lived happily ever after, eventually showing up in the fossil record as a completely marine reptile.

The side branch, the Sea Devils, got stuck in the semi-aquatic state and evolved in different directions - they got bipedal, got smart and became the Sea Devils.

I'm being sweeping here. Evolution isn't a conscious process. It doesn't have a specific direction in mind. It's just a random accumulation of traits that work, which can proceed further and further down pathways. Mammals start out as land animals, some become semi-aquatic like Otters, and some go from semi-aquatic to fully aquatic like Whales.

Anyway, my thinking is that the Sea Devil's ancestors were a transitional or intermediate species, whose relatives went fully marine. So to figure out where the Sea Devils came from, we need to look around for an aquatic, short tailed Reptile species, possibly a plant eater. Potentially one with poor thermal regulation.

I think we can broadly rule out Reptile lineages that were wholly land based. If they're not going to be spending time in the water, it's hard to get to a semi-aquatic species.

I'm going to write Dinosaurs off. Dinos, particularly the bird hipped, appear to have been overwhelmingly terrestrial, employed a very different form of bipedalism and had long tails. I don't think they would have switched over to primate/Sea Devil bipedalism. There is one Dino, Spinosaurus, that seems to have been semi-aquatic, but it seems to have been a short-limbed tail-swimmer. Let's rule that out.

For obvious reasons, writing off pterosaurs and pterodactyls.

Ichthyosaurs, Mosasaurs, Crocodiles and Tylosaurs - all tail swimmers. So nope.

Going straight for paddling Reptiles, the Plesiosaurs and Pliosaurs are well known as 100% aquatic. They appeared in the early/middle Triassic, so early on in the Mesozoic. The root lineage, Eusauropterygia was small headed and long necked, it also gave rise to the Nothosaurs who remained semi-aquatic. Poor candidates overall.

So what does this leave us for candidate lineages?

Turtles/Tortoises - sounds ridiculous. But if the Sea Devils split off before the carapace and plastron evolved then maybe. Turtles evolved between 210 and 260 million years ago, the middle Permian to the middle Triassic. The carapace and plastron seems to have evolved around 220 to 230 million years ago. So it's possible that a Permian Era proto-turtle went down a really different direction. Honestly, I doubt it, the limb configuration seems to be a sprawl, and not well suited for standing or walking upright. There is in some regards a facial resemblance. A Permian appearance would put them well before the Dinosaurs.

For my money, probably the best candidates were the Placodonts, another aquatic species that evolved to resemble sea turtles. The Placodonts were another line of Sauropterygian emerging in the middle of the Triassic. The Sea Devils might have evolved from a Proto-Placodont, semi-aquatic transitional species. The earliest known Placodonts were long tailed, but the tail reduced consistently as they transitioned completely to marine existence.

All of this would put the time period of Sea Devil evolution as likely Permian era, before the great Permian Extinction which gave rise to the Age of Reptiles, the Mesozoic. In the Doctor who universe, it's possible that the Sea Devil civilization resulted in or caused the Permian Extinction 259 million years ago.

Or possibly, they emerged as slate as the Triassic, and are responsible for the Triassic extinction, and the Triassic/Jurassic boundary.

I recognize that this dissection contradicts some aspects of Sea Devil Lore. For instance Sea Devil mythology suggests that they went into suspended animation as a result of a feared close encounter between the Earth and Moon. This seems to be nonsense.

The theory now is that the Moon was created when a Mars sized planet named Thea ended up in the same orbit as Earth and eventually collided with the Proto-Earth. Thea's core merged with Earth, the moon formed out of ejected residue. This was before life began on Earth.

Of course, in the Doctor Who Universe, there's a NuWho episode in which the moon appears to have a different origin as a giant cosmic egg, so go figure. The cosmic egg hatches into a monster butterfly which then immediately lays another egg which turns out to be another exactly identical moon, and then goes off into space. It is that dumb. It makes my head hurt, so I'll pretend it doesn't exist, and that the whole thing was a massive acid trip, where everyone was lying on the floor of the Tardis, twitching, drooling and buzzed out on hallucinogens.

It's given lore that the Silurians and Sea Devils are sibling species, with the Sea Devils being an offshoot. I'm not sure how correct this is. I think that they're related in both being Reptilian intelligent species from deep time. I'm not at all sure that they're the same Genus, or from the same evolutionary pathway.

It's possible that they are connected. They've been sharing the Earth for hundreds of millions of years, there's got to be some relationship, even if it's only a cordial sharing of the planet. Or taking turns.

It's quite possible that the show's lore is correct and that one is a direct evolutionary offshoot of the other. But within the lore, it's also possible one uplifted the other as an unrelated species to sentience. Or maybe they just arose independently and learned to get along. But overall, I'm not at all persuaded that there are sufficient morphological overlaps to suggest a close relationship to the Silurians.

Unraveling the Sleestak

The Sleestak are a race of Reptile men, sometimes described as having both reptilian and insect features, who were a recurring villain in the Kroft Series, "Land of the Lost" through three seasons and 43 episodes, from 1974 to 1976.

Sid and Marty Kroft were a pair of television series producers, mixing live action with costumes and puppetry, for children in the 1970s, with notable productions like H.R. Puffinstuff, Lidsville, the Banana Splits, and Saturday morning superheroes. Land of the Lost was one of their productions, and although aimed at children, this was not a normal kid's show.

Following the adventures of a family trapped in a pocket dimension occupied by Dinosaurs, Ape-men and lizard-men, it never talked down or was anything less than intelligent. Created by noted Science Fiction writer, David Gerrold, the show recruited Star Trek figures Walter Koenig and D.C.

Fontana, as well as famous science fiction writers including Larry Niven, Theodore Sturgeon, Ben Bova and Norman Spinrad. That's a powerhouse line up.

The world of Land of the Lost was a detailed landscape featuring stop-motion Dinosaurs, a hairy Human-like race called the Pakuni, and a reptilian race called the Sleestak, decayed descendants of the Altrusian creators of the pocket dimension. It became a cult classic.

The series was rebooted, 1991-1993, for two more seasons and 26 episodes. The new Land of the Lost featured a new family, but was otherwise a direct continuation, with more stop motion Dinosaurs, and the return of both the Sleestak and Pakuni. The Sleestak were revised into something between a dinosaur and a horned toad.

With intelligent scripts, well done stop-motion Dinosaurs, and imaginative world building the two series twenty years apart maintained a cult status and loyal fandom, being popular at Science Fiction conventions.

Finally, in 2009, with a few adjustments, they showed up for a big screen movie starring Will Ferrell and Danny McBride.

What's interesting about the Sleestak of the Land of the Lost is that they represent an extremely consistent morphology and history between original series and film. The movie tweaks that a little, but not much. Unlike the Klingons who changed radically with the relaunch of Star Trek, the Sleestak are largely identical.

We see a lot of them, and they seem to be important to the 'world' of the Land of the Lost, essentially a pocket universe that seems quite consistent between the two series, but which is slightly different in the movie. Well, if they take the show with a grain of salt, we'll return the favor in our analysis. We might refer to the movie, but we'll ignore inconsistencies from it.

There's a theory that they Altrusians, and their Sleestak descendants, may be alien - given that the 'Lost Land' has three moons and may have two suns. For myself, I'm going to assume that they're terrestrial Reptiles, most likely from the Mesozoic. Despite the weird sky features of the pocket universe, the Land of the Lost is chock full of Dinosaurs and prehistoric Reptiles, but fairly sparse on any genuinely alien life.

So, here we go, let's assume that the Sleestak are real animals/beings, from Earth's evolutionary history. How do we assess them?

Basic Anatomy: So, what can we tell of Sleestak anatomy. Let's start with this thumbnail description. Sleestak are bipedal reptilian animals standing approximately five feet in height. They appear to be covered in scales of various size, except for leathery padding on the abdomen.

They are characterized by a large head, proportionately larger than Human. The eyes are set far forward, completely black with no apparent structure, and apparently not mobile. Between the eyes and above the mouth there are two small nostrils, also not mobile. The nose is not prominent. There are small external ears facing forward. The mouth is extremely wide with minimal lower jaw; teeth are non-prominent or absent. In the movie version, Sleestak appear to display small sharp teeth and an apparent jaw within a jaw structure, but the canonicity is questionable. The Sleestak possesses a small horn located high up on the center of the head above the eyes.

The neck is extremely short and thick; the Sleestak head almost sits upon the torso. The neck does not appear to be all that flexible. There is, however, what appears to be a ruff of skin depending from the neck, possibly a display function. The back features a prominent spinal ridge ending in a vestigial tail about six inches in length.

The limbs seem to be of roughly equal length, with legs appearing to be longer due to high tarsal bones which elevate the stance. The Sleestak is literally perpetually standing on its toes. There are apparently three toes. Some specimens have two fingers, some three, the subordinate finger appears to function as an opposable thumb.

It is remarkable how closely the Sleestak resemble old speculative reconstructions of Humanoid Dinosaurs. Peculiarly, such reconstructions are now dismissed, with the belief that an intelligent Dinosaur would tend to follow the theropod body plan. Let's follow up with a more detailed analysis of their anatomy.

Eyes and Visual Function: The most arresting feature are the eyes. Huge unblinking eyes, without eyelids, eyelashes or nictitating membranes. No discrete eye structures are visible - no apparent pupils or irises. And no apparent eyeball movement. The area of the eye is approximately two to four times the surface area of the Human eye structure. One remarkable feature is extremely focused binocular vision. The Sleestak eyes are set so far forward in their skull that peripheral vision is extremely limited.

What does this tell us? The positioning of the Sleestak eye guarantees focused binocular vision, with likely highly developed depth perception. The size of the eye may imply nocturnal lifestyle, or low light situations. That poses certain problems of its own. Most nocturnal animals embrace that lifestyle to avoid predation, it's much easier in most other ways to be day walkers. Polar animals which experience protracted arctic 'nights' may develop nocturnal traits to continue to function, and indeed this feature was exhibited in Antarctic Dinosaurs. Behaviorally, the Sleestak appear to hate bright light and tend to be most active at night or dusk or dawn.

The lack of apparent visible structure or movement is puzzling. It is possible that what we are looking at is a transparent eyelid membrane similar to snakes. The function of such a membrane, obviously would be to protect the eye, potentially from grit, parasites, harsh light or sudden changes in the intensity of light. The uniform blackness may be a 'night vision' function, similar to the reflective surface of a Cat's eye. Alternately, we may not be looking at a protective membrane, but the eye itself. In such a case, the sheer size, lack of mobility and absence of pupil and iris are puzzling. How does the animal focus? How does it adapt to changes in lighting? The Sleestak do not appear to need to move their heads to orient their vision, they seem equally adept at day or night although they do seem to be intimidated by sudden light or high contrasts.

One very unusual feature is that the eye curvature appears to protrude above and beyond the face, which implies that Sleestak visual lens extends involves a complex field, perhaps similar to exotic camera lenses, or certain kinds of fish eyes.

As an intelligent species, we would expect a high degree of overall sophistication. Given what their visual coordination indicates, the Sleestak eye is either an extremely crude and limited structure, whose large size is required for minimal function, which seems unlikely. Or it is quite an elaborate and highly complex structure with adaptive and functional mechanisms we can only guess at. However, in our view, it seems unlikely that the Sleestak would abandon long successful evolved structures, such as pupils, iris and eye mobility for new and untried structures.

The most likely option is that the Sleestak retains normal eye structures under a snakelike but black transparent membrane. The Sleestak are almost certainly a predominantly visual species, particularly in comparison to their structures relating to other senses.

Ears and Hearing/Nose and Scent: The Sleestak do appear to have a modest external ear structure, but it is small and featureless even in comparison to the Human ear. In particular, the Sleestak external ear does not appear to be moveable, but seems oriented forwards. Like Humans, Sleestak ears sit on opposite sides of their skull, rather than above it. This means that there is a barrier to sound between the two ears, and allows sound to reach each ear differently.

In Humans, and presumably Sleestak, this feature allows us to distinguish with great accuracy the direction that a sound originates. It's likely that the Sleestak have reasonable hearing in Human terms, and that their hearing is oriented forward and is highly directional. There is no indication of any facility such as echolocation. The Sleestak are never heard to make clicks or high-pitched squeaks or any of the sounds that appear as lower registers of animal sonar or sonic radar.

The Sleestak seem to have no nose to speak of, merely a pair of nostrils located directly above the mouth. The nostrils are set close together, and do not appear to be mobile, they do not close or quiver. We can assume from this that scent is not a significant part of the Sleestak sensory web.

The Horn: The Sleestak horn may be an archaic remnant of a sagittal crest. Notably, the Sleestak horn does not appear to vary, but is found in apparent males and females, among young and old specimens, does not relate to social dominance and is found in archaic specimens. It is not clear what, if any function that the horn serves, or has ever served. In our view, it may be a biological relic.

However, the more likely explanation for the Sleestak horn is that it is a neotanous feature. Reptiles in the egg will develop a horn that they use to break out of the shell. It is likely that Sleestak evolution is marked by neotany, which is the retention of juvenile or infantile traits into adulthood. You see this with domesticated animals, but also with Humans. Basically, retaining juvenile traits seems to correlate with intelligence. So the horn is likely a retained juvenile trait.

Jaw and Dentition: Sleestak have an extremely wide round mouth with relatively immobile lips. Teeth, if they exist at all, are not prominent. There is some indication of a more complex mouth structure. In the movie, the Sleestak exhibit mouths lined with small sharp teeth, and there appear to be at least two rows of teeth and a multi jaw structure. The lower jaw is relatively flat with no real chin.

The jaw and dentition are puzzling because it raises the question of what the Sleestak are eating. In particular, we don't see any of the specialized dentition - cutting or shearing teeth, incisors or canines, that are prominent with evolved carnivores of any sort, whether crocodilians, Dinosaurs, Mammals or Sharks. The Sleestak's jaws and teeth do not seem to be consistent with major predators.

On the other hand, the jaw structure doesn't seem heavy or robust enough for a typical dedicated grazing or browsing plant eater. Most large plant eaters tend to have long or heavy jaws and/or large grinding teeth. We can pretty clearly determine that the Sleestak were not eating fibrous or woody vegetation such as grasses. Nor are we seeing the specialized features that occur with insectivores, scavengers, fish or filter feeders.

The jaw and dental structure seem atypical. Of course, there are many exceptions in nature. Frogs for instance, are insectivores but do not sport significant teeth. Sauropods had very small heads and jaws and dental structures for their food volume, most of the sauropod's 'chewing' took place through gizzard stones. Edentates such as Sloths and glyptodonts made do with few or no teeth.

So what conclusions do we draw about the Sleestak jaw and feeding patterns? The wide mouth suggests bulk loading of foodstuffs. The relatively small sharp teeth suggest cutting and shearing, but they do not seem to be large enough or well anchored enough for significant predation.

If the Sleestak were carnivorous, they likely restricted their diet to small animals and insects. Rather, the Sleestak were most likely specialized leaf-eaters and swallowers. They did not chew. They probably employed gizzard stones for digestive grinding.

Bipedalism and Body Morphology: Beyond that, overall Sleestak morphology is puzzling. The Sleestak appear to be slow moving bipeds with large powerful arms and hands, short necks and short almost vestigial tails. Given a reptilian ancestry, this makes very little sense. Almost all Reptiles have large heavy tails, used for swimming, balance, weapons or fat storage. There's very little fossil or contemporary evidence to suggest many species with a trend towards tail reduction (with the exception of the line that developed into birds). All biped Reptiles tended to rely on the tail as a balancing organ, and tended towards a 'birdlike carriage'. So there seems very little justification or explanation for the Sleestak to evolve towards a vestigial tail or a Human-like versus birdlike bipedalism.

Sleestak behavior, particularly their slow and careful movement, and certain peculiarities of anatomy give us clues as to Sleestak's evolutionary origins.

Essentially, the Sleestak were not the reptilian equivalent of primates, but rather, they were the reptilian equivalent of South American Sloths. They evolved first as large tree climbers and clingers.

They're not unique in this pathway. Koalas occupy a similar niche. The giant lemurs of Madagascar underwent convergent evolution to become very similar to Sloths, anatomically and in lifestyle. Certain prosimians, like Pottos, appear to be very similar in lifestyle and anatomy to Sloths. It may be that Tree-Apes such as Gibbons and Orangutans may be considered to be rough evolutionary parallels to Sloths.

If Apes and Sloths are essentially occupying the same evolutionary niche, this may explain why the new world

Monkeys of South America never evolved into parallel Apes. That niche was already occupied.

The environment of a large tree dwelling herbivore does much to shape its anatomy and behavior.

For one thing, trees are a dangerous place for a large animal. Life and death is all about clinging to the right branch. Climb onto a branch too small to support your weight, its death. Climb onto a branch that's rotten or cracked, its death. A branch that another animal approaches and adds weight to, its death. Fierce storms, anything that puts stress on the tree or branch, may produce death. Move too fast from branch to branch, the better the chance of making a mistake. Jump and miss, that's death. One limb hanging on, that's risky. Two limbs hanging on, not as risky as one, but still dangerous. Three limbs hanging on is better, four limbs is best. Movement becomes a deliberate careful matter of moving and setting one limb at a time. Gravity is a constant enemy, always pulling down. Even resting is a perpetual struggle against gravity.

So the large tree dweller's behavior orients towards moving very slowly and deliberately. They cling with all four limbs to support weight. They're stationary as often as possible. Movement involves one limb at a time, or two at the most. Movement is always deliberate and careful. We see all of these traits with Sleestak movement.

There is more, of course. Living in trees requires specialized adaptations. The movement ranges of limbs expand. They're more able to swing limbs out to the side, or in directions or angles not usual for ground runners. They adapt to hug or cling. The front limbs become as large and heavy and as important as hind limbs. Paws, particularly the forepaws become gripping structures. Digits lengthen, become heavy and powerful, a flexible wrist develops. These developments are well established with giant Lemurs, Apes, Sloths and even Koalas, Pandas and Bears to some extent. These are also traits that we find with the Sleestak.

Indeed, the Sleestak show definite Sloth-type adaptations. Sloths move towards reduction of digits, two toes and three toes. Multiple digits are not as effective in clinging as fewer large powerful digits, particularly if you've got weight. The Sleestak show the same reduction of digits, exhibiting two and three fingered varieties.

This may explain the biological reduction of the tail. For a large arboreal animal, a tale is a liability. It doesn't help balance, it hinders it. Sloths, Giant Lemurs and Apes have all evolved towards reduced or absent tails. We also see this reduction in other large tree climbers - Pandas, Bears and Koalas.

Given the reduction of the tail to a vestige, and given the enlargement and strengthening of forelimbs and digits, this would tend to bias a Sloth-like Reptile away from a birdlike bipedal posture, towards a more Human-like bipedalism.

Of course, the downside of tree dwellers like Sloths or Apes is that ground life becomes more difficult. Sloths' hind feet are turned inward, so they literally walk on the sides of their feet. Apes adapted a large long flat foot. The Human foot is little more than an adaptation of the Ape foot. The Sleestak foot appears to be an extended two claw arrangement, and the Sleestak seem to walk or perch on them. So Sleestak feet may have two stances: Gripping and rigid perching. The Sleestak, like Sloths and Apes, seem to be awkward walkers.

Habitat and Evolution: Assuming that the Sleestak were originally Sloth/Ape analogues, we can chart a rough sequence of steps. The Proto-Sleestak line were originally small tree climbing Reptiles who adapted or evolved into something roughly similar to Monkeys or Sloths.

We actually have a good candidate for a founder species – Suminia, a synapsid/therapsid amnodont that liked in the late Permian, about 285 to 252 million years ago, right up to the start of the Triassic, in the Mesozoic era. It was about the size of a large rat, but it shows numerous adaptations for tree climbing and tree living, and was well on its way to evolving towards a reptilian Monkey or Sloth, or Proto-Sleestak.

As these Proto-Sleestak evolved to become larger, their morphology moved toward the acknowledged form of mature Sleestak, an animal of roughly 150 to 200 lbs.

Beyond that, however, certain traits seem contradictory. Night vision and nocturnalism suggest predation. But a ground dwelling Sleestak species would have certainly adapted to rapid movement for predator avoidance. This, of course, is peculiar. There's another word for slow moving ground walkers. That's lunch.

Even nocturnal animals contend with predators and must move fast at times. Of course, the Sleestak may have combined a nocturnal lifestyle with large size and big claws to guard against predators. Size can guarantee safety all by itself, particularly if Sleestak retreated to the trees in the daytime for safety.

Of course, given the predators running around in the Mesozoic, a Human sized creature might be just a snack. Even being nocturnal might not be enough added protection.

So overall, I suspect that generally, predators weren't a big factor in a nocturnal lifestyle. Indeed, their ground movement, which is clearly driven by tree living, suggests that they are both relatively recently moved out of trees, and largely untroubled by predators at all. That implies a very peculiar environment, one without significant large animal predators. And that the environment poses some sort of advantage for nocturnal capacity.

Another interesting feature is that the Sleestak in the Land of the Lost appear to be a hibernating species, specifically, one whose hibernation is driven by temperature. The Sleestak go dormant in cold temperatures. They become active in warmth. Now, possibly this suggests an ectotherm, or cold-blooded species, which implies that the Sleestak may have evolved from lizards or are more closely related to lizards, turtles, snakes, crocodilians or the lower Mammal-like Reptiles, as opposed to being warm blooded and related to Dinosaurs, pterosaurs or higher Mammal-like Reptiles.

However, it seems difficult to reconcile Sleestak nocturnal habits with cold blooded lifestyle. A cold-blooded animal of this size would almost certainly be oriented towards daylight activity, and would tend to be dormant at nights. I'm therefore inclined to place the Sleestak as Dinosaurs or a form of advanced Mammal-like Reptile, again, Suminia seems the best candidate for an ancestral species.

However, Sleestak hibernation/reproduction appears to be tied to Altrusian moths, which would be a seasonal insect. This suggests that the Sleestak life cycle is highly seasonal. Strong seasonality, in turn, suggests that the Sleestak developed well away from equatorial latitudes, in temperate or higher levels. Some place where there were pronounced seasons, particularly spring and summer, autumn and winter.

Of course you do get seasons in tropical and subtropical latitudes, but these tend to have warm temperatures year round, with seasons distinguished as rainy or dry. So Sleestak seasonality may be tied to this. But their trait for hibernating in cold temperatures implies animals who may be winter adapted.

The nocturnal vision adaptations may relate to high latitude protracted nights and days. The further north or south you go, the longer the nights and days get in each season, until finally you have the Arctic or Antarctic midnight sun/month of night. But there's a contradiction there, since the long nights would be the coldest season and thus most likely for hibernation.

But then, polar light is probably the weakest light on the planet, so rather than true nocturnalism, we might be looking at polar animals adapted to very weak light. Or perhaps Sleestak's original habitat was deep rain forest with extremely poor light. In evolutionary terms, it appears that the Sleestak are much closer to their tree dwelling ancestors than we are to ours.

So, where does this place the Sleestak? My best guess is that they've evolved on a large island - something like Madagascar or New Zealand, or perhaps something along the size of Australia. Most likely, something intermediate - the Sleestak are more advanced than Madagascar or New Zealand creatures, but then again, Australia or South America sized 'islands' tend to evolve their own predators. The Sleestak evolved to be intelligent, so they need a lot of space, but they weren't a heavily hunted prey species, so their homeland wasn't too big.

Likely it was similar to Madagascar or New Zealand. The island or island continent was free of significant indigenous fauna. A large land mass free of animal life is either the product of a planetary mass extinction event, or has been the result of submergence/emergence. Take your pick. If we're looking at an extinction event, then the Sleestak evolutionary start has to take place at the border of the Permian/Triassic, the Triassic/Jurassic or the Jurassic/Cretaceous. Given that the Land of the Lost seems to sport late Jurassic (Allosaurs and Sauropods) and Cretaceous (Tyrannosaurs and Ceratopsians), but nothing earlier, we can probably rule out Permian/Triassic and Triassic/Jurassic.

On the other hand, if the Sleestak evolutionary line emerges from a continental emergence, then the most likely point is very late Jurassic, or somewhere in the Cretaceous, when continental drift was breaking up continents and pushing up land masses. Either way, we can fix the rough time period as the later part of the age of Dinosaurs.

The Sleestak evolution probably originates from the Jurassic/Cretaceous divide, since they have Dinosaurs from both eras. Likely they evolved in the Jurassic and survived into Cretaceous.

We can also make a decent guess as to location - high up in latitudes, either Sub-Arctic/Antarctic or actually Arctic/Antarctic. Despite the high latitudes, the environment would not have been Arctic or Sub-Arctic, it was still a very warm world. The climate was probably equivalent to our modern temperate: Warm summers, colder winters.

So what were the Proto-Sleestak and how did they get there? The same way that Lemurs made it to Madagascar or Monkeys made it to South America. The Proto-Sleestak, likely small tree-Reptiles, descendants of Suminia, were the Mesozoic equivalent of Monkeys, Sloths or perhaps Raccoons. They were uniquely suited to tree climbing and tree clinging, which made them uniquely suited to surviving sea voyages and rafting events.

As with New World Monkeys and Madagascar Lemurs, the Proto-Sleestak, find a virgin Island continent to populate and diversify into. The island continent is wet and full of rainforest. There's an adaptive radiation, similar to South America and Madagascar. They get larger, producing forms equivalent to the Ape/Sloth/giant lemur niches, or essentially the 'Ape-version' or 'cave-man' Sleestak.

Eventually, one form becomes ground walkers, like ground Apes or giant Sloths. There don't seem to be any significant predators. Or if there are local predators, the ground Sleestak are already large enough that they are not bothered.

Sleestak Intelligence: The big question is why or how the Sleestak made the jump to intelligence. That's tricky. Apes and Monkeys are very smart. Lemurs and presumably giant lemurs much less so. Sloths, Koalas, Pandas and presumably giant Sloths, not smart at all.

There are two theories to explain Monkey/Ape intelligence. One is that as frugivores (fruit eaters) we evolved a very complex lifestyle - not every tree in the forest produces fruit, not all of them produce fruit at the same time, and so in order to eat regularly, Monkeys and Apes had to produce very complicated mental maps and calendars of their environment, to know where to go and when. Lemurs' diets were a bit less picky, so they didn't need to be as smart. Sloths were simple leaf eaters and didn't need to be smart at all. Parrots, on the other hand, have a lifestyle very similar to Monkeys and are some of the smartest birds around.

Of course, that leaves Sleestak out. If they're simply bulk leaf eaters, then they don't have a lot of evolutionary pressure to develop intelligence.

Actually, regarding prospective bulk leaf eaters, or bulk eaters, here's an interesting anatomical clue. Sleestak are green, but their front abdomens seem to feature a large ridged yellow patch running up and down. What is that? Stretching folds. You see them on whales. Basically whales swallow immense quantities of water when feeding, their bellies stretch like balloons, and then they expel the water through their baleen teeth which act like sieves or nets, tonguing the small life trapped in their mouth.

The Sleestak don't do that, of course, but what they probably do is bulk eat so much that their abdomens distend. Maybe they do it for hibernation, or maybe they just feed infrequently but in huge quantities. Or maybe it's a holdover when their ancestral species were bulk, leaf eaters and not much more.

Flowering plants appeared during the Cretaceous, which is a little bit late for the Sleestak. I don't believe that fruiting plants evolved until the age of Mammals, so if the Sleestak and Proto-Sleestak had complicated rain forest diets that drove intelligence, then either this was extremely early flowering seed and fruiting plants, or they probably had to be eating something else.

It's possible that as the Cretaceous went on and flowering plants predominated, Sleestak took advantage of developing intelligence to maximize these resources. But right now, it seems a little early in Jurassic/Cretaceous history for them to evolve intelligence as frugivores.

Moths or soft-bodied insects might have been a part of the diet, their life cycle is tied to the Altrusian moths. That's a hell of a coincidence, it may be that the biological relationship to the moths is that the Sleestak have timed to wake from hibernation in time to eat them. So maybe in some ways, they might have been partially a hyper-specialized insectivore? Maybe the moths, heavy on protein, were the key diet component that provided enough nutrition, and required enough complex behavior to drive intelligence?

Of course, it might not have just been moths. Within scripts, for the series, the Sleestak were also described as eating insects and using tools to dig insects out of trees. So moths and insects are likely a significant, maybe critical, component of their diet. The Sleestak appear to be at least somewhat omnivorous/ carnivorous, they hunt Altrusian pigs. Those claws might have been good for digging out termites or insects. I keep thinking of them as reptilian Sloths, but they may also be loosely analogous to anteaters.

Humans in the Lost Land seem able to access various foodstuffs, but we don't know how much of that, if any, is in the Sleestak diet. Their population concentration (7000 individuals occupying a relatively small portion of the lost land) suggests some sort of agriculture or food production technique. The Land of the Lost is a relatively small place, and that's a lot of individuals to feed.

The other theory for intelligence is complex social organization. We were animals that hung around together in large groups, had complicated social lives, and had to keep track of a large number of prospective mates, rivals, peers, juveniles and oldsters. The jury is sort of out on that one. Herd animals aren't particularly bright. On the other hand, pack animals like wolves or lions tend to be very smart, because they're dangerous to each other and they need to work together.

Does this apply to the Sleestak? What we see of them suggests that they're extremely gregarious. The Sleestak of the Land of the Lost all seem to live communally and tightly packed in one community. The Land of the Lost, in any version, seems large enough that there could be Sleestak villages, suburbs, cottage country, rival communities... But there isn't. This implies a strong need to congregate, and possibly social complexity.

It may be that Sleestak intelligence was driven by some other unknown factor. Either of the going theories for primates suggest that it would be some kind of extreme environmental complexity that demands a lot of compartmentalization and sorting, and some form of memory, mapping and projection.

We do know that despite being slow moving, the Sleestak are past and present tool users, and even now appear capable of making complex tools such as nets, crossbows and periscopes. A number of animals, crows, otters, parrots and Apes use situational tools. It's believed that such applied tool use may have helped to drive Human intelligence, and this may be the same for the Sleestak.

The Sleestak also construct elaborate dwelling complexes, so they may also be similar to beavers or other animals which produce elaborate dwellings. It may be that Sleestak tool use and intelligence was an outgrowth of some hive or lodge building traits, or perhaps a similar sort of environmental manipulation that beavers practice. That would certainly drive complexity. We don't know about Dinosaurs, but we do know that some modern birds put a lot of time and effort into nest-building, both to establish safe places or to attract females.

One peculiar feature of the Sleestak is that they appear to have inherited memory, although it is comprehensive. The existing Sleestak do not understand and cannot manipulate the pylon system that controls the Land of the Lost. It may be that particular knowledge was bred out, or that individuals with that specialized knowledge died off without reproducing. Or perhaps it is blocked for some reason. Or perhaps it was not acquired long enough or deeply enough to 'take hold.' Or maybe inherited memory is limited and it doesn't work for everything.

Finally, it may be that the basics of pylon knowledge are there, but the Sleestak no longer have the education and training to take advantage of it, in much the same way that Humans are innately upright walkers, but ballroom dancing takes education and training.

It's not clear how this inherited memory works. If it's genetic or tied to genetic flow, that's pretty odd stuff. Or it may be the result of chemical information exchange. Possibly from the mother, or from chemicals permeating the egg surface.

Sleestak verbal communication doesn't seem very sophisticated, essentially atonal hissing. This may or may not mean anything. On the other hand, it may be that the true basis of Sleestak communication is chemical.

A communication key to the Hall of Skulls appears to be a mist which facilitates understanding or communication. Adults don't seem particularly chemically adapted, so the trait may be most prominent in youth or eggs. Sleestak society may be organized across generations in ways quite different than our own.

It's possible that this inherited memory, however it works, is the key to Sleestak intelligence. After only a few generations, the Sleestak would probably need to cope with some increasingly complicated information, and that would probably drive increasingly sophisticated neural wiring.

Finally, one last wild card - the Sleestak had a god, never actually seen. But according to series creator, David Gerrold, if he'd been around for the second season, the Sleestak God would have turned out to be the Queen. This is interesting. So perhaps a Queen in the sense of eusocial colonial insects? Where a dominant female does all the breeding and the offspring run the hive?

It's not impossible - Naked mole-rats, a Mammal, have this same hive/breeding strategy.

It would be easier for Reptiles for reptiles to develop colonial eusociality, more so than for mammals. Reptiles can lay a lot eggs and lay more rapidly, as compared to having to give birth like mammals. And some Lizards are notable for having offspring without males for fertilization – so potentially a capacity to produce drones or subordinate daughters like colonial insects.

Interestingly, the Sleestak have a communal egg-hatchery, indicating possibly a single egg-layer.

So maybe the Sleestak developed intelligence as eusocial colonial creatures, basically like ants or termites, but with a lot more neural wiring available?

A final riddle - the Sleestak, although they're clever enough to make sophisticated tools, aren't a patch on their ancient ancestors, the Altrusians. Ancient is a relative term, the Altrusians are only a thousand years earlier, which is nothing compared to the time frames we're dealing with. The Altrusians were smaller than the Sleestak, and gold rather than green. Altrusian throwbacks are born among the Sleestak, though usually purged. To complicate things, the Sleestak call themselves Altrusians.

We don't know what caused the Altrusians to deteriorate into Sleestak. Maybe some diet deficiency? Or a virus? An environmental contaminant? Possibly some kind of social revolution purging all the smart ones? Or maybe the Sleestak are right, they really are just Altrusians, but merely the trailer park, high-school dropout version.

Sleestak in the Context of Planetary History: The Sleestak were probably Earth's first intelligent species (not counting Silurians and Sea Devils - that's a different continuity), emerging somewhere between ninety and seventy-five million years ago and surviving an indefinite period of time. They do not appear in the fossil record, suggesting either that they were not widespread, or that their span of time was not actually a long one, their civilization might have come and gone quickly.

How far did they get? Did they venture into space? Did they colonize the solar system? Explore the stars? Did they meet other Aliens? There's at least one genuine Alien that appears in Land of the Lost. We may never know the scope of their civilization.

At the pinnacle of their technology, they were able to create or access a pocket dimension, and set up control structures for it, with doorways into space and time, which reached into our era and even beyond. By our time, it seems clear that this system was in disrepair and malfunctioning, but largely intact. It seems to have allowed at least some limited movement between past and future. The Human inhabitants of the Land of the Lost in both television series encountered other Humans from both the past and future, and in at least one episode one of them met a future self.

We don't even know if this was the pinnacle of their achievement, they may have surpassed it. On at least a couple of occasions, the series gives us evidence that actual aliens entered the pocket universe system.

What exactly was the pocket universe for? It seems to open into various places and times on Earth. So perhaps a time machine? If their evolution is in the Cretaceous, they may have been able to reach into the Jurassic to collect earlier Dinosaurs, although that seems unlikely. We don't know the range of the pocket universe in terms of accessing time and space.

It doesn't appear to open into other worlds or off-Earth places, so that might be a limitation But it's possible that there are gateways to such locations, but that these environments are so different that they're not accessible - possibly there are locks. However, without real evidence, it doesn't appear to have been a device to reach extra-dimensional or extraterrestrial locations.

Internally, the pocket universe appears to have experienced only a few thousand years of subjective time, allowing a population of Altrusians/Sleestak to survive, and preserving an assortment of Dinosaur fauna which is probably representative of their era. There are no prehistoric Mammals in evidence, except perhaps for the Pakuni. There are Mammals which seem to be from the same time period as later Humans, so, with the exception of alien intrusions, it appears that the gateways were mostly dormant for at least 65 million years.

So why is it opening now? The earliest new opening clearly allowed the Pakuni access. That's assuming that the Pakuni are on the Human line at all. They don't really resemble anything in the Human evolutionary lineage.

We can't necessarily rule out that the Sleestak/Altrusians didn't pick up some prosimian species and genetically modify them into a species that resembled Hominids.

Other openings from the pocket universe, however, extend into the future. The series recorded visitors from the Human future, including a future in which time travel and space travel had been mastered. It's possible that the gates have reactivated because it's been opened up by our own descendants in the next few hundred or few thousand years, and this has set up ripples backwards in time.

On that front, it's possible that the Pakuni may be where Humans are going to end up.

It's not clear how long they lasted. Anywhere from a few thousand to millions of years. It is likely that at their best, the

Sleestak civilization probably did not survive the mass extinction sixty-five million years ago. That implies that there was no significant extra-planetary population, barring a few space missions. Or that if there was, they did not return to resettle their home world. Evolution on Earth carried on without them, as if they were never there.

So in the end, perhaps the pocket universe that was the Land of the Lost was a genuine time capsule, a device to allow the Sleestak/Altrusians and a fragment of their world, the life forms of the Mesozoic, to transcend their era and reach out to some far future era, to meet us.

We know from the two series that in the future, Humans are able to travel to the Land of the Lost and repair it.

Perhaps there's really a future for the Sleestak. I wouldn't mind them coming back again.

The End

Observers and Aliens

Where is Everybody?

This is not going to be a rant about how tosh Humanity is, although we are pretty tosh. This is going to be a relatively thoughtful meditation on the universe, how big and vast it is, and the easiest ways to achieve a goal, which often doesn't involve a journey of a thousand miles.

Everyone knows what the Drake Equation is, and everyone's heard of the Fermi Paradox. If you haven't, go look it up, I'll wait here.

Boiled down, the Drake Equation suggests that the Universe should be brimming with intelligent life. The Fermi Paradox asks the question: If that's the case, where is it?

There may well be life elsewhere in the Universe, possibly in great profusion. Most likely, 99% of it will be microbes. Most of the history of life on Earth is just microbes. And after all the complex life dies off, it'll just be microbes again until Earth is crisped.

But even at 99% microbes, that still leaves an incredible number of planets left over with complex life. If even a microscopic fraction of that complex life results in intelligent species with technology, then there should be truckloads of them.

There may well be intelligent life elsewhere in the Universe, lots of it. We don't really know for sure. So far, we've got a sample size of one, in both categories. But the sheer profusion of stars with planets suggests that regardless of whether it's likely or not, it's not impossible.

I think though, that we overlook the vastness of the universe. There are a hundred billion stars, give or take, in this galaxy alone, and there are millions and billions of galaxies. Count those numbers up and you can go a little crazy.

But the distances are incredible. Right now, our nearest neighboring star is four and a half light years away — an unimaginable distance. But that's the nearest star. The light years pile up. Thousands. Our Galaxy is a hundred thousand light years across. The spaces between galaxies can be millions of light years. The universe is ninety billion light years across.

Literally millions of intelligent species could arise and coexist, all so unimaginably distant from each other that none of them would ever know that they weren't alone. Vast.

Our fastest vehicles would take literally tens of thousands of years to get to the nearest star. Our most feasible science-fiction scheme to get there would literally take centuries, and involve the expenditure of more energy and resources than all of Human history combined.

We don't have the technology or the energy to travel to another star on any basis, and while we have expectations and ambitions, there's no guarantee that the technology and energy to do so are ever going to be achievable, by us or anyone else.

It may simply be unachievable. Period. End of story. To posit that alien civilizations are able to travel from star to star or reach Earth, is essentially believing in magic. Sorry.

We also underestimate how vast the abyss of time is. The Universe, last time I checked, is 13.8 billion years old. Our sun is a mere 4.6 billion years old.

Life on Earth started up somewhere between 3.5 and 4 billion years ago, but most of that time it was just unicellular organisms not doing that much.

Complex multicellular life doesn't show up until roughly 1.6 billion years ago, and it doesn't actually get going big time until 541 million years ago. So basically, 1/8th of the history of life, and 1/9th of the history of the solar system.

It takes another hundred million years or so, 400 million years ago, for life to get up onto land, and complex vertebrates start to dominate. Another hundred million years to get to critters like the Dinosaurs, the Mammal like Reptiles, the bigger amphibians, the ambitious bugs to reach any level of size complexity and significance that maybe they could start getting smart? 300 million years ago. 65 million years ago we got Mammals running the show. Five million years to get to sophisticated primates. Two million years, give or take to get to tool and fire using hominids. Modern Humans at best a few hundred thousand years old.

Agriculture and the first Human civilizations round out to maybe 10,000 years ago. Or basically, one two-hundredth of the span of time that advanced hominids were around. One thirty-thousandth of the time that complicated sophisticated life was bopping on land. One fifty-thousandth of the time that any kind of multi-cellular life was kicking around. Literally one eight-hundred-thousandth of the span of life on Earth.

By the way, that little slice of 10,000 years, 99% of that time involved living in mud and stone huts, hitting our neighbors with rocks, and complaining about fleas. We've actually had a global civilization for roughly 500 years — defined as at least a few cultures able to send members traveling around the planet and loosely aware of all the major civilizations. We've had a technological civilization for maybe 200 years. A high-tech civilization, and that's ranging from radio and biplanes to us, for about a hundred years.

So basically a tiny fraction of one hundredth of Human civilization, itself one two hundredth of the hominid line, in turn one thirty-thousandth of complex life on land. Or roughly our history of advanced civilization is one eighty-millionth of the span of life on Earth.

It's mind boggling. My math is probably off. But its still mind boggling no matter what.

What this suggests is literally millions of technological species like our own, at levels at or better than our own could have come into existence and gone extinct millions of years before we showed up. Millions more may be waiting to be born. An intelligent species may amount to little more than a single heartbeat in the life span of a host star.

Of the vast number of possible intelligent civilizations that could exist in the reasonable time frame of the universe — say 12 or 13 billion years, only the tiniest sliver might exist in the same time frame as our century, or at least, exist in a time frame that we could detect from Earth, or that they could eventually detect us. A tiny sliver likely so incredibly widely distributed through an incredibly vast universe, that we'll likely never detect them, and they'll never detect us.

Sorry to rain on your parade. We're probably not being visited right now. There were probably no ancient astronauts. No Black Knight satellite in orbit. No alien pyramids on Mars. No watchful probes out in the Asteroid belt or Oort cloud. It's just us being lonely.

They Aren't Coming to Visit

But suppose there were Aliens? Wouldn't some of them actually be curious about other life? Possibly. Curious enough to search? Sure.

Wouldn't some come looking?

Why?

I don't think they would, even if they could.

They don't need to.

Here's the thing. Let's posit an alien technological civilization. Let's even posit that it reaches well beyond our level, to the upper levels of achievable science and technology as we understand and can predict it. No magic wormholes, no fantasy warp drives, no Bussard ramjets. Just the outer limits of physics and technology.

Such a civilization might well be able to build probes that could spend the centuries or thousands of years needed to get to the next star. An incredible investment of time and energy and technology. I think it's basically impossible, or at least at the far reaches of probability.

But would it actually need to do that?

Take a look at our own civilization, rinky-dink as it is. We launched our first space-based telescope only thirty years ago, which gave us our first unfiltered look at the Universe. Before that we were staring out the bottom of a coke bottle, a thick layer of atmosphere. The James Webb space telescope, the biggest one yet was launched in the last few years. We're seeing amazing things; we're peering back behind the curtains almost to the Big Bang.

We only started developing the techniques and surveillance to find our first exo-planet in the 1990s. Since then, we've begun to find them at exponential rates, as we get better and better at it.

We're literally at the beginning of this stuff, and we're already looking at techniques to detect if some of these exoplanets have water, we're beginning to sniff at the atmospheres of these worlds.

Extrapolate that with real science and technology progressing over a few decades or centuries. We'll be able to put up telescopes twice as big as James Webb, ten times the size. A hundred times the size. We could put up literally hundreds or thousands of Super-James Webbs across millions of kilometers, out past the orbit of Saturn, away from the light pollution of the sun, their data connected and integrated by quantum computers, so that for all practical purposes, we are looking at the universe with integrated light and radio telescopes millions of kilometers in diameter, with computing and analysis systems thousands of times more subtle than our best work right now.

I'll repeat: Right now, we're already detecting exoplanets, we're measuring their mass, orbit, composition, we're on the edge of detecting water, with the equivalent of stone tools compared to what is realistically feasible in decades and centuries.

So what could we detect with that feasible future technology? With dozens or hundreds of linked James Webbs coordinated so that they're functionally a single giant hundred-kilometer telescope?

We'll be able to map every extra-solar system to a literally fine degree, tracking every large rock. We'll be able to detail the atmospheric composition of alien worlds, measure water content, evaluate composition, detect large structures, and maybe even map alien continents.

We'll be able to detect the chemical signatures of biological activity and life.

Right now, from space, we can see the light from Earth cities, each city a pinpoint of light, outlining whole continents and coastlines, showing population densities. Have you seen those pictures, of Earth's night side lighting up from space? They're beautiful.

With our super-telescope array we might be able to see the light from alien cities in other star systems. Wouldn't that be stunning!

If there's a civilization out there within spying distance, we'll be able to spot it and even have a good read on what level it's at.

And we will be able to do it at a thousandth, perhaps a millionth of the cost of a single interstellar probe. The probe will go to one star, our hypothetical super-surveillance grid could survey thousands, possibly millions of star systems in the time it takes the probe to get where it's going.

So seriously, what would we do?

We'd do the cheapest, easiest thing that promises the biggest reward and return on investment. No interstellar probes. We'd build colossal super-surveillance grids and map the universe in incredible detail.

What would an alien civilization with those abilities do?

Probably the same, because if they got that far, then they're probably not stupid and understand things like cost effectiveness.

Which brings me to the Dark Forest hypothesis. This comes from a novel called the Three Body Problem by writer Liu Cixin. In a nutshell, the idea is that the universe is full of intelligent life. But everyone is hiding from each other.

See, basically, it's statistically inevitable that if there are aliens out there, one of them is going to be a crazy-ass set of genocidal bastards. The sort that would spin up an asteroid near light speed and send it out as a planet killer. The idea is not new, Fred Saberhagen wrote about Berserkers - a robot species dedicated to obliteration of all other life. There's no real way to protect yourself from someone sending an asteroid your way at 98% light speed, or making your sun go nova.

So there are only two ways to cope with this - one is to get them before they get you. And since you can't tell which civilization is the genocidal mofos, the only thing to do is to blow them all up. Which gives us a universe filled with genocidal mofos blowing each other up. Which may explain why the universe seems so empty - everyone got blown up real good, and we're just late to the bloodbath.

Or... hide. Damp down, don't do radio emissions, conceal everything. Just keep quiet and hide. Because the minute you start making noise and getting detected, you become a target.

I don't buy it. Very simple reason: It's not a dark forest out there. A dark forest has trees, it has cover, places to hide. The Universe out there, it's more like a brightly lit prairie. There's no hiding.

Folks, with a level of technology that's barely a few centuries past smashing two rocks together, look at what we're doing with space telescopes. In a few centuries at most, we'll be examining distant planets at micro levels. If there's life, we'll find it. If there's intelligent life, we'll know it.

Anyone else out there is going to build the same technology, have the same ability to scrutinize, and they'll know. Like I said, there's no hiding from that. And even if we decided to start trying to hide, we'd have left plenty of footprints out there before we declared silence. There'd be so many leftovers it wouldn't be funny. And given the outer ranges of detection technology, if we had a spaceship moving from one planet to the other on a non-natural course, the game would be up.

So most likely, there's no one out there looking to take a shot at us. The Universe is not full of paranoids pre-emptively armed and ready to off each other. And honestly, cosmic genocide seems like an awful lot of work for very little peace of mind. There's just no sign of it and any level. Maybe races that lunatic and paranoid self-destruct before they can cause trouble. Or maybe they just get toasted by their neighbors once they act out.

So most likely, if there are aliens out there, they're just doing what we're going to do. Build massive space telescope arrays, stay home, make popcorn, and just watch from a distance. Unless they invent technology which amounts to impossible magic, based on our knowledge, the most likely outcome is that the advanced civilizations of the Universe are Peeping Toms. Surveiling the Universe from the comfort of home, perhaps watching us right now. They might not even say hello, although if they think we're watching them too, they might wave.

If they are watching us right now, from thousands of light years away, they may just be noticing some infinitesimal shifts in the atmosphere or night light output, which suggests that someone here might be getting up to something. Early Hominids are lighting a lot of fires lately. Or maybe there's some tell-tale iron oxides in the air suggesting Roman and Chinese Empire metalworking.

It may be a few more thousand years before they're reasonably sure that some shenanigans are going around on Earth. And maybe in ten or eleven thousand years, assuming we last and they last, they might send us a message, halfway hoping that both sides will be around ten thousand years after that.

But even if they detect us, they're probably not going to bother showing up in person. No real point in it. And they certainly won't bother even trying until we hang around for a few thousand or tens of thousands of years and prove our staying power.

Otherwise the trip might not even be worthwhile. Would you risk a thousand-year trip if you weren't sure we'd still be here when you arrived?

I think that they, and we, would be in it for the long haul. Maybe they're out there, watching silently, knowing that any information or help they could send us would be useless by the time it arrives. So they just watch and hope, crossing their fingers that we'll make it. Maybe all we'll ever get, is their silent well wishes from depths of space.

But ultimately, our destiny will be our own. It's a nice planet we've got here. It could be a lot nicer if we made the effort. Maybe we should.

Maybe they'll mourn us if we don't make it.

Maybe, just maybe, they'll have faith in us. Maybe somewhere deep in the Abyss, someone is cheering for us to succeed.

That's actually kind of encouraging.

The End

More Books by the Author

Thank you for taking the time out to read my little book.

If you did like these excursions, might I recommend other books in the series: **The Dawn of Cthulhu, The Fall of Atlantis** and **The Bear Cavalry, the True (Not!) History of the Icelandic Bear.** In addition, I'll also recommend the two-part alternate history chronicle of World War II in South America – **Axis of Andes** and **New World War.**

What else do I have to offer? Well, I have trilogy of collections of horror stories, starting with **Giant Monsters Sing Sad Songs,** and a pair of funny fantasy collections imaginatively titled **Drunk Slutty Elf,** and a fantasy murder mystery, **The Mermaid's Tale,** and a kick-ass splatterpunk slasher novel, **Squad Thirteen,** and a literary collaboration – **Twilight of Echelon.**

For non-fiction, I have **Starlost Unauthorized** about the Cult series created and abandoned by Harlan Ellison, three kick ass **Doctor Who Pirates Histories,** and **LEXX Unauthorized,** the four season chronicle of a cult Sci-Fi series.

Leave a review. Mention it on your blog, or your Facebook. Say nice things. Toss me a couple of stars. Appreciation is a wonderful thing and it can get hard to get noticed. Reviews help.

www.denvaldron.com

SQUAD THIRTEEN

A FEROCIOUS SLASHER/HORROR NOVEL

Our greatest weapons are our worst nightmares

Slashers are real,

they can't be stopped,

so we used them.

The come. They Kill. No one survives. God help us all!!!

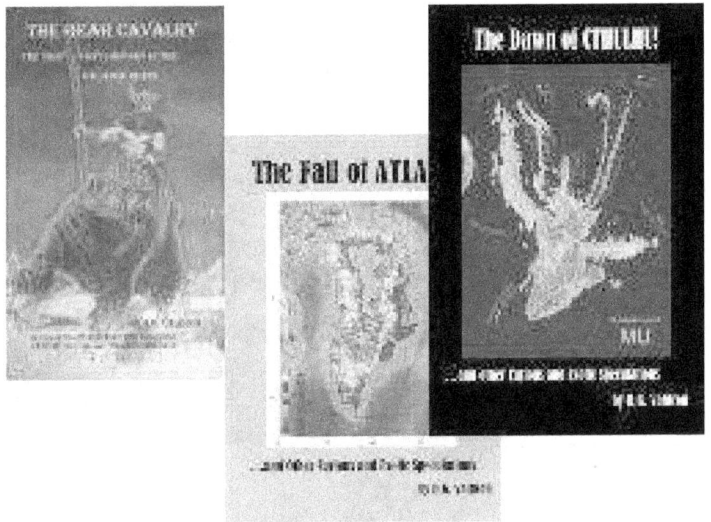

MORE CURIOUS AND EXOTIC SPECULATIONS

The Dawn of Cthulhu - The Secret History of H.P. Lovecraft's Cthulhu Cult; Lost Continents Found – real and legendary; The Monsters of Sesame Street, is a light hearted examination of Muppets as if they were actual animals.

The Fall of Atlantis – Retroverse, An Accidental Cinematic Universe of 50's Sci-Fi movies, Greenland Without the Ice, Rome Crosses the Atlantic, and the Rise and Fall of Atlantis, an ecological catastrophe.

The Bear Cavalry, the True (Not!) History of the Icelandic Bears, an off the wall, short novel about the Viking domestication of bears, their evolution into a medieval cavalry *Bonus novelette,* ***The Sharebear Apocalypse.***

AXIS OF ANDES
NEW WORLD WAR
A History of WWII in South America

Berlin, 1937, Adolph Hitler and his cabinet meet with a strange delegation from Ecuador. The delegates from the small South American nation beg for help, fearing an impending invasion from their rival, Peru. What happens at that meeting sets in motion a chain of events that lights the entire continent on fire. Nations are in ruins, and the map of Latin America will be changed beyond recognition.

HEARTS IN DARKNESS
A Trilogy of Horror Collections

Giant Monsters Sing Sad Songs – The connection between the author of the Necronomicon and a boy in Providence; a girl who meets the last Sasquatch, a poet who shares abandoned Tokyo with a Kaiju…

What Devours Also Hungers – The unkillable killers in masks are recruited into the army, vampires and their hunters, serial killers, monsters and more.

There Are No Doors in Dark Places – A childlike cancer that talks to its owner; A single mother drawn into dark magic; A man who turns into a different monster each night, a pregnant woman finding her body being stolen from her; and many more.

Drunk Slutty Elf

and Other Stories

Hilarious Science Fiction and Fantasy

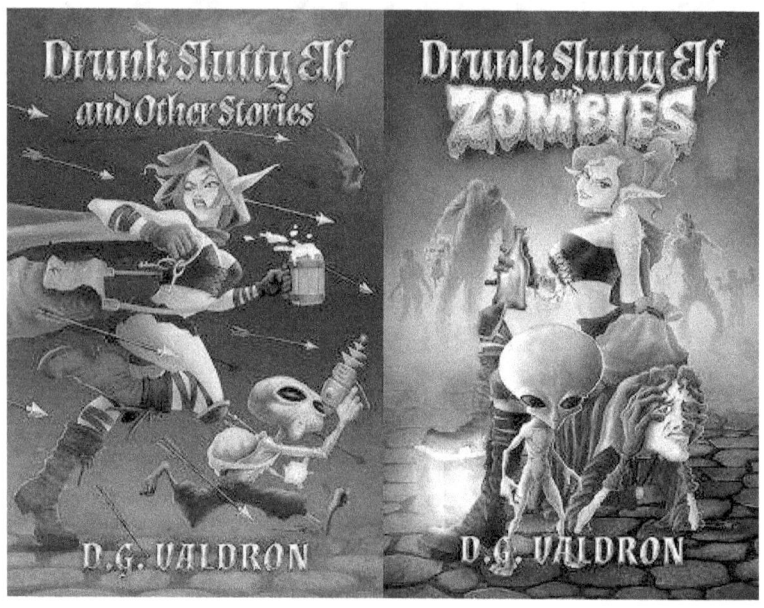

plus the sequel

DRUNK SLUTTY ELF

AND ZOMBIES!!!

Two volumes of savage, satirical, subversive wicked, funny, frantic science fiction and fantasy. Demented ghost hunters, frustrated aliens and many more.

STARLOST UNAUTHORIZED
And the Quest for Canadian Identity

The series that was Harlan Ellison's nemesis. The most
controversial series in the history of Sci-Fi television. This
exhaustively researched book, based on interviews with some
of the stars and writers, brings a fresh new interpretation of
the Starlost, and a re-evaluation of the series and its themes in
the context of the 1970s crisis of Canadian nationalism.

The Pirate Histories!

What's a Pirate's History, you ask? They're things that they don't want you to know about, or that they don't care about, things that are great and marvellous and intriguing... but unapproved.

It's a history of secret and forgotten corners of the Whoniverse. The first woman Doctors, the first black Doctor, animations, audios, stage plays and fan films.

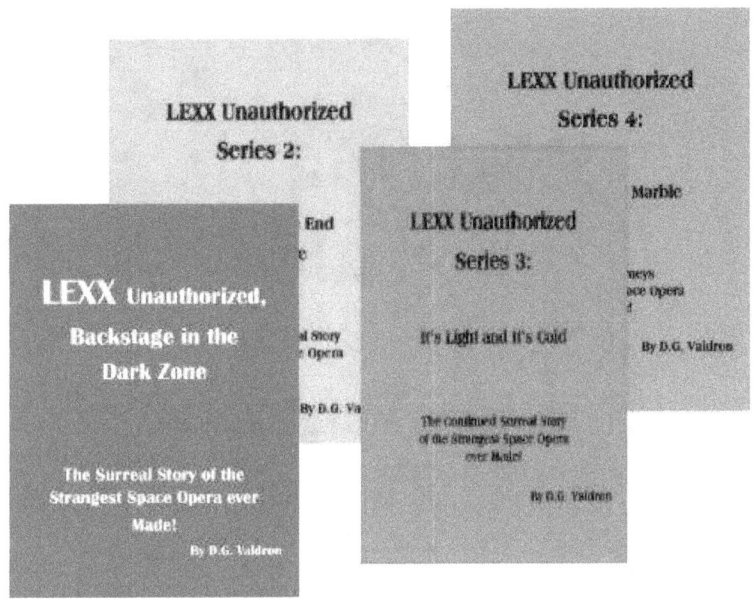

LEXX UNAUTHORIZED

LEXX Unauthorized about the making of a show about a giant space bug that blows up planets, the cowardly security guard who is its captain, and the undead assassin, runaway love slave, and robot head who form its crew.

Originally billed as 'Star Trek's Evil Twin,' the cultiest of cult Sci-Fi, LEXX's forte was black humor, startling visuals, big ideas, and a sensibility that had more to do with surrealists like Jodorowsky or Bunuel than mainstream science fiction.

As unconventional as it was onscreen, the story of how it came to be is even more bizarre.

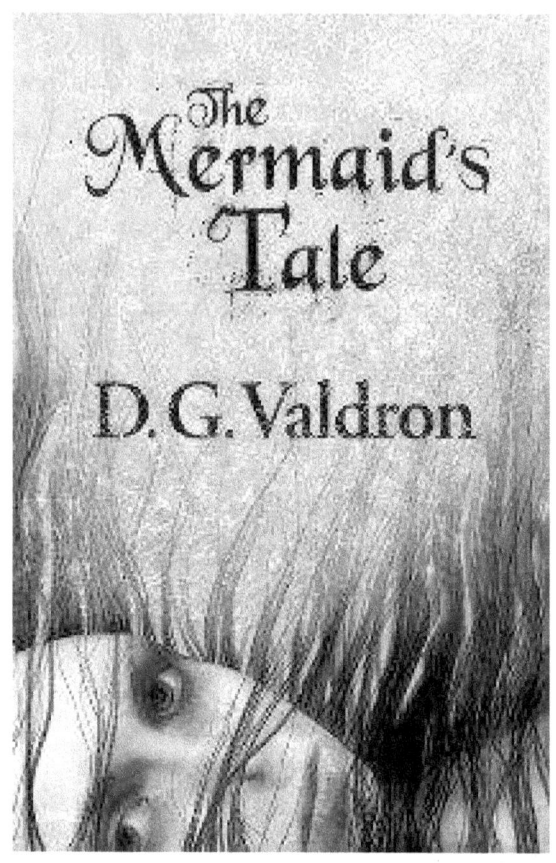

A Dark Fantasy of Murder and Redemption

There's a City where all the races come together uneasily, descending into civil war. There's a Mermaid, murdered cruelly her people distraught and crying out for justice. There's an Orc, her mission: Solve the murder, before it all comes crashing down. And something else... the world's first serial killer.

TWILIGHT OF ECHELON
Published by AT BAY PRESS

Based on the work of famed artist Robert Pasternak the book features paintings from Pasternak's Echelon series, accompanied by stories written independently by D.G. Valdron, Lovern Kindzierski, Alex Passey and Blaise Moritz.